Trial By Terror

and Other Short Stories

GREGORY J. CHRISTIANO

PublishAmerica
Baltimore

First printing

Softcover 9781462643615
PUBLISHED BY PUBLISHAMERICA, LLLP
www.publishamerica.com
Baltimore

Printed in the United States of America

CONTENTS

Trial by Terror

When a young American couple took refuge from a violent storm in an exclusive French hotel, little did they realize that they'd be accused of a grizzly crime, and endure a harrowing—trial by terror.

Peggy and Matthew Barnes had been in France only a few hours. Renting a car, they were driving along a deserted stretch of countryside when a massive storm struck. It became a flash flood, brightening the summer sky with fierce streaks of lightning.

"Matty, we'll be killed. We have to stop at the first place we find," said Peggy, glaring at the road ahead. She was twenty-five, beautiful, her eyebrows well marked like delicate wings, giving her face more definition. Her clothes were fashionable and perfectly tailored. Matthew was handsome, in a conventional way, dressed in a suit and blue tie. He was well groomed and had a pencil mustache to accent his squared jaw and soft brown eyes.

"Looks like a hotel to the right," said an excited Matthew Barnes. Peggy shuddered, blaming it on the grim, gray, raw and cold day rather than her nerves. "Looks like a real plush hotel Matty."

"We haven't much choice, dear. Anyhow, it'll be nice to splurge just this once!"

It was a massive structure, styled in an elegant French Imperial period. Mansard roofs and ornate windows framed the three wings of the three story building. The couple parked to the side and briskly ran in through the entrance. Brocade curtains fell almost from the ceiling to well below floor length, gathering up the rich swaths that demonstrated wealth. The curtains were excellent at keeping out winter drafts, but it also excluded some of the golden summer light. The furniture was massive, and where the wood showed, it was deeply carved oak, darkened by generations of overpolishing. The surfaces were clean; there were small portraits of people on the wall of various ages all posed solemnly.

The couple was greeted in the lobby of the great house by a well dressed gentleman in his early forties. Long sideburns, jet black hair, rather tall and very somber. "Je m'appelle Yves, monsieur, madam. Votre baggage…?" He said.

Matthew glanced at his wife, "I think we've run into a language barrier."

Peggy pulled out her dictionary, "That's what dictionaries are for, dear."

"Monsieur, madam?" again came the inquiry from the gentleman, who was either a desk clerk or the manager. Matthew struggled with a few words of French translated from the dictionary, "Une salle, s'il vous plait."

"Monsieur," said the clerk somewhat bewildered, "vous ne comprenez pas. Ecoute…" Obviously he didn't understand Matthew's pigeon French. The manager of the Hotel de Fou tried to speak again to the couple, but furtively, since they didn't understand a word.

"I think he's trying to tell us he has no room, Peg."

"Well, I'm not going out in that storm, even if I have to sleep in the lobby."

Something in Peggy's voice struck a sympathetic cord in the manager. Moments later, they were escorted by a bellhop into a nearby room, up a grand stairway. Without saying a word the bellhop led the couple across the chilly hall past the study, perfectly in keeping with the somber grandeur of the drawing room. Beyond the massive front desk they passed a bookcase crammed full of matching volumes. A stag's head hung high on the wall, its glass eyes staring into space, a bit like the paintings and photos in the other room. On the wall opposite the desk hung a large portrait of a lady dressed in a formal afternoon gown.

Peggy and Matthew passed several hotel guests as they ascended the stairs. Peggy whispered her concerns, "Stuffy old lady, ignoring us as if we weren't here. Ugh? This place gives me the creeps."

"I told you it's an exclusive hotel," reasoned Matthew, "She must be an aristocrat and we're intruders."

Later, curiosity led the couple to mingle with the wealthy looking guests gathered in the drawing room. An adventure that was to turn the evening into a nightmare ordeal.

Shortly they were approached by an elegant looking lady. The lady bore a close resemblance to the portrait in the lobby. Her hair was white and neatly swept upward. Her features were enhanced by the soft light from the window she was facing, her eyes clear and wide, her winged brows accentuated.

"Ah! I speak not much the English," she said with a warm smile, "But welcome." She extended her hand. "I am Contesse Louise de Rochaud."

"How'd you do!" said Peggy shaking her hand, "We're Peggy and Matthew Barnes.

“Come,” gestured the Countess, “I fix champagne. We dine together, non?”

They returned to the luxury of the Countess’ suite for a glass of champagne.

“We finish la champagne. Then I mus’ dress. I meet you dans la sale a manager, eh?”

“She must mean the dining room, Matthew.”

The American went down to the lobby to wait for the Countess, but soon a stony faced committee march stiffly down the grand stairway to confront the couple.

“Monsieur, Madame,” said one of the guests, “Allons.” He pointed toward the dining room.

“He wants us to follow him, Peg. We’d better, I guess.”

They were met by a grim-faced mob of people. The Barnes’ didn’t need an interpreter to grasp the horrendous accusation hidden in the language. The ghastly corpse of the Countess lay in a pool of blood on the dining room floor.

“Assassins!” shouted the manager of the hotel pointing a finger at the couple, “Vous aves tue la Contesse!”

An incredulous look appeared on the face of Matthew, “Are you trying to tell me we killed the Countess? My God! She was alive when we left her. Why would we do it?”

The manager stepped forward and presented a suitcase and showed the couple the contents. It was filled with precious stones, gems and other jewelry. “That’s my suitcase,” gasped Matthew, “This whole thing is a frame-up.”

“Aha,” said the manager with a scowl, “Il faut les mettre en jugement.”

“They must be brought to trial,” was the literal translation. Peggy and Matthew Barnes were herded into another room to face their accusers. To them it was a frightful absurdity, but there they were facing a judge and surrounded by a jury.

“Notre verdict, coupable!” said the man in robes. A chorus of, “A la guillotine!” came the reply from the surrounding throng.

“Guillotine!” cried Matthew, “You call that a trial? We weren’t allowed to testify, no interpreter, no lawyer. This is some kind of sick joke, isn’t it?” He rose from his seat and pointed at the ‘judge.’ “You stole the jewelry, murdered the Countess, and pinning it on us.”

He turned to Peg and whispered, “Let’s get out of this madhouse. Look, the door’s open—run for it. GO!”

Amid wild shouts and shrieks the Barnes’ made a life-or-death run for their car. They tore down the stairs, followed by an angry mob.

“Arretez eux!” they shouted, “Capturez—eux!”

“Keep running Peg, we’re almost to the car.” They made it to their auto and somehow Matthew shoved the key into the ignition. Approaching voices were drowned out by the roar of the engine as the coupe sped away.

“They’ll call the police,” said Peg, out of breath, “There’ll be roadblocks.”

“Listen. We didn’t kill anybody. We’ll go to the embassy, demand a lawyer…”

About two miles away, Matthew abruptly pulled over to the shoulder and stopped. “Why are you stopping,” asked Peg, “It’s so dark here, I’m scared Matthew.”

“The name of that place, there’s something about it, Peg. I’ve got to look it up.” He opened his guidebook and thumbed through the listing. “Hotel de Fou…insane! Maison de fou is the real name, and it’s a madhouse. But the inmates were nobility, so it’s called a Mad Hotel!”

Peggy glanced at the book, “They’re all insane? They murdered that woman just to put us on trial?”

“Seems so. But those lunatics seemed so normal to me.”

“I’ll never get over the shock,” said Peggy, looking back down the dark road.

* * * * * * * * * *

There was such gaiety back at the Hotel de Fou. The shrill laughter led by the Contesse Louise de Rochaud herself…

“I wish more strangers would come here. Their trials are such fun,” she laughed combing her long, white hair.

“Yes,’ said the manager, “And those two were such a delightful couple.”

A.P.B. (All Points Bulletin)

I

At the state prison a new inmate took up residence in a cell with a hardened criminal. The corrections officer led him into the cell to meet his new cellmate. The officer was addressing a fat, dumpy-looking man with a bald head and round, chubby face. "Here's your new home, bud, the warden told you the rules and from now on you'll live up to them!"

"Okay screw," the fat man answered, "Got ya. Ya don't have to gimme no sermons."

The man in the cell was in his forties, tall, a full head of dark, wavy hair, large hooked nose and a pencil mustache. He was smoking a cigarette. "The upstairs bunk is yours, chum," he said to the new inmate, "Make yourself comfortable, haw!"

"Put him on to the routine, Griggs," said the guard, "I don't want any trouble." With that final spiel, the officer locked them in. The fat man had a last word, "Aw, can it! I've been in stir before, I know the ropes!"

"Yeah? My name is Eddie Griggs, what's yours pal?"

The fat man introduced himself, "I'm Luke Canfield. They just hung a ten year rap on me, but if they think I'm gonna serve it, they're off their rockers."

“Hummph!” said Griggs in a ho-hum manner. “That’s big talk palsy! What’s the rap for?”

“It was a heist in an insurance company office. My partner fouled us up. It was like this…” Canfield flashed back to the day of the crime…

‘Louie, Canfield’s partner, was busy jimmying the lock on the insurance company’s doors…”Come on Louie,” said an anxious Canfield, “Hurry up with that lock. You want us to get pinched before we even get in?”

“Aw, take it easy. I ain’t no Houdini…” Louie got the door unlocked, “Ah, there she goes!”

‘They headed right for the office safe—a huge, six-foot high massive cast iron monster. “There she is,” pointed Canfield, “Ought to be loaded. This is the end of the week. They’ve been collectin’ premiums like mad!” [In 1953, most people paid in cash]. “Hey, that looks pretty solid,” said a worried safe-cracker, Louie. “It ain’t gonna be easy knockin’ that over.”

‘Canfield knelt down in front of the lock mechanism, “This is gonna be a lot easier than it looks! It’s just a fancy tin can.”

“Yeah, well I hope what’s inside ain’t a load of tin too! Ya ready to knock the tumblers out?”

‘It was only a minute or so before Canfield had the safe open! “See?” he beamed, “What’d I tell ya? Nothin’ to it! I coulda knocked this over with a plain screwdriver.” Louie was just a little nervous, “Oh boy! Lets get the dough and scram. This is too good to be…”

‘Before he could get the words out the office door flew open. The uniformed night watchman had his revolver drawn, aiming at the two crooks. “Okay boys,” he shouted, “The party’s over…reach!”

Louis and Luke raised their hands and didn't move a muscle.

"Keep 'em up there and don't move."

"Okay, okay!" said Canfield, his voice trembling, "Don't get trigger happy. We ain't goin' nothin'"

"Yeah!" said Louie as he grabbed his automatic and started blasting the officer…"Not until I blast your crummy head off!"

"Louie, you shot him!" cried Canfield.

'The watchman returned fire and Louie fell dead with a scream of pain. In an instant, Canfield ran out the door passing the watchman. On the way downstairs, Canfield was thinking, "That jerk Louie cases the job and doesn't even find out when the night watchman makes his rounds—I'm glad he got it."

'Canfield continued to tell his story to Griggs…

'I was real anxious to get outta there…

"Maybe I can make it before the coppers get here! I don't want to do anymore shooting. One's enough for one night."

'But my luck ran out. Two cops were waiting for me at the foot of the stairs. "Drop it mister," ordered one of the officers, "Or we'll blow you to pieces…"

'I was stunned, "Why you…I'm comin' through. Out of my way flatfoot."

'One grabbed my arms and the other cracked me over the head with the butt of his revolver. I was knocked unconscious.'

Canfield turned to Griggs and finished his story…

"They gimme ten years. The watchman didn't croak or it would have been the hot seat for sure. What's your story?"

Griggs sat down on his bunk, his cigarette dangling from his lips… "Me?" he said, "I got hooked in the Wells Fargo armored car stickup three years ago. Maybe you remember it?" Canfield nodded.

Griggs continued: "The plan was nifty but with our lousy luck…"

'My boss was giving me the run down…"Rickie, you're gonna handle the push cart. You sure you can handle it now?"

"You know me, boss," I said, "I ain't never flopped before, have I?"

"Okay then," said the gangland leader, "But watch yourself. One slip and you're gonna be givin' our regards to the boys in the morgue."

'He turned to the rest of the guys in the room…"The rest of you will be with me. Remember, there's half-a-million if we make it!"

'One guy answered confidently, "Don't worry boss, we know what to do!"

'The next day," continued Griggs, "I was on the spot and the armored car turned into the street just like we figured…I was pushing the vegetable cart, pretending to be a peddler. I watched the car turn the corner and thought, "…them monkeys are gonna get the surprise of their lives!"

'They backed up near the bank entrance and began to unload the loot…I thought…"Huh! Look at 'em. Them halfwits are so busy bein' important they ain't even looked this way. This'll wake 'em up all right!" I approached them with my tommy-gun cocked and ready.

"Up with them," I shouted, "Wise guys, and don't make a fuss. I got a nervous finger." I signaled the rest of the gang, "Come out boys…" Four others had come out from around the corner. The boss held a pistol on the security men, "Okay, you guys," he ordered, "Get away from the truck if you wanna live!" He motioned with his gun to move aside.

"Holy smoke," said one of the guards to his partners, "They brought an army!" As he was speaking, his partner drew his service revolver, "Yeah, duck Tom…" and fired at the boss. Two more security guards jumped from inside the truck with automatics and a gun battle started. We never counted on extra guards in the truck. Every one of my cronies got it—I tried to hightail it outta there but was cornered. They handcuffed me—and here I am.'

"From now on," Griggs vowed, "I'm workin' only for me. No prize schmoes are gonna trip me up."

"The same goes for me pal," reflected fat Canfield, "But like I said, they ain't keepin' me in here."

Eddie looked out through the steel bars, "Maybe ya got somethin' there! Luke, this joint is more crowded than a New York subway. That's why we're doubled up, besides, the joint's rotten—fallin' to pieces!"

From that moment on the two hoods spent every spare moment scheming to get free. One day in the carpenter shop where both men worked…

"Hey Luke, come here a minute, I need a hand…" Luke dropped his load of 2 x 4's and got permission from one of the guards to go over to Eddie. He marveled at what he saw. "Holy smoke. A gat! Where did…" Eddie had what looked like a .38 snub nose. "Sh," cautioned

Eddie, “It ain’t no gat…It’s carved out of celluloid I managed to swipe. I didn’t want to show you till I finished.” Eddie showed it to him up close. ”Looks good, eh?”

“So, what good is it?” asked Canfield.

“Listen, they’re repairing the wall an’ if we can get near it…we can force our way out.”

Early next morning:

Both men were carrying lumber to the spot near where the outer wall was being repaired.

Eddie whispered to Canfield—“Make it look like we got orders to take this lumber to the wall. If we get stopped, we’re through!”

“Well, we fooled the screw in the shop. The rest should be easy,” commented Canfield, confident their plan would work.

There was a hole in the wall where a man could just about squeeze through. “Halt!” ordered the guard, “Where are you going with that plank?”

“Okay,” whispered Eddie, “this is it!”

“I’m ready,” answered Canfield.

They dropped the board and Eddie pulled his phony gun.

“Okay screw, stand back like nothin’ was happenin’ or I’ll let ya have it in the belly!” ordered Eddie.

The stunned guard moved back, while flabby Canfield relieved him of his automatic, and then slugged him over the head with the gun. They squeezed through the opening and ran for the road about fifty yards away. They came upon a car parked a little ways down the road, overpowered the driver and stole the vehicle.

II

Back at the prison…

"Warden, Caruthers's is dead!" panted one of the guards as he reported to Warden Drake.

"This is very bad, men," said an angry Warden as he addressed his correction officers in is office, "This makes it twice as imperative that these men be apprehended. Call the police to send out a three-state alarm and an A.P.B."

"Yes Sir, right away," said another guard.

In a matter of minutes, police in every city in the area were on the alert for the escaped men.

"Five foot eight, dark hair, mustache, in stolen car…" repeated a local police officer, "They won't get very far. Breaking jail is no cinch these days," assured his partner.

Meanwhile:

As the two hoods sped towards town in their stolen car…"Yeah and we gotta ditch this jalopy," said Canfield, "By now every cop must be watching for it. They probably got the make on it, an' know it better than their own mother!"

"The first thing we need is clothes and dough," extorted Griggs. He continued, "There's the joint we're looking for." pointing to a local clothing store, "Let's get some clothes and clean out the till. Two birds with one stone, eh?"

"Yeah," laughed Canfield, "Then we'll hijack another jalopy and head for the coast."

The two hoods entered the store, "Yes, gentlemen?" said the clerk, "Er…er…" stammered Griggs, "We were out of town camping and we lost our duds. The boat turned over…heh…heh!"

"Yeah," added Canfield, "We had to borrow these rags from a farmer. We want new outfits." The two men were still wearing their prison garb.

"Too bad…too bad," remarked the clerk, "Well, you've come to the right place! I can give you everything from soup to nuts!"

They followed him to the clothes racks. No other customer was in the store; the two hoods were alone with the clerk. "That's fine mister," said Griggs as he continued to put the clerk off guard, "We sure need it!"

Then Griggs suddenly changed his tone of voice…"Yeah, and we also need dough. All you got!"

The stunned clerk turned, "Why…why…you…you're crooks. Stand back! Keep away from me." He ran behind the counter and pulled an automatic from the drawer.

"…raise your—yiiii!" Griggs wrestled the gun from his hands, "You asked for it Bud. Guys like you shouldn't play with guns—it ain't safe."

"Yeah, palsy. You need a goin' over," added Canfield, gleefully.

"Help! Help! Aaghhh!" cried the terrified clerk, as Griggs shot him in the chest.

"Well ain't that too bad! He went and shot himself!" laughed Griggs.

"Grab that gat, the clothes and dough. We ain't got too much time to play around!" said Canfield.

The pair quickly cleaned out the cash register and changed into suits right off the racks. Canfield was admiring himself in a full length mirror near the fitting room.

"Hey, not a bad fit without alterations," crowed Canfield as he adjusted his jacket, "It sure feels good to wear real clothes again!"

"Yeah," said a very disappointed Griggs, counting the money he'd taken from the cash register. "The crum only had ninety bucks in the till. Well, that'll hold us for a day or so…come on, stop admiring yourself Canfield. Let's scram!"

Griggs continued as they exited the store, "Let's leave the jalopy where it is. We'll register in the local hotel do the street and hop a train in the morning. The cops will never suspect we'd stay near a crime scene…it's perfect!"

"Good idea. Them coppers will be hunting for two cons from an abandoned car. Nice figurin' Eddie!"

Across the street a suspicious dentist looked through the blinds…

"Hey, that's funny," he thought to himself, "Those guys coming out of Harry's shop with new suits and he's got his 'Back in Thirty Minutes' sign up. I'd better take a look and see if everything's all right." The dentist left his office and spotted the two crooks going into the local hotel.

"There they go—into the hotel," the dentist muttered under his breath, "Maybe I'm wrong, perhaps—but, I'll say hello to Harry anyhow."

At the hotel:

"Nobody seen us come outta the store," a confident Griggs said, "We're okay. Now don't forget to put on the act."

"Sure, I got it. Don't worry 'bout me Eddie. I shouldda been on stage."

They walked to the front desk to register.

"You say your baggage is coming later?" asked the hotel desk clerk, as the two cons signed the register. "That's right Bub. We had a breakdown and its at the garage right now." answered Canfield.

"That's right," added Griggs, "We're traveling salesmen…bushed. How's business here?"

Meanwhile at the store:

The dentist discovered the body of Harry, the store clerk, and frantically phoned the police…"I knew something was wrong the minute I saw those men come out and that sign up! Poor Harry." After the police arrived…"Tough break," said one of the officers, "He was a fine man. You say they went into the hotel?

The dentist took the policemen outside and pointed down the block. "That's where they went, all right. Probably thought no one saw them. I'll…"

Another officer interrupted, "Here's some old clothes chief. Prison outfits. Found them in the back room."

The chief grabbed the clothes, "Prison outfits! Those birds must be the two escaped cons. Radio headquarters Bill and tell them to surround the hotel. We've got a little business to attend to."

It wasn't long afterwards that a dozen policemen had the building surrounded and prepared to go in."

"Watch your step," cautioned the Chief, "And shoot to kill. These rats are armed and dangerous, especially when cornered. You three take the back entrance."

Four of the officers entered the hotel and found out what room the two hoods were hold up. In the room, Griggs was at the window staring down into the street.

"Luke! Luke! Com'ere! The coppers got the joint surrounded! They've been tipped off 'bout us!"

"Huh? Why, I'll blast every last one of them dirty flat footers. How…how'd know we was here?"

"Hey," Griggs grabbed Canfield's wrist to stop him from firing the stolen gun, "Lay off that you stupid cluck! What are you tryin' to do, get us blasted fulla holes? Put that rod down."

"Aw, them coppers drive me off my nut! I hate their guts!"

Both men bolted out of the hotel room and ran down the corridor.

"They don't know what we look like. Maybe we can walk through and—too late—there they come!" hollered Griggs, holding the gun he'd taken from Luke.

"They ain't gonna take me Eddie, I ain't gonna burn. Come on!" They ran for the back exit.

"We'll bust our way through," cried Luke.

The police shouted for them to halt. One officer intercepted them coming down the emergency exit stairwell. "Drop 'em!" the officer hit Canfield across the back of his bald head. Griggs dropped the gun and raised his hands. "Don't shoot. I give up."

"Good work boys," said a relieved Chief of Police. "Took them without firing a shot. Take them away!"

EPILOGUE:

Griggs cagey scheming was to no avail. Eight months later they settled in at the Death House, convicted and sentenced to pay the supreme penalty. Their vicious criminal careers had been brought to a permanent close.

Book Him!

Troy Reynolds faces a cold-blooded murderer and proves to everyone that books are not only tools of knowledge, but weapons of justice as well!

Troy and his friend Jerry were passing a book store one Saturday afternoon, noticing a poster—"Boys Wanted for Part-Time Work". J.J. Adkins was the proprietor. An elderly man, tall, slim, white hair and mustache. The boys entered. Troy was all of fourteen, so was his friend Jerry.

"I think you two would do very well for the job…" said Mr. Adkins, after a brief interview.

"That's swell, Mr. Adkins, when can we start?" asked Troy.

"Right away. I'm afraid your first task is dusting off all of these books!" Mr. Adkins pointed to a row of shelves and asked Troy to dust them off. "Troy, you can do that and familiarize yourself with the stock. Meantime, I'll start Jerry on something else."

Mr. Atkins took Jerry to the cash drawer and safe. "I have this weeks receipts all ready to go to the bank…do you know how to make a deposit, Jerry?"

"Sure," said the young boy answering with confidence, "I'd rather run errands than dust!" Mr. Adkins gathered the checks, coins, cash and credit receipts and placed them in a money pouch. He had already filled out the deposit slips which he kept separate for Jerry to give to the teller when he arrived at the bank. "There's quite a good deal of money in that bag, Jerry. So be careful."

Jerry was a bit nervous carrying all that money, but he was delighted with a new found trust and waved to Mr. Adkins and Troy as he left the store to walk to the bank. A few minutes later, Jerry enters the bank. As coincidence would have it, a bank robber entered at exactly the same time! The thief was a well dressed, heavy-set man in suit, tie and fedora. He was carrying a satchel and brandished a .357 magnum revolver. He knocked out the guard with a blow to the back of his head, and then went to one of the teller booths.

"Out of the way, squirt, or you'll get hurt," he said as he pushed Jerry aside. "Okay Bud…this is a stick-up. Put all the cash in this bag. Hurry!" he demanded. The frightened teller quickly did as he was told and in a matter of seconds loaded the satchel from the money drawer. Even Jerry's deposit doesn't escape the crook's notice! He grabbed for the money bag. "Oh, no! Please don't take that!" pleaded Jerry.

"Shut up and hand it over!" said the heartless thief as he held the gun on the rest of the crowd in the bank. "The rest of you stay where you are!" The crook leaves and the police arrive minutes later and immediately go into action. Before an A.P.B. could be announced, a description of the culprit must be given. The video cameras were on, but it would take a while before they could be rerun, so an on hand identification was required.

One officer was gathering information, but the eye witnesses gave differing descriptions. One lady said, "Oh, he was horrible, officer! He had a red tie and…" She was interrupted by a young man, "No, he had a maroon tie!"

"Just a minute," said a frustrated policeman, "One at a time. Just answer my questions, please. If we can get a good idea of what this fellow looked like, we'll catch him sooner! Now, what color suit was he wearing?" An old gentleman with a hearing aid raised his hand, "Uh—brown! Wait, no, it was dark gray!" Another man hollered, "No, it was beige. I remember."

Jerry approached the officer and got his attention, "I can tell you…I noticed particularly when I realized he was a thief! He had a light grey fedora, a beige suit with grey stripes, brown tie, brown shoes, and white shirt." Amazed, the officer thanked and complimented the young boy as he jotted down the details onto his note pad. "Now that's more like it."

Jerry continued, "When he told the cashier to put the money in the bag, I noticed that the top of his hat came right up exactly to the bottom of that glass partition."

"Almost my height," said the tall policeman. "He took a bag that had hundreds of dollars from me! I was going to deposit it for Mr. Adkins."

"Carl, go with this boy and explain what happened."

"Don't worry son, we'll get the money back for you and your boss," said Officer Carl.

"I hope so," said a very worried Jerry, "This was the first time I ever deposited the receipts for Mr. Adkins. I'm sure he needs the money."

Meantime, the robber finds the police cordon's too tight for him... *"Cops everywhere! I'd better slide into one of these stores and lie low for a while."*

"That's one of my favorite books, Troy," said Mr. Adkins, "Why don't you take it home with you and…"

"Okay—get your hands up, grandpa; you too kid! And don't make no noise!" The crook pointed his gun at Mr. Adkins and Troy. However, Jerry and the police officer can be seen approaching through the front window.

"Come with me gramps! You, kid, go on as if nothin' was wrong or I'll plug the old geezer!"

"Y-yes!" said a stunned Troy. The officer and Jerry entered the store. "Troy," said his excited friend, "Where's Mr. Atkins? Something awful has happened." He grabbed Troy's shoulder, while the officer stood close by. "The bank was robbed," blurted Jerry, "The thief stole thousands of dollars, and took Mr. Adkin's money too!"

"Where's the owner, son?" asked Officer Carl, "I've got to explain for this boy."

"He—uh, he went out." Explained Troy in a nervous tone, fidgeting with the book Mr. Adkins had given him. "I don't know when he'll be back…he didn't say. It's too bad about that money Jerry."

"Gee—you don't look sorry!" said a puzzled Jerry.

"Don't worry, I'll wait for a few minutes," said Officer Carl.

"We'll have to get these books…" said Troy, but he was fixing the shelf as some volumes fell, "Hey, grab them!"

"Look out;" cried Jerry,"They're falling!"

"Officer, would you please give me that big book in front of you?" asked Troy. Officer Carl picked it up and immediately noticed…"Huh? Say! What kind of a book is this? Better let me put this in place."

"That would help..." said Troy motioning with his eyes to the back room, then pointing to a spot on the book shelf. "It goes right there, thanks!"

"Well, I'll be running along..." said the officer in a firm, strong voice, "I'll come back later to see Mr. Adkins." But alert Officer Carl strolls casually past the curtained doorway. He suddenly drew back the curtain while pulling out his service revolver. "No funny moves Buddy...the game is over!"

"What!" cried the crook, "Get out of my way."

"Oh, no! You're not going anywhere but jail." They grappled with one another. The officer landed a solid blow to the thief's jaw, but the crook kicked him squarely in the head and knocked Carl to the floor. The thief made a dash for the front door of the store, as Troy grabbed the heaviest book he could find and flung it at the running hood. His aim was perfect! The book struck the criminal in the side of his head, knocking him unconscious! Officer Carl recovered and raced to nab the fallen hoodlum. "Nice pitch, kid. He's out cold!"

"Boy, I was sure he'd get away again," said a relieved Jerry.

The officer disarmed and handcuffed the bank robber and called for backup. "Troy, that was about the slickest tip-off I've ever seen—you certainly used your head."

"But you were on your toes, too! I was afraid you might not get it!" Mr. Adkins looked confused, "Get what? I don't understand! Do you mean Troy told you the thief was in back? But, we heard everything..." The officer smiled and pointed to the bookcase. "Just take a look at that shelf," he said, as he winked at Troy.

Jerry and Mr. Adkins went over and saw five books arranged in order...the titles were:

"Behind the Iron Curtain"
"Man Trap"
"Crime and Punishment"
"20,000 Years in Sing-Sing"
"Under Cover"

An amazed Mr. Adkins said, "My goodness…I certainly was lucky to hire you two boys today!"

"The bank'll be glad, too!" said Officer Carl.

Troy made one last observation, "But…look at the mess those books are in now!"

Card Sharks

There was no warning...the victim in the crooked card game made a lunge for the card sharp—Curly! A blow was struck, then another... and Richard Crine looked down at the man on the floor! Crine hadn't struck him...but he was one of the trio who'd cheated him of his cash!

Mr. Crine was of slight build, brown, wavy hair, light complexion which turned even whiter as he knelt near the lifeless body of Dutch Williamson, "Yuh hit him too hard, Curly! He ain't breathin'."

Walt Peters looked on from the card table just as horrified. "I'm getting' outa here. I didn't expect this!"

Curly was a stout, burley fellow with a billiard-ball bald head, heavy eyebrows, and sporting a tattoo of an anchor on his muscular bicep. His fists were still clenched as he spoke, a cigar dangling from his lips, "Hold it Crine. You're as guilty as I am! We all cheated him outa his dough…more than a thousand bucks! That's a felony, see!"

Crine held out some of the cash he won, "That's right," he said nervously, I've got over two hundred here, but I won't keep it."

"It's too late," snorted Curly, "Yuh took part in a felony…a man was killed. That makes you guilty of murder too!" He reached out and snatched the cash from Richard's hand. "Gimme the dough," he continued, "You go home to your wife and keep your mouth shut. Forget this ever happened."

Richard Crine didn't go straight home. He walked the streets for hours, trying to get up enough courage to go to the police.

"It's not fair," he thought to himself, *"I didn't cheat anyone in that game...they did! I didn't know there was any cheating until Curly admitted it. If I tell that story to the police, they'll never believe me."*

He couldn't console himself in any way. *"I won that money...the game was crooked. The cops would never believe me. I'd better do as Curly says!"*

Richard Crine, fairly well off insurance broker, was miserable for a month. Then, just as he thought this was all behind him, the letter came.

One evening after arriving home from work, his wife gave him the day's mail. He opened one of the letters—it was from his old playmate, Curly…just a clipping from a month old newspaper!

Mr. Crine read it intently, deep in thought," 'Unidentified man found in river. Police have been unable to locate any next of kin. He was a middle-aged man of…' His face turned white, *"The description fits the man Curly hit! Wait! Here's a phone number to call!"* Curly had written his phone number in the margin. Curly was waiting for this phone call. He knew it would come.

"Hello Richard. Bad business, eh? Yeah! Walt and I, we're stayin' outa sight. That's just the trouble. Me and Walt can't work. We need dough, and plenty of it."

Crine was careful not to let his wife overhear the phone conversation. Curly paused, then continued, "We'll get out of town Richard, but we need loot—at least fifteen thousand bucks. That's right, fifteen grand, and you'll never hear from us again!"

That first payment wasn't too hard to raise, but it nearly cleaned out Mr. Crine's savings account. He brought the money to Curly and his pal Walt the next day.

"I told yuh Richie-boy wouldn't let us down, Walt!" crowed Curly as he counted the cash.

"He'd better not," snorted Walt, "If he squawks, we'll all do a murder rap. Understand, Richie-boy?"

"I, I understand!" replied a very distraught Richard Crine, "Well, goodbye, gentlemen," he continued, as he backed cautiously out of the seedy hotel room, "Have a nice trip."

After Richard left, an elated Curly turned to his crony Walt, "Did yuh hear that? 'Have a nice trip.' He says! Wait'll I call him next week!" He pounded the table with his fist and laughed.

One week later, Richard Crine got another call. It was then he knew the bitter truth. It was blackmail and he was helpless. He met Curly again at a different flop house. After handing Curly another five thousand:

"I have no money left now, Curly. Don't call me again."

"Yuh'll raise some Richie-boy," Curly demanded, "You're a clever guy."

Richard was in despair as Curly continued, puffing away on his reeking cigar, "Your wife's got a fur coat, right? Sell it! Sell your car. You got a responsible job and you can put your hands on a lot of that insurance money. Steal it! You've got to or go to prison for a long time!"

It went on and on. Richard Crine paid out another twenty-six thousand before he hit a snag.

One night, working late at his office, he was altering the books, *"I thought my boss would never go. I've embezzled another two thousand for Curly. I'll cover the shortage in the books over time."*

His boss, Mr. Larkin, suddenly returned, catching Crine in the act of embezzling. He wasted no time and called the police. Finally, after Mr. Crine's story was told and retold, Lt. Detective Ted Randall of the Racket Squad took charge.

"You should've come to the police at once Mr. Crine. Let's see that clipping. And describe the dead card player to me once more."

After hours of questioning, Lt. Randall took Richard for a drive. He parked out in front of Fazzio's Pool Hall.

"What are we comin' here for, Lieutenant?" asked a very confused Richard Crine.

"I've got a surprise for you," answered Lt. Randall, as they exited the unmarked police car, "Just peek in the window, that's all, and tell me who you see."

Mr. Crine squinted through the seamy glass. "It's…it's him! It's the guy they killed! But how? He was shocked to see the very same man, Dutch Williamson; he thought was beaten to death by Curly, months before! Yes, it was the same man! Lt. Randall had a plan. He and Richard made a phone call.

Mr. Crine made the call to Curly. Curly happened to be with Walt again and was discussing his conversation with Crine over the phone, "Listen, Crine's gonna pay one last time…five thou, and it's the last one! Whaddya say we let him meet Dutch again! It'll be good for a laugh!"

After hanging up, Crine turned to the Lt., "I'll be glad when they're in jail."

"Don't forget," reminded Lt. Randall, "You broke the law too! The D.A. could indict you if he wanted to, but your boss, Mr. Larkin didn't press charges. He's willing to have you reimburse the firm. He understands the circumstances."

Next day Crine met Curly in the same hotel room. As Crine laid the money on the table, Dutch, the 'victim' came out of an adjoining bedroom, all smiles and waving to Richard.

"Okay Richie," said a rather smug Curly, "the game's over. We got your dough. Look at him," pointing to Dutch, "Here's the corpse! Well, say somthin' Dutch, so he won't get scared of a ghost!"

"Hiya chump. Nice haul," said a grinning Dutch Williamson staring down at the loot Crine had placed on the table.

It was then, Lt. Randall and three uniformed policemen burst into the room, guns drawn, "You're all under arrest." He read them their rights as they were being disarmed and handcuffed.

Later, at headquarters, Richard Crine learned he hadn't been the blackmail ring's only victim. There were several other men present.

The lieutenant addressed the group, "You all had one thing in common, fear! Fear of scandal, fear of jail. And Curly's gang traded on your fear!"

Lt. Randall reassured them, "None of you will be prosecuted for failure to report a crime. You've all been punished enough. The court has issued subpoenas so you'll have to testify against those three, of course. But if one, only one of you had come forward at the beginning of the shakedown, this affair would never have continued. You can go!"

<u>Clash of Armies</u>

It was an invasion! Somewhere in our galaxy, one life form was attacking another! Somewhere a valiant army was being crushed by an overwhelming might of a vicious invader! Michael Trent is the only man on earth who witnessed it!

It happened on a Sunday afternoon when I was watching the Yankee and Red Sox game on cable TV. "Atta boy Bernie, slice a single to left…"

Suddenly the TV screen grew snowy, and then it flickered to diagonal lines, as if the signal was being scrambled. "Aw, fer cryin' out loud…there goes the picture. I paid my cable bill this month!"

I fooled around with the dials and tightened the cable connections… "It won't come on again! Wouldn't you know this'd happen on a Sunday…when I can't call the TV repair man from Cablevision." Moving the set out from the wall…"I'll just have to try and fix it myself."

I spent the next half hour monkeying around with the set. Finally I finished. I turned the TV on again.

"Now I can see the rest of the ballgame."

But instead of the ballgame:

Fuzzy images in silhouette flickered across the screen. The images looked alien, with antenna and segmented bodies. There were hundreds of these figures, rank after rank, indistinguishable, yet clear enough to make out their odd-looking shapes. They seem to have six legs and square shaped heads with antenna and what appears to be serrated jaws. It was a frenzy of action, yet they kept and ordered line, row after row. I could barely make out some faint noises as well—almost like the sounds of a multitude of reed instruments playing in a discordant tone all together at the same time.

"Hey, what's this?" I muttered, "The picture's blurred…I can't make out these figures. They don't appear human. It must be some kind of science fiction program!"

I fooled around with the dials but the picture was still out of focus. The sound wasn't clear—seems to have been garbled, yet I can sense it was a foreign language of some sort. It appears to be an army lining up for battle!

"I must've mixed up the stations when I was fixing the set! I'm tuned into another channel! But that's funny, I don't see any science fiction program listed about a story like this!"

I checked another TV guide. Same thing. No mention of any 'War of the Worlds' movie.

"I don't get this at all. Why isn't this program listed? I'll call Dave and Bill. Maybe they know what this show is." But when I spoke to my friends…

"B-but that can't be! Are you sure? You are? Okay, Bill, thanks…"

Dave and Bill switched to every channel, but they couldn't find this show! My television set must be the only one that has it." Because, when I used the remote to change the channel, the same picture came on—all stations! There was definitely something screwy going on here.

"This is weird! How can my set be the only one, unless—unless it wasn't a show! That must be it! That must be the answer. By monkeying around with the TV, I've accidentally tuned into something that's really happening!

There was a furious shudder on the screen, high-pitched screeches of pain and shouting. Still not in any human tongue or sound. Hand to hand combat with no visible weapons. They were tearing each other limb from limb. It was all too realistic to be any special effects!

"But there's no war like this anywhere on earth…and these monstrous figures, they're certainly not human. Then it must be coming from somewhere else! Maybe from some other world or dimension. I could never be sure!"

I watched the battle continue. Line after line, row after row of invaders and defenders ripping each other apart. It was such a scene of savagery that it made me tremble with disgust. It was all too real! Maybe an interstellar conflict of some sort. But taking place—where?

"This is just incredible…and yet it was the only logical explanation. Somewhere in time and space an alien race is fighting a vicious battle and through a one-in-a-billion accident, my television set, and cable connection, picked up the images!"

The enemy was breaking through the defenses and the defenders couldn't stop their onslaught. They were losing the battle. The attackers seemed to have overwhelming numbers and they were slightly larger than their opponents!

"But where is this happening? Is it on another planet? Is it past, present, future?"

I watched the screen intently. The invading army was routing the defenders—there was a scramble to regroup—so they retreated to a trench. I could see the hordes descending on the beaten army.

"If the picture wasn't so blurred…if only I can get a clearer picture. Maybe I can figure out where this is coming from."

I pulled the set out from against the wall again, and tried to fine-tune the images. Here was a conquest in progress and I didn't even have the presence of mind to videotape the damned thing! For the next several minutes I worked frantically.

As soon as I finished, I hurredly turned on the set again! But when the picture came into focus, I saw the ball game again!

"No—I've lost it! I've got the ballgame on again."

After that, no matter what I did to the set, I was unable to tune in that conquered alien world. Finally, I gave up.

"I must have been the first man on earth to see life struggle on an alien world. But I can't prove it. It sounds so incredible that no one will ever believe me…"

So Michael walked away, for how could he have known the mistake he had made.

How could he have known that outside his house, on a small mound of earth, a furious battle had just ended?

And that one-in-a-billion accident caused his cable connection to pick up the final moments of an insect drama.

A drama in which a colony of black ants had been invaded and conquered by an army of red ants, right beneath his window!

Double-Cross

Being a cargo handler on a freighter has its advantages for John Fahraday. He was working his shift one early morning when he discovered a stowaway! No, two stowaways, an old man and a young lady.

The old man seemed agitated and yelled to the cargo handler—"Arrest this hussy—she tried to rob me!"

"P-please," said the little slip of a girl, barely five foot-one, brown eyed, brunette, "Listen to me. This old devil beat me. He knows where a treasure is buried! He owed it to me!"

"Liar," cried the old man, "Have her arrested. She tried to steal my map."

"You have a map?" questioned Fahraday.

"It's been a nightmare, Mr. Fahraday," said the young lady. "Kill him and we'll share the treasure!"

"Make me out to be a villain!" shouted the old man, his voice crackling with emotion—balding, with long, stringy hair down to his shoulders, craggy, cracked face and an aged look about him. He sprang for her and grabbed her throat. "I'll teach you…"

Startled, Fahraday struck him across the head with an iron hook. The old man was dead before he hit the floor of the hold.

"H-he's dead! Y-you killed him! Thank you." Sighed a grateful woman. "It must have been destiny that brought us together." She fell into Fahraday's arms. "H-how can I repay you?"

"We'll talk about it later," he said to her. He grabbed the limp body of the old man and retrieved the map. Was it a genuine treasure map?

They dragged the body behind some crates and hauled it out through a back hatchway near the stern of the huge ship. Unseen, undetected, they left the dock and hastily walked to Fahraday's apartment. He'd been a longshoreman for twelve years and never knew a moment's rest. Hard work, calluses, aching muscles, with constant overtime! It is a god-send if all this was true! Linda Grey was her name and she would be his meal ticket, if all this was indeed true!

She warmed up to Fahraday and convinced him to help her get that treasure. In the next days they planned their move.

"Every dime I have is tied up in this venture, Linda. I have killed for you! You're my love, my dream come true." He fell head over heels, hopelessly in love with her.

"Mmmm…that lipstick of yours makes my head swim! It's delectable. It's sweeter than nectar."

"You're an answer to my prayers, John."

They rented a skiff, brought a week's worth of supplies and made off toward a northern island off the coast of Newfoundland. They sailed for two days.

"Look baby!" said an excited Fahraday, "We've sailed right through some of the busiest shipping lanes and you've gotten through this without even getting your lovely hair mussed!" He noticed she was scribbling notes in her diary! "What's that you're writing, dear?"

"Just…just some notes on our journey. Sort of a chronicle of what we've done!"

"Trying to keep secrets from your sweetheart?" he said as he reached for the diary. "C'mon, let me see what you've really written down." She pushed his arm away, "D-don't, darling! A gal's got a right to some privacy…even from the man she's going to marry!" She smiled at him—her usual seductive glance—one which he couldn't resist. "You'll learn what's in my diary soon enough, darling!"

They spotted the island.

"The…the boat's wobbling over this current!" said Fahraday. "Hold on, we're going in."

Down through a strong undercurrent, the skiff managed to navigate over a shallow reef till they made landfall at the eastern end of the island.

"S-so, this is the island where the old man had a treasure of stolen loot buried!" exclaimed John.

"Burrr! It's cold here. The old fool picked a real out of the way spot. Let's find the crystal pillars—a spot near an abandoned mine."

An hour of hiking over forest and glade brought them to a clearing where two pillars about forty feet high marked the spot where they were to dig.

"I'll start digging right away," said an anxious Fahraday.

"Don't be greedy, pet! We've got all the time in the world. Let's get back to the boat and celebrate our love and luck first! Come on, be a good boy. I've got a surprise for you!"

He agreed, and they headed back to the boat. "Guess this does call for a celebration baby. Heh! Haven't had a bottle of Burgundy in years. You think of everything, don't you?"

Linda was prettying herself up and put on the lipstick John loved so much. "I've tried, dearest, for your sake. Get your knife and open up the bottle."

The jubilant pair drank and drained the bottle of wine. Their heads spinning; intoxicated with their triumph, they clung in a passionate embrace.

"Press your lips against mine darling. Tell me how much you love me, John!"

"I've killed for you baby…and I'll do it again!"

It was a long, passionate kiss. John's mind was racing…"Yes toots, it's going to be a memorable kiss. Your very last!" He plunged the knife squarely in her back between the shoulder blades so it would penetrate the heart!

She screamed from deep in her throat as she slowly fell to her knees and collapsed on the floor of the cabin.

"Foolish woman thought I loved her," thought John Fahraday, *"She'll never know I've just been using her to get my hands on that treasure!"*

"Die, my sweet," he whispered, "you'd never have suspected your beloved John would double-cross you, eh? Goodbye, baby, you sweet, innocent fool!"

He chuckled a bit, but something was wrong. Something was very wrong.

"F-funny taste to that lipstick! My…my throat…feels like it's on fire! T-that lipstick…it must have been poisoned! That double-crossing witch—she knew I'd taste the stuff after I kissed her…and…and…"

He gasped, couldn't catch his breath! He stumbled, grabbing at his throat…"She…she planned it…this way! Of all the dirty, lousy…Arrrggghh!"

When the police found the dead couple they discovered a last entry in Linda's diary…

'This fool John really believes I love him! He'll never know I was just using him to get the treasure…"

Face to Face

There is nothing on earth more personal as battle, and still nothing less personal. It is personal because it involves human beings in mortal combat, and non-personal because the opposing soldiers regard each other as merely objects to be overcome on the way to victory, or defeat! There is rarely any personal enmity, any selfish point of view brought by one soldier against his foe. But what happens when two enemies, unknown to each other come…face to face?

It was one of the fiercest engagements of the Spanish-American War, and one of the few times when the enemy gave the Americans a fight to a standstill! The ranks held on both sides, each attack was driven off, and valor claimed its toll! The tide turned, then back again. Attack and counterattack. The loses were heavy on both sides. The armies had had enough and both retreated from the battlefield. And with the retreat, the officers counted their survivors.

"Didn't Sgt. Blaine come back with us?" asked a recruit.

"Last time I saw him, he was shot in the leg, but I thought he made it back." Answered another soldier.

"Blaine lost the company banner," said a third, "And he won't come back without it, wounded or not."

Between the two forces stretched the ruin and desolation of no man's land, peaceful and quiet now, a place marked with the ravages of battle. And here, while he crawled among the ruins, looking for the company standard he had dropped, Sergeant Blaine prayed that the wound in his leg would let up until he found what he was looking for.

"I can't go back," was his thought, *"without the banner. It was in my charge and I dropped it when I was hit. I've got to find it."*

Off in the distance, maybe fifty yards away, he spotted the torn company standard. He was crawling towards it when, *"Blast it! The enemy!"* He saw a Spanish soldier peering at him from behind the rubble of a deserted adobe.

"Looks like he's wounded too," thought Blaine, *"in the shoulder. All he's got is a bayonet while I have one bullet left in my rifle! I've got to get him before he gets me, and I can see he's thinking the same thing."*

Blaine managed to get up on one knee and aim his rifle at the Spaniard, who was maybe twenty-five feet away, half exposed from behind the jagged adobe wall, holding his bayonet, ready to throw it at the Sgt.

And so the two enemies watched and waited for each other to make the first move…the move that would spell disaster to one…because neither would have a second chance, if the move failed!

"He's getting set to come at me! I've got to make my one shot count." Blaine aimed the rifle at the soldier, *"Take my time, aim right, and then..."*

Blaine was trained to think of the enemy as a faceless foe to be destroyed, but it must be done carefully and without recklessness, because the enemy would do the same to him. And so he waited, patiently waited, his finger on the trigger, while the Spaniard stumbled forward, weakly, now fully exposed!

"Got to admit, he's got courage!" he said aloud.

The Sgt's finger tightened around the trigger, *"Can't wait any longer, can't let him get any closer...the time is...now!"*

But just as the American was about to squeeze the trigger, the Spaniard stopped, leaned over, and...

"Well, look at that!" He whispered to himself, "Seems we're both here for the same reason. He's after his company's flag too!"

"Hey, Americano!" shouted the Spaniard, tossing the American standard over to the Sergeant, while he picked up his own standard.

And so both soldiers limped off the field of battle, two enemies on missions that each one respected and honored...and accomplished.

As they walked back to their own lines, with banner in hand they turned and waved at each other from a distance.

Glamour Boy

Like any other patrolman, Jim Donovan dreamed of the bright lights and action in mid-town...of a beat where things happened and a young rookie could distinguish himself. Then he got his break and half-wished it never came along!

"Donovan, come in my office," said Captain Barnes, "I may have a job for you."

As Donovan sat down the Captain continued, "How's your dancing, Donovan? Do you get along with the ladies? Don't laugh—this is business!"

Donovan squirmed his 6 foot frame a little. He had dark hair, handsome features and eager to please. "I…I guess I get by, Sir," came the answer, "Why?"

The Captain, a man in his fifties and looking to retire soon, explained his plan. "The midtown squad is having trouble with these socialites. They show a fortune in jewels in the swank nightclubs, then complain when someone fingers them and they lose their precious trinkets!"

Holding his fingers to his chin, Donovan responded, "What will I be doing, sir?"

"Go undercover, hang around with them. Drift in and out of the night spots and get a line on the gang behind the robberies. Pose as an out-of-town playboy. You got the looks! The job shouldn't be too hard to take!"

The boys in the locker room roared when Jim Donovan confessed about the new assignment. 'Glamour Puss' was the mildest term heard!

Donovan was changing out of his uniform to his street clothes. "Lay off, I didn't ask for the job—but I'll do my best while I'm on the case!"

He had a robust expense account and a new, well-tailored suit for the occasion. It took some time at first…young Donovan drifted around the better places, feeling his way, gradually getting to know the usual crowd.

He entered a ritzy nightclub one evening and was called over by a gentleman he had met before.

"There's Jim! You remember, Clair. I introduced him last night. Come over Jim and join us."

"Thanks," answered Jim, straightening his bow tie, "Hello Gordon."

Clair Stevens was a stunning blonde, dressed in a silky red gown and wearing a breathtaking necklace, loaded with precious gems. Gordon, her brother, was a rich lawyer frequenting this spot as a regular.

"You're a man of mystery," said Clair, "You never tell us anything about yourself, Jim."

"I didn't want to bore you," Jim said, dryly, "Care to dance?"

As he waltzed around the dance floor, a pleasant thought entered Jim's mind, *"If the boys could only see me now."* He turned and spotted a shady-looking man staring intently at Clair's jewels. *"That character,"* thought Jim, *"I've seen him around somewhere, and always near people with money and jewels."*

The man approached Gordon, "I met you at the club Gordon, didn't I? Good evening Miss Stevens. I see you're wearing that gorgeous necklace again!"

"Why not?" she responded with a subtle smile, "It's no use to me in the jewel case at home."

It was a casual meeting, but young Donovan heard enough to make him think and suspect the man was up to no good. He said good night to all but didn't go home.

The suspect, Channing, offered a ride to Gordon, his sister and Gordon's date, a red-head with an expensive fur and bracelet. "Don't bother Channing," said Gordon Stevens, "we can get a cab.'

"Don't be silly Gordon, I'll be glad to drop you off."

They accepted his offer and got in. Meantime, a half a block down the street, Donovan hailed a cab, showed the driver his badge and told him to follow Channing's car.

It was nearly three hours of waiting in a dark alley opposite the residence of the Gordon's, after Channing Drake delivered the threesome to the door. Donovan's patience was rewarded.

He saw three, well dressed men pull up in the same car Channing Drake had driven the socialites to their high rise.

"Drake isn't with these characters. I'll have to follow them." Donovan waited till the men entered the elevator.

Checking the apartment directory at the concierge's station, he found the apartment number and floor of the Gordon's. All was quiet on the eighth floor, but when Donovan tried the knob, Gordon' apartment door was unlocked. He opened it slowly and entered.

Drawing his revolver he overheard one of the men. "They're all tied up, including the maid! The chief said the ice is in the jewelry case—probably in the bedroom."

"Okay boys, this party is over, we start the next one down at the station house."

"It's a cop!" cried one of the hoods, "Someone fingered us!"

Donovan was just beginning to read them their rights and disarm them, when—he was struck from behind and knocked cold. The third member of the gang had slipped around a bedroom and came up on Donovan from behind.

Next day, feeling like a fool with a terrible headache, he reported to the precinct headquarters and Captain Barnes.

"So, I bungled the job! They got away before I could get to my cell phone and call for backup. Want me off the case Captain?" Donovan's head was bandaged and it was still throbbing, but he suffered no concussion!

"You're stuck with it, Donovan. The boys who made the actual take didn't know you. Channing wasn't there either to identify you, as you reported, so you can go on eating caviar with the big shots and nab that gang!"

Gordon, his sister Clair and Gordon's date were sworn to secrecy about Jim Donovan's real identity…and they introduced him around to help in his assignment.

On one such evening in a plush night club, Gordon Stevens introduced Donovan to a very rich widow.

"Mrs. Lacey," said Clair, "this is Jim Donovan, a friend of mine from out of town."

"I've heard of you Mrs. Lacey," said a rather overwhelmed Donovan, "and your famous jewel collection!"

Naturally, there was Channing Drake, hanging around the night spot. Donovan, recognizing him, turned to say, "Foolish, isn't it? Tempting fate wearing all that jewelry!"

"You're too suspicious Donovan," replied a rather coy Channing, "No one would bother Mrs. Lacey."

The rookie had another hunch; this time he was determined to do the job right. He was deep in thought as they bid each other goodnight. *"She must have more than a hundred thousand in diamonds around her neck right now!"* He noticed Drake and some of his henchmen outside the nightclub climbing into Channing's car. Looks very much like they planned to follow Mrs. Lacey's limo. Donovan hopped in a cab. *"They're the same boys that jumped me! I have a hunch Drake is going along on this job himself. I hope he does, I'll be right behind him and we'll get the whole gang!"*

He was right! Drake and his gang forced Mrs. Lacey's limo off to the curb, jumped out with guns drawn, "Start taking off the rocks lady! These guns are loaded!"

Suddenly, a rather nervous crony yelled, "Lookout boss, we got trouble." Before he could utter another word, Donovan disarmed him and punched him in the jaw. "Drop your weapons," Donovan demanded.

"Hey, Drake," shouted another of his cronies. "…it's the same guy—a cop…ugh!" Donovan socked him as well.

Drake, his face covered with a neckerchief, wheeled around and pointed his automatic at Donovan. "So you're the snooper who tipped the last job. You won't get in our hair again!"

"Take it easy, Drake. You're done for and you know it."

Young Donovan wasn't bluffing as Channing Drake's game was up. Two uniformed officers grabbed Drake from behind. Donovan made sure he had time to call for backup. Later Drake and his men were booked at the precinct.

"You look a little sloppy, Jim," joked the captain, "the girls in the bright spots wouldn't know you now!"

"I guess not, Sir," quipped Donovan, "By the way, when do I go back in uniform?"

"Not a chance, Jim," said the Captain, "that boyish charm of yours would be wasted on an ordinary shift."

"What luck! I'll probably spend the rest of my career getting ulcers with the celebrities or from undercover work." Donovan smiled, hands in his pants pockets, bouncing back and forth on his heels.

"Someone has to do the job, Jim," reasoned Captain Barnes, "I used to pound the beat ages ago and even I had to put up with all the small talk."

He's Coming!

Jay Prescott got the phone call early that morning.

"Listen, Prescott…the story hasn't leaked out to the press yet, but I heard it from one of the guards. Peterson just escaped from the state pen! You know what that means."

Prescott began to shake, tremble. He was an elderly gentleman, wealthy, wearing an expensive hand tailored suit, vest, gold chain, button-down collar with a diamond pin as big as a thumb nail fastened through the middle of his silk tie. His temples were gray but he sported a full head of hair. He cringed as the caller went on.

"Prescott, are you still there?"

"Y-yes, th-thanks for the tip! Sure I know what that means. It-m-means, he's coming. He's coming for me!"

Moments later…

Prescott phoned the local precinct. "Police headquarters, Sergeant Ryerson speaking…"

"This is Jay Prescott, Sergeant. I just received some disturbing news that Peterson has escaped from jail. He swore he'd break out and come and get me. I want a police guard at my house. I demand it!"

There was a knock at the door.

"Hold on Sergeant, someone's at the door!"

Prescott peered cautiously from his second floor bedroom window and was relieved to see two police officers knocking on his front door. "Open up, it's the police," came a loud voice.

A surprised Prescott ran down and met the officers at the door.

"I was just talking to headquarters…" he began. "We beat you to the punch Mr. Prescott.

Word of Peterson's escape came over the wire immediately after they found his cell empty. We're here to set up a twenty-four hour guard on your house."

"Not that'll do much good!" said the other officer.

"Wh-what do you mean?" asked a nervous Prescott, his voice trembling.

This was no ordinary prison break, Mr. Prescott." The officer went on, "Peterson made himself invisible!"

The first officer continued, "Only an invisible man could have slipped by the guards at the gate! He was discovered experimenting with chemicals in the dispensary. Notes and a partial formula was discovered. He's a brilliant chemist and we know he was attempting this sort of thing, but ignored the possibility. Well, he seems to have succeeded!"

"Impossible," cried Prescott, "Y-you you're just trying to scare me. Right?"

"No sir," said the first officer, "We don't crack jokes about serious matters like this."

"Right," agreed the other officer, rather dryly, "There's no guarantee that he won't slip past us, but you stay inside, and let's hope for the best."

Prescott was thoroughly shaken. *"Peterson is coming for me,"* his mind raced, as he walked back up the stairs, *"They'll never be able to stop him. He'll get me sure!"*

His thoughts went back to the events that led up to his predicament:

"I framed Peterson, sure. I wanted all the rights to his chemical patents. The only way I could swing it was by trumping up a false charge that would land him in jail. I never knew he would develop a way to make himself invisible. I know he is a genius—but this!"

He peered from behind the curtains on the second story bedroom window.

He was thinking hard about the scene in the courtroom, the day Peterson was convicted.

"You did this to me Prescott! But I'll get out sooner or later, sooner than you think! And I'll come back for you! I'll come back for you, Prescott. You can take that to the bank."

Peterson was allowed to continue his experiments in prison, being a licensed chemist, he helped the dispensing of drugs to the inmates from the prison hospital. The prison administration kept a close eye on him, but he managed to evade their scrutiny and secretly developed his invisibility formula.

Prescott realized his hopeless situation. He decided it would be best to clear out of town altogether, so he began to empty his wall safe and gather all incriminating evidence of the trumped up charge he created. His briefcase was filled with patents he had stolen. Suddenly, he heard the door downstairs creaking open!

"Th-the door downstairs just opened by itself!" cried Prescott.

"S-somebody's coming up the stairs! I-I can hear him. No! No!"

He fainted.

A few moments later. "What happened?" asked one of the policemen.

"I don't know," answered his partner, "I used a skeleton key to get inside and see if everything was all right! When I got up here, Prescott was yelling his head off."

The policeman opened Prescott's briefcase…"But it look at his briefcase, it's stuffed with documents about the Peterson case—and what appears to be falsified patents! Looks like they'll reopen that fraud case now that they have fresh evidence!"

As the officers were calling an ambulance for Prescott and gathering up the spilled contents of the briefcase—back at the state prison…

Just moments earlier…A guard passing Peterson's cell hollered down to another guard to come over.

"L-look!" he shouted as he pointed to Peterson's bunk.

"It's Peterson!" exclaimed the other guard. "He's taking on form in thin air!"

Sure enough, Peterson was ever so slowly materializing. The guards opened his cell as Peterson came to and explained to them what happened.

"Yes, I made myself invisible so I could escape and prove Prescott was guilty. But the formula is imperfect. It made me black out as soon as it took effect and I've been lying here in my cell ever since!"

Over the Wires

In 1829, Samuel Finley Breese Morse, an art student in London, wrote home to his mother in America…

'I wish that in an instant I could let you hear my arrival, but three thousand miles are not passed over in an instant, and we must wait four long weeks before we can hear from each other…'

All the time he worked at his painting, Samuel Morse also studied electricity. Returning to America on the packet ship *Sully,* Morse shared a table with a passenger who had been studying electricity in Paris.

"Tell me, Mr. Jackson," said Morse, "How far can electric current be sent? How fast can it travel?"

Jackson was a tall man with gray hair, clean shaven, wearing a black suit with ascot. "We did one experiment where a spark jumped out of one end of a long coil of wire the moment it had been started from the other end. I do not see why a wire laid around the world would not act the same way."

For the rest of the voyage, Morse stayed in his cabin, thinking and scribbling in his notebook.

"*I can control the electric current,*" he was thinking to himself, "*and break it up into long and short flashes. If I used a code, these flashes could spell out words!*"

By the time the *Sully* docked, Morse had notebooks full of model telegraphs. He also had the Morse code of dots and dashes.

Speaking to the Captain as he was disembarking, "One of these days you'll hear about the invention of an electric telegraph, Captain Pell. Then you can say the idea was worked out aboard your ship."

Samuel Morse taught art classes at New York University. He lived in a small room which served both as art studio and science laboratory. Alfred Vail, one of Morse's students, became his partner. They begged Alfred's father, Judge Stephen Vail, to invest some money in Morse's invention. Morse showed the Judge a model, "These springs and wheels come from and old wooden clock. A current of electricity makes the pencil mark dots and dashes on a moving strip of paper."

Judge Vail speaking to Morse and the Judge's son in his office, "It's probably a fool idea, but let's try it out. I will give you two thousand dollars and not a cent more. If the machine works, you might ask Congress for more money."

The two men fitted a shop in the corner of Judge Vail's factory in Morristown, New Jersey. Here they improved their model and got a patent on it. One day they asked Judge Vail to come and test it.

Judge Vail asked his son, "Send this message over your wire son, and we'll see if Professor Morse at the other end can tell us what it says."

The message was sent.

Morse repeated it, "It says, 'A patient waiter is no loser.'"

The Judge was duly impressed, "Well, well! I'll be darned! It works!" He patted Morse on his back.

In 1843, when the men were able to send a message through three miles of wire, they took their instrument to Washington, D.C.

"If Congress would appropriate $30,000 we could connect Washington with Baltimore. A telegraph can work over forty-four miles, as well as over three!" Morse explained to a Senator.

"Thirty thousand dollars to string a wire between Washington and Baltimore? Why not a stairway to the Moon?" an incredulous Senator said to a colleague.

"Maybe we should grant half the sum to Mr. Morse and half to that other crackpot who wants to experiment in hypnotism," the other Senator said with a hearty laugh.

Feb. 23 was the last day Congress would meet that year. Morse sat in the Senate all day long. At eleven o'clock at night, with only one hour of the session left, there were still one hundred and forty bills waiting to be voted on.

Morse walked back to his hotel thinking to himself, *"I might as well go back to New York. After I've paid the hotel bill and bought my railroad ticket, I'll have thirty-seven cents in my pocket!"* It was a cold, snowy night which made things seem even more hopeless and dismal.

The next morning, when Morse came downstairs, he found a visitor waiting for him. She was Annie Ellsworth, daughter of The Commissioner of Patents.

"Your telegraph bill was passed, Mr. Morse! My father saw President Tyler sign it! Congratulations!"

Morse was so shaken he could not speak…then…he grasped the lady's hand with both of his and said, "You and your father are my true friends. Now I ask a favor. When our telegraph line is ready, will you be the first to send a message?"

"I shall be proud and happy to have that honor," Anne said with a wide grin.

Morse hired workmen and started constructing the line from Washington to Baltimore. His plan was to lay the wire underground. But, to his chagrin, he found the current ran out of the wire into the earth. Morse tried to wrap the wire in cotton, to insulate it so the current could not escape. This proved to be too expensive. In dismay he spoke to his friend Ezra Cornell—"We have only insulated five miles of wire, and have already spent over twenty thousand dollars. What can we do?"

"Why not run the wires overhead instead of underground? Then the current cannot leak out. We can keep the wires from touching the poles by stringing them through necks of broken bottles."

Weeks passed while the long thin line of wire stretched on wooden poles between the two cities. Many people were frightened by it. They were worried about getting electrocuted!

Finally the line was finished. On May 24, 1844, a distinguished group of citizens met in the Supreme Court Chambers in Washington, D.C. They watched in awe as Samuel Morse sent Anne Ellsworth's message to Alfred Vail in Baltimore…

W-H-A-T H-A-T-H G-O-D W-R-O-U-G-H-T-!

Rendezvous with George Mara

James Kendrick seemed to act strangely whenever the jolly little man was close by. James Kendrick behaved as if one thing he dreaded most of all in the world was a—"Rendezvous with George Mara."

James Kendrick was in the midst of a busy morning at the office when he receives an unexpected call:

"W-what's that?" Kendrick said shocked, "Good old Louie Templeton passed away last night? I…I can hardly believe it!"

Kendrick hung up the phone and walked slowly out of the office. He was a tall, lean, sandy-haired fellow with a touch of gray at the temples, clean shaven wearing a tan business suit this day.

"It must've been quite a shock," said a female colleague of Kendrick to another coworker, as he passed them by, "Lou Templeton was one of his closest friends."

"Poor Jim," replied the younger gentleman, "It's as if he lost his own brother." They watched him as he left the office.

The next day is a melancholy occasion for Jim Kendrick.

At the gravesite he thought to himself, "I've been so upset about this whole mess that I never even thought to ask how this terrible thing happened to him!"

He approached a friend to inquire—"Tell me, Dave, what happened to Lou? He was in perfect health when I spoke to him a few days ago."

"Thought you knew," his friend answered, "Car accident. Broken neck. Poor old Lou never recovered consciousness. It's a real tragedy."

Kendrick suddenly noticed a curious-looking man lighting a cigar with a broad grin on his face. He stood, maybe, 5' 2", stout, with a loud plaid jacket and light-colored bow tie. His hair, parted in the middle was straight and cropped short about the ears.

Kendrick commented about this character to his friend Dave, "There's one person who doesn't seem to think it's a tragedy. That pudgy little feller…he seems to be enjoying himself. Who is he anyway? I've never seen him before."

"Oh, that guy," responded his friend, "Name's George Mara. He was with Lou when the car piled up. Mighty lucky little man… climbed out of the wreck without a scratch!"

"George Mara, eh?" said Kendrick, rather dryly. "Don't recall Lou ever mentioning him. Know anything about the guy?"

"Not a blessed thing. He's a complete mystery Jim. Where he's from…who he is…nobody knows."

They watched as the short, stout man with the funny grin walked away.

"You seem awfully interested in this Mara fella, Jim. Any particular reason?"

"He…he puzzles me," answered Kendrick, "A man who grins like that at a funeral might be a real whacko or a sinister character or… who knows?"

The next day, having thrust all thought of the pudgy little man from his mind, Jim is on his way to the office…when someone yelled—"FIRE!"

The adjacent building was in flames and many people trapped on the upper floors. The aftermath claimed many lives.

Kendrick spoke to a stranger "Do you know how this terrible fire started?"

"There isn't even a hint about what caused it," said the young woman who saw the incident from the very beginning and was still pretty shaken.

Kendrick turned to leave when he bumped into Mara! "Ooops! I—I'm terribly sorry…"

"Entirely my fault Mr. Kendrick," said Mara, "We seem to be fated to meet at the most melancholy times, don't we?" It was Mara alright, same smug grin, same cigar dangling from the corner of his mouth; same bow tie and jacket.

Without another word, Kendrick walked quickly away.

Several days later, Mr. Kendrick was at his desk in the office when a co-worker showed him the morning paper. "Hot item from San Francisco, Mr. Kendrick. A bridge collapsed on the coast…every single pedestrian and driver lost. Here, read about it."

Kendrick was even more stunned when he saw the front page photo. The *San Francisco Call* had a picture of the collapsed bridge and there was George Mara being interviewed by a reporter.

“It can’t be,” Kendrick cried aloud.

“You look like you’ve just seen a ghost,” the startled colleague said.

A week passed, Jim Kendrick was enjoying an evening at home watching TV when a bulletin broke: “We interrupt this program for a special news bulletin, just received. A derailment on the Rock Island line just outside of Chicago. It is one of the most costly in railway history. A head-on collision destroyed two passenger trains with at least several hundred dead. No survivors!…”

The correspondent was interviewing an eyewitness…

“It’s George Mara,” said a shocked Kendrick…”That grinning little twerp is everywhere, wherever there’s a disaster. Who is he anyway?”

In the days that followed, Jim is visibly shaken by what has happened. His work is affected until his boss realizes Kendrick needs an early vacation.

“You’ve been working too hard lately Jim. I think a brief vacation will get you back on track, and so I’ve arranged for you to represent us at the Consolidated Conference in L.A. Go by boat. Take an extended cruise. It’ll relax those jangled nerves or yours.”

Delighted by the chance to forget his forebodings, James Kendrick prepares to enjoy himself thoroughly.

He was boarding the cruise ship with two red-cap porters carrying some of his luggage. As he approached the dock entrance he stopped short to see George Mara waiting by the entranceway!

“This promises to be a most interesting trip, Mr. Kendrick! I’ve looked forward to your company for a long, long time!”

Kendrick, in a panic, ran from the dock.

"Mr. Kendrick," shouted a porter loading his suitcases on a dolly, "Where are you going? Whatta ya want us to do with the luggage?"

"T-throw it overboard for all I care! I-I'm not going on that ship!"

James Kendrick flees in terror, stopping only when he reaches the safety of his own apartment.

His thoughts are racing, *"Am I acting like a fool? Or is this man Mara a deadly omen...the 'Kiss-of-death?' All I know is that I hope I never see him again."*

Huddled in the security of his apartment, James is too frightened to make any plans for the conference. Then, two days after the ship departs…

A news bulletin on the radio…"The cruise liner *'Constellation'* has been lost at sea. No communication since yesterday morning. The Coast Guard reports officially the ship has disappeared with no trace. All aboard presumed dead. They will continue air-sea rescue for another few days…"

"T-that includes George Mara! At last he's gone!"

A quick phone call and James is able to make an air line reservation…

"This flight can still get me to that conference in time, "thought Kendrick, as he got in the ticket line, "There's a terrible weight off my shoulders with…with him out of the way!"

Despite his resolve not to worry, James finds himself searching the faces around him.

"This is stupid," he was thinking, "I know he was lost at sea, and yet…yet"

Though there is no trace of the man he dreads, James Kendrick is unable to relax as he takes his seat on board the plane.

"We're about to taxi for take-off, Sir," alerted the stewardess, noticing Kendrick was outwardly apprehensive, "Is everything all right?"

"It will be…" answered a visibly shaken Kendrick, "As soon as we get into the air!"

Suddenly the plane stops, reverses back to the hangar entrance to pick up a last minute passenger. A V.I.P., no doubt!

The door swings open and a shadowy figure enters the plane.

To Kendrick's relief it was just another businessman with a first class position. Being in first class also, the man asks Kendrick, "Is this seat taken, sir?"

"Huh? Why—why you're not…" said Kendrick nervously, but with a relieved sigh!

"Please sit down, my friend. It's a real pleasure to have you aboard."

Relaxing at last, James Kendrick prepares to enjoy his trip. A moment later the jet soars into the sky—the voice of the captain greeting the passengers.

"This is your Captain speaking. I'm pleased to welcome you on flight 519. In another moment…you will be enroute to your…uh destination!"

Kendrick knew that voice, as he shuddered in horror. There was no mistake—it was George Mara piloting the plane!

Sidney Chester's Wife

It was no wonder that Lucy Chester stood on the long lonely stretch of sandy shore, listening to the dirge of the March wind, to the fierce dash of green waves on the beach, to their rolling thunder as they foamed in a fury at her feet—no wonder that she had been standing there almost an hour, listening and watching the sullen clouds scurry through the sky, for the day and her surroundings were in perfect accord with her spirit, that restless, tempted, rebellious spirit of hers that all her life, had led through such gloomy ways.

She had dressed herself in a black woolen dress, clinging material that draped gracefully around her slender, well-rounded figure. She wrapped a thick scarlet kerchief over her hair—lustrous dark hair that waved from a white parting in loose bands back to a coil above her neck.

Her face was not beautiful, despite the warm redness of her lips, the dusky glow of her eyes, the tender tint of her complexion—at least, no one but Sidney Chester, her husband, had ever thought her perfect beyond compare, and he was of such a different mould from her that all his compliments and rough, honest flattery never could bring even one thrill of glad pride or shy delight to her heart. Yet she had married him, knowing that every fiber of her being was at variance with him, knowing that he never would be anything to her, and that she gave herself to him simply and solely because she was so heart-sick and heart-sore with her never-ending fight with her destiny—a destiny that forced her to such hard work to make a living. He had a comfortable income and home, and when he had awkwardly asked her to "have him," she had thought anything was better than such never-ending misery as hers.

So she married him. And now, three years later, Sidney Chester's wife was standing on the ocean beach, this raw windy March day, with pale cheeks and sad, unrestful eyes into which occasionally came sudden gusty looks of passionate recklessness, followed by cold, pitiful resolution, and wild, anxious desperation.

For the crisis in her life had come to her. Into her hands fate had "thrust the disposal of her future," to her, that day, was permitted her choice, her awful choice between—the dark, monotonous, joyless life that had never been so unendurable as very recently—simple endurance, until death released her, with Sidney Chester, or—such delirious happiness as took her breath away to think of Leonard Pennington. Poor Lucy! She had met him, and casual acquaintance had ripened into friendliness, and then—somehow, she never knew exactly how or where, they had come to understand that they loved each other. Leonard Pennington, the rich, idle, aesthetic man of the world, who was able and determined to do just as he chose, and do it well, whom women loved, who men envied, and she, obscure, shyly retiring, not beautiful, and Sidney Chester's wife!

It was one of those problems whose solution was impossible—why these two should have been allowed such terrible entanglement; why, with her peculiar nature, her romantic, morbid disposition, her intensely. She longed for that appreciation and exquisite tenderness and masterful devotion as Leonard offered her.

He was a very handsome man—just as the moment when Lucy turned her pale face down the shore, his blue eyes were all lit up with simling eagerness as he hurried up his rather leisurely walk, and went up to her.

"Well, Lucy, I'm really surprised and delighted to find you here, as you promised to be!" He took her gloved hand in his, and he could feel their trembling coldness through the cloth.

"What's the matter, darling? Is the sea breeze too strong, or—"

He wistful eyes went up to his face in a searching glance that pierced him to his very soul.

"Oh, Leonard, why did you come? Why didn't you stay away, and leave me to battle this alone? What am I to do?"

The wistfulness was gone now, and a wild excitement was in her eyes, that matched the rising passion in her voice.

He drew her closer to him, still holding her trembling hands in his strong grip. He smiled indulgently, tenderly. There was something of self satisfaction in the smile on his face.

"My sweet child, is it a fight between a deluded loyalty to him"—he nodded carelessly towards a group of houses far inland, one of which was Sidney Chester's home—"and—what your true, loving heart wants you to do. Darling, you'll never should regret having chosen between us—do you think you will? Do you think if you come to me that you will be unhappy? Think of it, Lucy—forever with me!" and gazed earnestly into her eyes.

"Oh, yes. But—the sin, the awful, awful sin—adultery!"

"I cannot think so dearest," he returned, in a patient, tender tone. "You are excited and morbid or you would look on this as we've done before when we discussed it quietly. You know you have said it was right, that we belonged together. It's a divine right of love, that ours would be a true marriage. That you would divorce Sidney. My darling, you asked me to meet you here to tell me you're ready to go through with it. I'm waiting for the answer that'll make us both the happiest lovers in all the world."

Stake-Out

When Dave Renaldi was appointed a detective and assigned to the Safe and Loft Squad, he was jubilant! Dave thought he'd see excitement every day—instead he spent endless hours doing nothing but watch a warehouse! He and detective Sam Keonig were on a 'Stake-Out.'

Patrolman Dave Renaldi read the police bulletins every day! As a result, he spotted Max Sigrid entering a liquor store:

"Drop the gun max," ordered Officer Renaldi, "You're under arrest. Let's go." Max was a three time loser.

Back at headquarters, the following day, Patrolman Renaldi, on the force for two years was congratulated on a nice neat job and collar… as a result, he was made Detective, Third Grade.

"You'll work with Sam Koenig, Dave," said Chief Lawson, "He's with the Safe and Loft Squad!"

The two men met and went out on their first assignment. "How do we operate, Sam," asked a very excited Renaldi.

"We mostly sit in our squad car somewhere waiting," answered Sam, rather dryly, "Sometimes we waste a lot of time waiting. And sometimes the waiting pays off!"

Koenig took Renaldi to headquarters first. He showed him the known criminals who specialized in safe and loft robberies first.

"We watch for these men, tail them when we get a line on them to see if they're going straight or not," advised Sam.

He showed screen projections of the criminals—"This is Jimmy Webber," said Sam, pointing to his profile—He was a real rugged looking character, with a full head of black hair, square chin and a nose which was broken and had a bump in the middle. "The boys call him *Shiv.* He just quit a job with a furrier. I've been watching him and his pals."

The two detectives hopped in their unmarked car and sped down to the seedy part of town. "Where are we going?" inquired Dave, "Is this Webber's neighborhood?"

"No," answered Sam, "He worked near here. We're going to watch the furrier's place. He may come back with a few of his pals!"

Sam checked his revolver then continued, "When he does, Shiv'll carry a gun on this job. He's a three time loser. The next time he goes to prison, it'll be for life!"

Dave Renaldi got to hate that building. They spent most of their time in the next week parked outside. On the second day, they answered an "Assist Patrolman" call on the police broadcast.

They apprehended the thief and that action earned Dave Renaldi a commendation—but it didn't interrupt their stake-out…their wait for Shiv Webber.

"You did a nice job, Dave…but remember," advised Sam, "Don't give Webber any free shots. Webber doesn't miss."

Finally, after twelve days on stake-out, they got results. A dark sedan stopped outside the building at ten thirty p m. Several men got out and entered the building.

"They're the ones we want Dave. But let's wait a while."

"Hurry it up Shiv," said one of the hoods.

"Relax, Butch. The alarm is off…we're in the money!" Said Shiv, grim-faced as usual.

Webber blew the safe expertly. They cleaned out eleven thousand in cash, and then picked out the most valuable furs to take with them.

As they came out with the loot and goods, Dave and Sam moved in, after calling for back-up. Webber fired one shot, and then ran! He ran, but Dave Renaldi was faster and caught up with him.

Sam reported into headquarters. "Yeah! We got Webber and his pals. Tell the Chief that Renaldi tackled Webber even when being fired at!"

Yes, Dave Renaldi learned that waiting was the biggest part of his job—but he learned that it usually paid off in arrests

Street Fighter

Middleweight contender, Charles (Chuck) Frawley, standing alone in his corner, was ready to mix it up with the second rank Middleweight, Smasher Ramos. Chuck's thoughts were racing back to his past, to the events that landed him in this unlikely place. He was heir to his father's company, worth millions of dollars, yet he chose the life of a brawler, a professional prize fighter.

* * * * * * * * *

It was only three years ago when it all started. Charles, his memory shifting back to a dark alley, was medium height and build, blonde hair, hazel eyes. He was taking a short cut on the Lower East side in Manhattan. Three hoods approached him as he walked through the narrow lane.

"Hey, man, what ya got in your pockets?"

Chuck stopped cold and turned.

"Who wants to know?"

Suddenly the three jumped him and worked him over. He desperately tried to fight back but they overpowered him, kicking him senseless. They stole his money, jewelry and his fancy jacket and left him bleeding and near unconscious in the gutter. The police arrived moments later in their patrol car. They warned him about the neighborhood and advised him to return to the safety of Scarsdale where he lived.

The next day he was at his father's office. "You let those muggers beat you for a dollar?" his father said, sternly, sitting behind his huge oak desk. He was a tall man in a three piece business suit, dark tie, sandy colored hair, deep, penetrating eyes with a wrinkled free complexion for a man of fifty.

"Charles, you're a hard-headed fool."

"It was a matter of principle dad!" Charles explained, rather matter-of-factly.

"Principles are for boys at Harvard, not Greenwich Village. Son, you need a keeper!"

The next day, the household had a new chauffeur, Herbert. He was big, solid, husky and wiry with a pushed-in nose, cauliflower ear that gave away his former profession.

"I'm going to New York, Herbert, I won't need you…"

"Sorry, Mr. Charles…I have orders to stay with you."
"So, you're my keeper…a bodyguard! I can't believe my father would do this to me."

"Your dad worries about you. He hired me to protect you."

"You're an ex-pug, aren't you, Herbert?"

"I had a few bouts!" he said modestly. But Charles knew he was a seasoned professional.

"Once I boxed Rocky Fletcher for the Middleweight title!" he boasted.

"Then teach me to protect myself! Teach me to box!" implored Charles, touching Herbert's arm.

Herbert reluctantly agreed and set up a gym in their three-car garage. He equipped it with all the necessary boxing items—punching bags, skip-ropes, barbells and a small ring.

For the next several weeks, they spared. Charles learned to punch from the shoulder, throw left hooks, jab straight and jar a man's head back…how to slip punches, weave and bob…and all the useful tricks a wily pro picks up in a decade of ring work.

* * * * * * * * * * *

Charles made his college boxing team and went on to win the Inter-Collegiate title…and guaranteed himself a scrapbook full of impressive clippings!

"You've done well in college Charles," his father said one day at his office. "Now its time you came into the firm. Some day you'll take over the mills."

"Dad, you've been watching over me like a mother hen all my life! I want to get out on my own. I want to go into the ring—to be a professional boxer."

His father was stunned. "A common fighter?" Charlie's father clicked his tongue in disgust, "Charlie, you're heir to a fortune! Why this—this return to the jungle?"

"Boxing is a science, dad. It's the most independent thing I can think of. In that ring, it's just me against another man…any man."

His father couldn't talk Charles out of his chosen career. Eventually he signed a contract with Phil Mario, who managed a couple of contenders, and soon he was living in the sleazy, sweat-filled world of the prize fighter.

"Charles Randal Frawley…what kind of moniker is that for a fighter?" said Mario as he laced up Charles gloves in the gym. "Let's see…" He thought a moment. "We'll call you Chuck Grabowski… now, there's a name with respect!"

With Herby, the chauffeur, in his corner as well, Charles made the circuit of small clubs around the country, dropping some decisions, winning most. He learned the trade well. 'Chuck Grabowski' was becoming a headliner.

Now, facing his biggest test, Chuck was up against Smasher Ramos, the number two contender for Middleweight. He would fight him at Madison Square Garden.

* * * * * * * * * * *

His thoughts returned to the ring where he faced a great challenge. Smasher was rough, strong and crafty with over fifty fights under his belt and winning most of them by knock-out. But Chuck made him miss a lot, with his inside jabs and lateral moves. Smasher kept coming in, bobbing and weaving, ducking, like a smaller version of Rocky Marciano. He peeks out of his shell and for a split second his head is an open target.

That's all Chuck needs to flash his solid right, straight from his shoulder, with his entire body weight behind the blow!

Smasher goes down—and he never heard the referee count to ten. The crowd roars. It was deafening. Chuck had won the big won. After the fight, Charles walked into the dark city and returned to the alley where he was mugged many years before. He walked through the dangerous streets with a cocky self-assuredness—with confidence. He strolled down the lane, he feared before.

Again, as if he expected it to happen, he was approached by a lone character. "Got a cigarette buddy?" came the raspy voice from a seedy looking creep.

"I don't smoke," said Charlie, tensing for trouble.

The man moved forward, sticking his hand inside Charlie's jacket pocket. "Aw, come on, man, what you got in there? A little bread, maybe?"

Charlie grabbed the man's arm and pushed him aside. "Get your filthy hands off me, you bum."

The punk began to push Charlie around. Charles shoved him away, threw a punch, and it starts all over again. The blow only made the crook angrier. The man lowered his head and rammed into Charles' stomach, and then suddenly stood up catching Charles' chin with the back of his head. The man bit, wrestled and squirmed around in this fierce struggle. The bum was a street fighter. Charles couldn't get a solid blow in because of all the head butting, shoving and kicking.

And when the police sirens sounded, Charles heaved a sigh of relief! The creep fled down the alley out of sight.

The next day, Charles headed for his father's office.

"So, you're coming into the business after all. I didn't expect it… you were becoming very expert in the sweet science of prize fighting." His father said, delighted, as he faced Charles with his arms folded. "What changed your mind?"

"I thought fighting was a science too dad, until I came up against a common street fighter, a hoodlum! In his own way, he had more science than I did, and I couldn't put him away!"

"Ha," said a gratified father, "He wouldn't fight according to the rules, eh? Well, some businessmen are like that too! How will you get out of the contract with Phil Mario?"

"I had a clause in there allowing me to quit whenever I chose. It was Herb's idea. He had enough experience to know how to drop out of the terms of a binding agreement. But now I'm more interested in learning the business. Sounds like a challenge. I've got a lot to learn too!"

His father smiled. "You've learned a lot already! I have a feeling that you'll make it son, right to the top!" He turned over the picture of his son in his boxing pose. He planned to replace it with a picture of Charles in a three-piece suit!

The Rescue

It's 1952 somewhere in Korea. The Chinese communists have a lone tank pinned down...

Left behind when their engine quit, marooned for a day while the tide of war swept past, Lt. Jerry Wilkes' main battle tank finally got rolling again, but by then the commies had driven the 8th Army backward. The crew of the tank knew they had scant hope of ever making contact with their outfit again.

"Don't miss those cross-eyed apes," the tank commander ordered to his machine gunner. Tony was firing from atop the turret. A Chinese Communist tank was cresting the hill directly in front of them.

"The Red infantry's on the slope up there!" shouted Tony. "When they reach us, we'll be cooked!"

"Try to get headquarters or any aircraft in the area," Terry yelled over to Claude, the radio operator and driver.

"...we're hit and under attack. Heavy tank fire! Request immediate air cover. Home in on my signal!"

The Communist infantry stormed downhill. Lt. Wilkes' tank thundered and a stream of death erupted toward the enemy. Shells shattered steel as the Communist tank's 96mm shells erupted on the turret.

As Tony gunned down the wave after wave of soldiers—"Man, we ain't got a prayer. They're only seven shells left…almost no fifty caliber ammo left…"

"We're not surrenderin'. I don't like the idea of eating with chopsticks," shouted Jerry.

Meantime the radio operator, Claude, continued his transmission, "We're under attack near the MeKong River! Unable to move…"

Suddenly a response! "Hang in there buddy! I'm on my way…" The fighter pilot radioed back. The men could hear the vroom of the jet engine clash through the noise of battle!

Kaskovich was loading one of the last shells when the jet descended strafing the Communist troops. One of the reds got onto the turret ready to lob a grenade down the portal when he was swept off with the fighter's blast.

The F-86 Saber jet swooped down low enough to clear the Red soldier's swarming onto the tank.

"That's the first sweep! Button up, you guys…I'm going to drop napalm just past your tin can…and then make a run on that T-34 tank!" The pilot radioed as he got into position.

The jet came down for another run! A streaking rocket ripped through the Red tank's armor and erupted inside! But the Chinese infantry was still advancing…but the napalm and .50 cal slugs and small caliber fire from the tank turned them back. The air force pilot took another long look and then made a transmission to headquarters.

"One of our main battle tanks is about six miles inside the commie's perimeter! Still full of fight…but they won't last long without air support!" Again, he transmitted…"Silvertip three to silvertip leader…

We've got a customer six miles behind Red lines! Heavy tank disabled, needs the following…"

Meanwhile the crew of the trapped tank took a breather. Lt. Wilkes began, "You guys better move out. Let me stay here, the Reds'll find me and their doctors."

"Nothin' doin' Lieutenant. Knock it off skipper. We're all stayin' put," said the gunner.

Back at field headquarters, the Colonel had a talk with the pilot who saved the tank and its crew.

"You say the tank had a broken tread? Any other damage?" asked the Colonel.

"It's really beat-up! But I think the tread is the only major damage."

The pilot continued, "I've got the photos from my wing cameras. Let the photo lab develop them and have a close look."

In the darkroom one technician examines the photos:

"Linkage pin is shot, that's for sure! A couple of tank tracks are torn up…and maybe a new bogie wheel on the right side, forward!'

The Colonel phones the quartermaster, "Deliver the parts to this field in twenty minutes or I'll have you before a court-martial board! We're going to get that tank out, do you hear?"

Meanwhile, in the bitter cold, Kaskovich was determining the damage and the other crewman, Ira Lanski, heated up some chow.

"We'll have some hot chow, then start hightailing it south, Lieutenant," commented Ira.

“Too bad, if we had some spare parts we could ride outta here in style,” the Lt. observed.

The Colonel got his delivery—and the needed parts were put aboard a C-82 transport…in addition to 90 mm ammo and cases of .50 shells were brought along. Gasoline, naturally.

“Volunteers will parachute in there!” The Colonel continued, speaking to the loading crew, “They’ll stay with the tank on the way back to our lines.”

Fifty minutes later, the C-82’s were over the crippled tank. Parts were gently landing near the tank…ammo, reinforcements and spare parts.

The tank crew looked up amazed as the paratroopers and supplies landed! A tank maintenance expert landed with the spare parts. The paratroopers provided needed firepower to keep the enemy at a distance.

A firefight was beginning at the crest of the ridge. The maintenance crew worked feverishly to repair the damage. While the paratroopers took the pressure off the fighting tank crew, and with the Master-Sergeant, the damaged tank track was repaired.

“Better get below, skipper,” advised Ira.

With the sky saturated with U.S fighters and piston-engine bombers, Lt. Wilkes sent his tank south toward home. The slow moving armored vehicle ground out slow mileage, but the Communists didn’t get much of a chance to attack the tank again.

The tank finally made the six miles through an infuriated enemy with an umbrella of U.S. fighters and bombers. No one gave up, no one surrendered. It was a successful rescue operation.

The Hand

Charlie and Mike ran a small curios shop in a small Mid-Western town. Two more opposite partners you couldn't imagine! Charlie was kind, honest and hard working, while Mike was selfish, lazy and a constant griper. Mike always complained. "Business is rotten," Mike always said, "and it won't get better till you stop goldbricking and make up new signs like I told you—yuh!"

"But Mike, I'm doing all I can," said Charlie meekly. "Why don't *you* do some work too?"

"How many times I gotta enlighten you? I'm the brains of this outfit! You think I'm just sittin' here loafing, but I ain't! The wheels are goin' round and round all the time—thinking up new ideas!"

Charlie just turned away, frustrated as usual, "Sure, Mike…sure!"

One morning, when the partners opened for business:

"Boy, I coudda slept another couple of hours!" Mike said as he stretched and yawned.

"Good Lord!" cried Charlie, startled.

"What is it Charlie?"

"What is it? Look! See for yourself!"

Mike gasped, “I can’t be seein’ what I think I’m seein’! I mean, it just can’t be possible…or…or is it?”

“L-lets touch it, and find out if it’s real, or if we’re just dreaming!” Charlie said inching closer.

It was a human hand suspended several feet above the floor in the shop’s back room!

“It—it’s a real hand, all right!” Charlie exclaimed as he carefully touched the back of it.

“But where did it come from? And what’s holding it up in the air?” a terrified Mike bellowed.

After a pause, Mike continued, with a scowl on his face, “I don’t know and I don’t care, ‘cause this is our chance to strike it rich! We’re gonna make this floatin’ hand the main attraction…we’ll exhibit it and charge admission!”

Charlie, still in shock, disagreed. “It’s wrong to exhibit this hand. I mean, whatever it is, it doesn’t belong here. Maybe it’s in trouble and needs our help. It’s certainly alive!’

“Well of all the batty ideas! Look, jerk…that hand will make us rich and that’s all that counts! Understand? Now just let me do the thinking.”

But Charlie just couldn’t ignore his qualms about the mysterious hand.

Late that night, Charlie stood by and watched the hand closely…thinking…and found himself addressing the hand as if there was a person attached to the other end of it. “I keep wondering about the way your fingers are bent, as though you were desperately asking for something! If only you could talk. But wait! If you can't talk…"

Charlie got a pen and pad and approached the hand…"maybe you can write!"

He held the pad firmly in both of his own hands and placed the pen into the mysterious floating hand…

"You're doing it! You're writing!"

In beautiful flowing script, the hand wrote…

"Help me! I am not of your world, but a scientist trapped between dimensions. Please follow these instructions…"

Charlie read the note—"…set up and electrical generator and circuit breaker six feet from me!"

The following evening…

Mike found Charlie setting up the apparatus as instructed. "Hey, what do you think you're doing?"

"I'm setting up this machinery to free the hand and send him back to his own dimension!"

"What?" cried Mike, his expression turning fierce and angry, "Are you nuts? That hand is our meal ticket. What d'ya wanta get rid of it for?"

"It's wrong for us to keep him here against his will." Charlie set the machinery in motion.

"No Charlie! Don't do it! Don't"

But Mike's cry was too late!

Electrical sparks flew around the clutching hand as it slowly faded away!

"There! I've freed the hand. Now he can return to his own world!"

"You fool! You blasted idiot! You got rid of the best exhibit anyone coudda dreamed of. Now we'll be struggling and penniless again!"

Mike ran to the front room office and opened the safe taking out all the cash that they saved. He came back pointing a revolver at Charlie. "Well, you made this mess and you can live with it. But not me. I'm takin' all our dough and clearing out. And don't try to stop me or I'll plug ya!"

But Charlie didn't make a move. He was only too glad to get rid of his shiftless, miserable partner.

Mike ran off muttering to himself.

Seconds later—Charlie heard a voice, faint, mechanical, a voice from another dimension…

"There is something in our world which is valueless to us, but you humans value it greatly. I will give you much of it…"

Once again the mysterious hand appeared, as though by parting a veil in space.

A stream of three inch square gold ingots poured out of the portal onto the floor!

Meanwhile, some distance away, Mike had hopped a train heading out of town:

"Two thousand bucks! It ain't much, but it's better than what Charlie got! Ha—but, that's the way it is! Suckers like Charlie never get anything in the end!"

The Hidden Room

Scott and Martha Harris were a sickly old couple, well into their seventies. Life had passed them by! Like so many people, their plans, especially travel plans were never realized. The daily demands of life had always interfered with their plans. Their health had deteriorated and their dreams were never fulfilled. The years had slowly passed like a tide eating away at a shore. Their youth was gone; their strength was gone. So they decided to move into a smaller house to spend their remaining years in some sort of comfort and peace.

The real estate agent, Mr. Azinger, thought well of himself. Here was a dilapidated house that was on the market for three years. It needed a lot of repair, was in an isolated, desolate area of town, and was a property that no one wanted. The Harris' wanted it. It's all they could afford.

Azinger closed the deal and dropped off the 'lucky' couple the day of the closing. He was pleased as he walked away, waving at the two old people standing near the doorway.

"I should thank them!" Azinger thought to himself as he took away the 'For Sale' sign, "But I guess I should thank my own shrewdness for sticking these old geezers with a lemon. I couldn't give away this rotten old hovel. Glad to get it off my hands!" He drove off with a huge smile.

The couple stared at their new home. It was a long, hard, sorrowful stare. The wood frame house was in a Victorian style but small, only two bedrooms. It had a circular, four pane window above the second floor which led to the attic. The wood shingles needed repair; some shutters were even off their hinges. What furniture left in the house was old and worn. The plumbing and electrical wiring, although it passed state regulations, still needed a complete overhaul.

A sigh came from Mr. Harris, "It's not much of a house for us to spend our remaining years in Martha."

"Now don't you fret, Scott. A little work and it'll be nice and comfy. It's not a house that makes a home, it's the love and companionship of the people who live in it—that's what counts most. And that's why we'll love it here!"

Still, Scott saw the realistic side to it. "We've come to this." His face sour and drawn. "…the sum of our lives, Martha. And when you think of the dreams we had, the places we wanted to see…"

"Dreams?" she said softly, "Dreams are for the young. Our dreams have passed."

They set to work, and cleaned up the place. Within a couple of weeks the house was as neat as a pin. "If only we could get rid of this damp, musty smell," Martha complained.

"The house is old, Martha, like us! It's decaying and dying!"

"Scott, you mustn't speak like that. I know you're disappointed, but we mustn't be morbid about it. Tch, tch—look—this geranium is dead. It's the mustiness in here!"

"Here," Scott grabbed the dead plant. "I'll throw it out."

"Don't bother," she said, just put it by the steps and you can throw it out in the morning." He laid it near the stairway and they went off to bed. In the morning, after breakfast, Scott went to throw out the dead flowers.

"Martha, look here!"

"What is it dear?"

"These flowers…they were dead last night…now look at them!"

It was a wonder that stunned them almost speechless.

"That's odd!" said and astounded Martha, "They're more beautiful than they've ever been! I don't understand it. How could they have rejuvenated?"

As Scott reached to pick up the pot, he felt a rush of air coming from beneath the floorboards near the steps. He held his hand out to feel the breeze. "There's air coming from under the steps, Martha! Fresh air…clean, fresh air, not moldy. I can smell it…it's fresh air all right!"

He ran his fingers along the wooden planks abutting the stairway. "There must be some hollow part under the steps, behind the paneling." He felt along the entire length with the palms of his hands.

"Must be a room or something. If there is a room under the steps there must be a way in!" he reasoned.

"You mean a hidden door?" queried Martha.

"That's just what I mean!"

As he spoke his next words, a door unhinged and flew open into a darkened space!

"Look…" said a startled Scott Harris, "I pressed the left side of the paneling and…a door! And there's something beyond—an empty room of some kind."

A strange feeling swept over them. It became euphoria almost! The feeling grabbed them both. It seems to emanate from deep within the room.

"Scott," exclaimed Martha, "There's something very strange about this. I…I'm afraid!" They both peered into the dark, straining their eyes.

"At our age, my dear," commented Scott, "What in the world is there to be afraid of? Let's peek inside."

"The air is sweet. I can feel a gentle breeze. It smells like roses," said a mellowed Martha.

"As far as I can make out, Martha, there are no windows, yet the whole room seems to be filled with a radiance."

Timidly, clinging to each other like two children lost in the dark, they hesitantly stepped into this hidden room. Suddenly, a great howling wind pushed against them—like a million tiny, tingling shots of pellets against their bodies—stopping them just over the threshold. They searched each other's eyes and saw something they couldn't put into words. A sort of calm, serenity overwhelmed them. Their bent, stooped bodies straightened. Their limbs felt strength again. Suddenly the wind ceased and a soft, warm light bathed them!

"Martha, something is happening, something miraculous!"

"Scott! You're changing, you're getting younger!"

“So are you dear! We…we’re regaining our youth! Just like those geraniums—they bloomed again!” said an overjoyed Scott Harris.

“Scott…” Martha said thoughtfully, “The things we wanted to do, travel, see the world…it’s not too late! Our night has changed into morning. It’s a new beginning. A second chance!”

“Listen,” interrupted Scott, “Someone’s pounding on the front door.”

“Let them pound away. We mustn’t leave the room.” They held each other’s hands, looking all of twenty-two again!

The knocking continued. It was Mr. Azinger, the realtor. He opened the front door and walked into the foyer. “Hey, Mr. Harris…anyone home? Hmmm…that’s funny.”

“We’re in here,” cried Scott.

Azinger made his way to the open door under the stairway. He peered into the room but couldn’t see them clearly. It was still pretty dark.

“He didn’t see us. He doesn’t hear us either!” noted Martha.

Azinger walked through the house searching for the couple.

Later that afternoon:

Azinger was speaking to a policeman sitting in his patrol car outside the Harris home.

“Nope, Mr. Azinger, never saw them move out. Didn’t see anything happening here,” said the officer.

A puzzled Azinger, standing near the driver's side of the patrol car, spoke to the policeman, "I don't understand it. That old couple just disappeared. I searched the house from top to bottom, even a musty old room under the steps. But, they're gone!"

He bent down to give the officer a brochure he found at the foot of the room.

"Not a stick of furniture," Azinger continued, "Not a bit if baggage. Why it's as if they never moved in! Only thing I found was this…on the floor of that hidden room under the steps."

He handed the glossy brochure to the patrolman. It was a travel catalogue from a local travel agency.

The Magic Landscape

(The Ever-Changing Countryside in My Mind's Eye)

If, standing on a place I would call the Rock, I would allow my eye to broadly wander over a fair landscape and through a mental vision range through the long vista where is revealed wonderful pictures as I gaze! The busy city streets fade away into the mingled copse wood and forest of a prehistoric time. Lakes that have long since vanished gleam through the woodlands, and a rude canoe pushing from the shore startles the red deer that had come to drink.

While I look, the picture changes to a polar scene, with bushes of stunted Arctic willow and birch, among which herds of reindeer browse and the huge mammoth makes his home. Thick sheets of snow are draped all over the hills around, and far to the northwest the distant gleam of glaciers and snow-fields marks the line of the Highland mountains.

As I gaze further, the scene appears to grow more Arctic in aspect, until every hill is buried under one vast sheet of ice, 2,000 feet or more in thickness which fills up the whole valley and creeps slowly eastward into the basin of a northern sea. Here the curtain drops upon my moving pageant, for an enormous gap occurs before becoming an Ice Age!

Once more the spectacle resumes its movement and the scene is found to have utterly changed. The familiar hills and valleys have disappeared. Dense jungles of a strange vegetation—tall reeds, club-mosses, and tree-ferns—spread over the steaming swamps that stretch for miles in all directions. Broad lagoons and open seas are dotted with little volcanic cones which throw out their streams of lava and showers of ashes. Beyond these, dimmer in outline and older in date, I descry a wide lake or inland sea, covering the whole midland valley and marked with long lines of active volcanoes, some of them several thousand feet in height. And still further and fainter over the same region, I can catch a glimpse of that still earlier expanse of sea which in Silurian times overspread most of the land.

But beyond this scene my vision fails. I have reached the limit across which no geological evidence exists to lead my imagination into the primeval darkness beyond.

I have tried to recount, in the best manner I could give, an illustration of what I saw—I return now to the green hills and grey crags that gave to me in boyhood a joy of life! To these visions, amid the changes of scene and surroundings, my heart ever fondly turns, and here I desire, gratefully, to thank their influence. I am indebted to such a peaceful countryside.

The Miracle Baseball Bat!

Mickey Cooper was a center fielder for the Centerville Lumberjacks, a semi-pro team. He was no more than 19 and had glue in his glove. Nothing in the outfield got past him. He was the pride of Centerville. The team had a loyal following and many businessmen donated uniforms and equipment. But the team wasn't winning big… there weren't enough top players on the team and Cooper was one of its worst hitters. His batting was really anemic!

The Memphis Green Stockings came into town one day and the manager had to bench Cooper. The coach had to put a slugger in the lineup. It was a few nights later that a county fair came to town and a featured performer was a magician—Roscallini—with a very popular act. He claimed to have occult powers.

Mickey Cooper was enjoying the performance, when one of the townspeople yelled out, "Hey, Roscallini—make a hitter out of Cooper, why don't you!"

Embarrassed, Cooper approached the magician and half-jokingly asked him—

"I really enjoyed your show tonight, Mr. Roscallini. Is there anything you can do to make me a better hitter?"

Roscallini was a tall, imposing figure with dark cape held together around his neck with a brilliant yellow-metal medallion. He wore a well-trimmed mustache and a full head of black hair.

"Are you the one they call Cooper?" he asked as he led Mickey to his trailer.

"That's right, sir. I'd give anything to be a .400 hitter! Anything..."

"Would you give your immortal soul? I'll come up with a solution to your problem—right in here boy." He pointed to the entrance.

The magician's trailer was decorated with mysterious objects, one, of course, was a crystal ball! Soon he was conducting a strange ritual before the hopeful eyes of the young Cooper.

"I call from the far reaches of eternity the greatest hitter of all time...the Master of Swat, Babe Ruth!"

Suddenly the crystal glowed brighter and a cloud appeared behind Roscallini. He spoke again, as the image of Babe Ruth could be clearly seen in the foggy mist. "Ah, great Babe, would you impart a token of your prowess upon this poor, suffering lad?" A searing flash of light blinded the young Cooper momentarily—and then—a bat appeared—seemingly hovering not far from his reach!

"A baseball bat!" Cried Cooper, "Babe Ruth's very own bat!" It was real all right! Louisville Slugger trademark and all. Cooper grabbed the bat, thanked the magician and went home with this precious prize.

From that day on, young Cooper was a batting sensation of the league. He became the scourge of all pitchers. His batting average soared to .425, unheard of in the history of the league. He took his bat with him wherever he went. The two became celebrities. "The bat is charmed, enchanted, magical!" people said.

With Mickey batting over .400, the Lumberjacks had come up from the cellar to tie for first place in their division. Now Cooper was in the playoff game for the championship and Big Asa Royce was facing the lead off batter. Bryant and Sylvester went down, Cooper up next.

As Mickey reached for his bat he noticed it was cracked, useless! His face went pale. “My bat! It’s cracked! Who cracked my bat?” He looked accusingly at Pete Rhodes, “Pete! You used my bat, didn’t you? You worm—you cracked it. It’s ruined!”

“Sorry, Coop—I—I figured if it did such wonders for you, it would work for me too. I’m real sorry!”

The manager was standing nearby and called time to the plate umpire.

“It’s time we told him guys!” the coach said dryly.

The coach approached Cooper with a revelation, “Coop, it was all a gag about that bat. It’s just an ordinary, run of the mill, Louisville Slugger. Nothing special about it at all. We bought it in New York!”

Cooper was perplexed, “But—what about the magician, Babe Ruth? I saw it with my own eyes!

“All tricks and a movie camera,” admitted the coach.

“The magician you said was from the east…” Cooper began.

“East New York!” interrupted the coach, “The Great Roscallini is an actor. We paid him to pull off this magic act.”

Clay Barton, the batting instructor joined in the conversation, “I figured you just needed confidence and it turned out we were right! You’re a natural hitter Coop! You didn’t need a charmed bat or magical tricks to get a hit!”

Young Cooper was stunned for a moment and then turned and sheepishly picked up another bat off the rack, swung it a few times to get the feel of it.

He stepped up to the plate, the pitcher, Big Asa Royce winding up. They faced each other, the best pitcher versus the best hitter, just like it should be. This is for all the marbles; this is for the championship!

Writer's Block

Here's a man who found a way to conquer writer's block—hide away in the mountains where there are no distractions. Here in this peaceful setting he hoped to get inspiration. He sure did!

Just suppose…he was a writer up here in a cabin in the woods, far away from the city where he was growing stale. He still couldn't think of a story plot! But he would soon…oh, yes, he was right on the brink of a terrific story.

He stood at the window, listening to the woods' sounds, looking out into the night. He was struggling to get an idea…something new, something fresh, different, and maybe even weird.

"A shooting star…wish upon a star! I wish I could think of a plot! Hey, wait a minute!"

His eyes followed the path of that meteor and an idea hatched. "That star…just suppose it wasn't a star. Suppose it was a spaceship coming down to earth! And suppose a writer, like me, saw it coming down close by…a writer trying to think of a plot…"

He walked out of the cabin.

"He'd hurry out of the cabin in the woods, the one he rented to get away from the city…and he'd hurry toward the spot where the spaceship had landed…" He found himself deeper into the forest.

"Just suppose the spaceship landed about…here!" He stopped in his tracks. "This writer would reach this spot and he'd find…what?" He pondered his own question for a while, rubbing his chin and looking all around him.

"The obvious thing would be to find the spacecraft. But that's too obvious! It's got to be something else…but what? I'm stuck again!"

That was when he heard a rustling in the underbrush.

"Whoa! It gave me a start! I'm beginning to believe my own story! Just a dog…but is it just a dog?"

It wasn't. The creature was exposed to the bright moonlight…it seemed to be a cross between a kangaroo and a large rabbit with a long snout, short fur, spotted white belly, large plump torso with a spiral tail. An animal not native to this neck of the woods, for sure!

The writer stared at it. It stared back with its almond-shaped dark-black eyes.

"Looks really strange…" He approached it…"You're a strange looking beast, but friendly, aren't you? Where did you come from?" He petted its long narrow head and laughed! There was something so warm and friendly about the creature! And all the time he was wondering what kind of an animal it was.

"Well, since we've met each other this way, I'm inviting you into my cabin. I'll see if I can rustle up something to eat. Someone will come looking for you, I'm sure!"

He then remembered the agricultural laboratory in the valley and the stories in the newspapers.

“That’s it, of course! You must be one of those scientific experiments they’ve been doing on animals at the lab…producing mutant by radioactivity or something. Somehow you got free and have been roaming the woods trying to find someone to take care of you! That must be it!”

The strange pair walked back to the cabin together.

He fed the beast and it ate with a voracious appetite! It even ate the cans the food came in.

“Boy,” said the author, looking on in astonishment, “They really got a mutant this time! Looks like you’re part goat too! What an appetite. I’d better phone the lab and tell them I found you.”

The animal came up to the writer and licked his face with friendly affection.

“I forgot…no phone! I wanted complete isolation. I’ll have to walk down in the morning. Haven’t had a dog in years; always liked them. You’re as friendly and appealing like a dog!”

It slept next to the writer’s bed that night, and there was a comforting feeling that he couldn’t explain. “Maybe they’ll let me keep you for a pet. I can sense that you like me just as much as I like you…”

In the morning when he awoke, the first thing he saw was his pet! It seemed to have grown during the night.

“Either you’ve grown or I need a pair of glasses! Say, I had an idea during the night. Just suppose this writer found a strange creature, not a freak like you, but a real being from another planet and he takes it home and makes a pet of it…”

He went to work on his story. Of course he forgot to go down to the Institute in the valley…he was too busy now. A strange bond developed between him and the creature as days passed, a sort of mutual love.

"I'm stuck again! Just suppose this writer in the story DID bring home this being he found and it ate everything in sight and grew at an alarming rate, just like you! Then what? What happens next?"

The creature was nearby all the time, like a faithful dog. The writer got up from his chair to give his mind a time-out. "I'll let the story rest for a while." Then, turning toward the creature, "I'll build a cage for you. You're getting so big, I'm afraid you'd scare someone to death if you went wandering off." He proceeded to build a cage of wood and wire mesh.

"Y'know, as much as I love you, I'm afraid I'll just have to go down and notify the Institute that I found you. You're getting just too big to keep around…and you eat too much too!"

By nightfall the cage was finished and he brought it indoors and put the pet inside. He noticed that the creature had grown as little more since that morning.

"Hey, don't look so sad. I'll let you out when it's bedtime. Gee, I hate to part with you. Maybe they'll let me keep you after all."

A moment later:

"Well, I'll walk down to the valley and tell the folks I've found you…and ask them to let me keep you."

As he turned to go out he heard a whirring noise and looked out the cabin window. It was almost the same as it had been the first night when he found the pet. There was a shooting star.

"But," he thought, *"stars don't make that kind of sound!"*

The shooting star vanished. The whirring stopped. Then, out of the woods…

The writer looked on in astonishment. "No, it can't be!" There before him were several of the same types of beast. He stood there frozen in a daze as the creatures brushed by him as if he weren't there and went to the cage that held his pet.

"They're unfastening the cage door!"

"They're prostrating themselves as though the pet was some kind of royalty—a prince of some strange race, just reaching maturity!" The writer's thoughts were racing.

With their spindly arms and tiny tentacle-like fingers wrapped around his pet, they led the creature out and closed the door behind them.

"It—it's unbelievable!"

The author rubbed his eyes. Was he dreaming all this? There before him was an empty cage.

"Wait a minute…the story! There's the ending! The spaceship comes back; the creatures from another world come for their young prince, and then take him away…"

He thought a moment, *"And it's true. No…it won't do. It's too trite! I've got to have a twist to the ending."*

But before he could finish his thought, the cabin door opened. There stood two of the creatures, nine feet tall. They grabbed him like a rag doll and one carried him under its arm.

"Hey! Wait! Put me down. I didn't harm your prince. We were friends. I liked him, he was my pet!"

Ignoring his pleas, they took him into the woods to a…yes, it was a spaceship; an interstellar conveyance, and what was more incredible, it was shaped like a flying saucer! His pet was there, tears streaming from its eyes, but smiling at him. It held him close, making crooning noises as the ship rose from the earth and swooshed skyward. Then, the 'prince' spoke, its voice halting, but kind.

"I…I could not leave you! I love you so much. I could not go back to my home world and leave my pet behind! I will love you and care for you well, my wonderful pet."

Then the thought flashed across the writer's mind, a thought that brought a wry smile to his lips, checking the screams of hysteria that trembled there.

"The perfect ending," said the writer, "The twist ending for the story that will never be published. And I'd have called it…'Writer's Block'."

Shoot the Works!

In a large eastern city in the late 1940's, a gang war broke out that had all the earmarks of the old Capone days. Buff Moran's gang had a stranglehold on the narcotics racket, while his rival, Arnie Driscoll, boss of the west-side mob was trying to maintain his territory.

Dannie Rivers, a torpedo for Driscoll just came back from a gun battle on the east side of town. "Evening, folks!" he said with a broad smile as he entered Driscoll's apartment. Kay Templeton, a strikingly beautiful blonde was Driscoll's girl, was standing with him as Rivers entered the room. "I've got good news for you boss," continued Rivers, dressed in a light green suit and red tie. "We just caught two more of Moran's boys. Somethin' tells me he's gonna be real sorry he started all this."

"Good work Danny," replied Driscoll. He was a tall, handsome middle-aged man, slightly gray at the temples, with a full mustache. He was dressed that evening in a smoking jacket and holding a glass of whiskey, which he liked to drink straight up. "Maybe now that we showed him," continued Driscoll with a slight grin, "we can play as rough as he can, some sense'll seep into his thick skull. Maybe he'll call it quits."

Rivers moved over to the bar and poured himself a drink. He was about the same height as Driscoll, clean shaven, in his twenties, with a full head of wavy yellow hair.

"I don't like all these killings, Danny! It's bad for business," explained Driscoll, a grim serious look cross his face, "The cops are starting to breathe down our necks. What I don't understand is how this started in the first place." A brief smile flickered across Kay's lips, some oblique, inner humor she didn't want to share.

A sudden, heavy knock at the door. "Oh-oh—we got company," remarked Kay. She approached the door, and opened it to find Buff Moran standing there with two of his hoods. Moran's husky, solid-built frame filled the doorway. His bushy tuft of brown hair was combed forward which made his rough features look even more menacing. The scar down his right cheekbone gave a finishing touch. He was dressed in a brown double-breasted suit and red bow-tie.

"Well, well," said Kay with a sneer, "If it isn't our little playmate Buff Moran!"

"Cut the comedy act sister," said Moran with obvious contempt on his face. "Tell Driscoll I wanna see 'im."

Rivers had is automatic pointed at Moran. "You can put that away Rivers. We came here clean. You can frisk me if it'll make you feel better."

"Excellent advice Moran. Go ahead," said Driscoll nervously, "Make sure they mean what they say." They were unarmed all right. Moran and his henchmen approached Driscoll.

"I'm willin' to make a truce if you are! I never would have bothered to start this war if a pack of uncut stuff wasn't heisted from my safe. It's worth a hundred grand, an' I thought…" Driscoll interrupted sharply, "And you thought I did it. Well, I didn't. You better start looking in your own back yard."

"It was one of my own boys," admitted Moran, "He did it for some dame. I ain't found out who she is yet but I will, an' when I do, she's gonna join her boy friend in the river where we just threw 'im."

A wince crossed Kay's face, unnoticed by all in the room. She whispered to herself in deference to the possibility that someone would overhear her, "I'd better put my thinking cap on—but quick." She took a couple of drags on her cigarette.

Later that night Kay goes alone to Danny River's apartment. She made advances towards him and he took the bait. "Geese, baby, you knew for a long time how crazy I was about you. If you felt the same way why didn't you let me know before?"

"Arnie is the boss, remember?" she said simply. "I had to string along until the right moment. I found out tonight what I needed to know." Rivers pulled back from her embrace and turned to go to the bar to pour a couple of drinks, "I don't follow. What did you want to find out?"

"Well," she replied, "for a long time I've suspected we were taking in a lot more than Arnie was letting on. And tonight I found Arnie is keeping two sets of books, one of which he shows us, and the other nobody sees."

Rivers looked at her curiously. "So what set of books nobody ever sees? Is it important?"

Kay leaned closer to him, "Nothing, except the organization is getting gypped out of, maybe, forty percent of the take! That's how much Arnie is holding back and feathering his own nest with!"

River's eyebrows rose and his eyes widened, "What? Is that the truth baby?" He became a bit incredulous, "Arnie wouldn't have the nerve to hold out that much from the gang." He grabbed Kay's arm, the tightness of his grip made her wince and pull back. "Oh, wouldn't he? I've got news for you sweetheart, I've been up to Arnie's place more than once and did a little snooping around. He's got a safe that contains a cool half million. He didn't get that from pinching pennies!"

A rage began to build in Rivers and her words made sweat prickle on his skin. "That rat. That smilin', no good rat. Holdin' out on us. What do you think we oughta do about it?" She returned an answer with a smug look on her face, "You're the best gunman in the business Danny, so that's a silly question to ask me." He turned to meet her beckoning gaze, "I'd love to rub him out right now, but it's out of the question. We got to take it up with the ring first."

Kay frowned very slightly, "Why? They'll just order you to do the same thing—then split it up. This way, it'll be just the two of us." She felt a surge of pleasure just seeing his face and knowing he would do whatever she wanted him to do. Her deep, long kiss reinforced it. "Yea, you're right," he admitted, and then a thought crossed his mind, "Say, could you get hold of his files on how he brings in the dope? If you could, we'd be in the driver's seat. The rest of the gang would have to ride along with us if they wanted their split."

Kay smiled, "That's easy darling. Just leave it to me." They left the apartment and began to drive to Kay's house. "When I get home," she told him, "I'll call Arnie and tell him I must meet him some place. He'll show up because he trusts me. But instead of me, you'll be there. And if you're so worried about the boys, well, we'll just let them think Buff Moran is their guy!"

Rivers smiles, "Sure, they'd never believe Moran. Even the cops will try to pin it on him. Baby, you're sensational. That's real clever!"

After reaching her apartment she called Arnie Driscoll and told him to meet her at Third Avenue and Grand Street in twenty minutes. "He's all yours, darling, on a silver platter!"

The plan was for her to go to Arnie Driscoll's apartment and come back with the information on how the drugs were smuggled into the country. "Now get going to Arnie's apartment," said an anxious Danny Rivers. "When you're finished meet me back here at your place."

But Kay wasn't through making phone calls. Right after Danny left her apartment, she telephoned Buff Moran, "Hello, Buff, in exactly fifteen minutes Arnie Driscoll and Danny Rivers will be at Third and Grand picking up package of uncut dope in *your* territory." Moran fell for it hook, line and sinker. "Why that double crossing four-flushing rat," came the reply.

Kay waited a few minutes then made an anonymous phone call to the precinct in that neighborhood. "Hello, police? I overheard there was going to be some shooting at the corner of Third Avenue and Grand. You'd better investigate right away."

What a sweet set-up she thought. *"Danny will kill Arnie, Moran's men will get Danny and the cops will close in on Moran. That'll leave me in the clear with half a million in cash!"*

At precisely the right time Arnie drove up to the corner of Third and Grand. From the doorway in which Danny was crouching, he could see Arnie Driscoll straining to catch a glimpse of where Kay might be standing. The street was deserted and dimly lit. Danny suddenly leapt out of the shadows as Arnie slowed down to a stop. He fired three shots at close range killing Driscoll instantly. At that very moment, Moran and his hoods came barreling down the street firing at Danny Rivers. The wounded Rivers ran off as the police patrol cars came on the scene, sirens blaring. The patrol cars came in at either end of the street trapping the Moran mob. Kay Templeton's plan was almost complete. Moran gave up as the cops put the hand cuffs on him and his men. Rivers escaped, wounded, and aware he'd been set up. It wasn't long before he made it back to Kay's apartment uptown.

He entered the apartment, bleeding from his shoulder. "Danny, you're hurt," Kay said in a pretense of being concerned. He locked the door behind him and drew his gun. "Hello baby, I got Arnie just like you figured, and Moran got *me* like you figured too—but I'm a hard guy to kill."

He pointed the gun at her as he staggered back, "Before I crawled away from your little death trap, I heard Moran tell the cops a dame had tipped him. Now, who do you suppose that dame could be?" He began choking.

She kept a bewildered look, "You've got it all wrong honey. All wrong. Please let me explain." Just as she began to rant her phony explanation, Danny collapsed dropping his automatic. Without hesitation, Kay picked up the gun, "All right, wise guy. I don't think you're such a hard guy to kill. I'll prove it to you." She pulled the trigger but the gun jammed. Acting immediately, she ran to the kitchen and grabbed a steak knife. As Danny tried to get to his feet, she drove the knife into his chest as close to the heart as possible. His blood curdling scream filled the air in high crescendos, knowing his own death was at hand. She could feel him struggling for his life, as he trembled in his death throes. While she was thinking of what story to tell the police, there was a hard knock at the door and a twisting on the door knob.

The police had followed Rivers and were led to Kay's apartment. They broke the door down. Kay had picked up the gun again and tried to figure out how to get it unjammed. "Drop it lady," ordered one patrolman. Startled, she threw the gun to the floor. "But how?" she cried.

"We trailed this bird, but it looks like we arrive a minute too late. You've killed him." After handcuffing her they discovered the half million Kay had taken from Driscoll's safe. One of the policemen turned to Kay, "Something tells me lady, you're the one that tipped us off about the shooting tonight. Whatever your plans were, they've gone wrong. Let's go, you got a date with headquarters. Come on."

Kay Templeton kept her date—a life sentence behind bars!

Date with Destiny!

It was a bright moonlit night; the stars were glittering like diamonds as Charles Reynolds reached Salisbury Fork. He'd been driving over an hour and turned down the country route. "Let's see, I'm supposed to take Grissom Road." The signpost was poorly lit, so Reynolds slowed down a bit to read the sign. Grissom Road led south, Harvard Drive to his right led southeast. Grissom Road was a typical tertiary route—narrow, part gravel, part dirt, some portions paved. He had to travel very slowly, "At this rate I ought to be at Barry's place by midnight."

Reynolds was still dressed in his business suit. He planned to spend the night at his friend's house in Rosedale. Grissom Road was narrow and winding and it was slow going. The clear night suddenly grew stormy. A howling wind arose. The sky grew darker, as the moon disappeared behind blackening clouds and the stars twinkled out.

"Oh, brother, a storm coming up! Hope I don't get caught in a flood." Harsh rashes of jagged lightning split the sky accompanied by the rolling, rumbling of thunder. The rain came, a blinding rain drowning the earth in its torrential downpour!

"This is murderous, I can hardly see." Reynolds drove on, hardly able to see the road ahead, but he was able to make out a railway crossing. Another car came out from behind him, passing on ahead. As it approached the tracks, it slowed down and apparently must have stalled out, rolling to a stop right over the railroad tracks. "Someone else caught in the storm. Must've stalled out. What an awful thing to happen—stalling out right on the crossing!" Reynolds stopped some yards behind the stalled vehicle. He got out of his car to see if he could help. As he opened the door, a blast of a horn and train whistle came from the distance! In the garish glare of the hurtling train's headlight, Reynolds could see the driver frantically trying to start the car. There was a woman in the car as well. Reynolds ran to the driver's side of the car and got a pretty good look at the couple trapped inside. "Get out you two. Get out before it's too late!" he shouted. One of them must have pressed the lock button on the doors because they were struggling to open them.

It was too late. Reynolds dove away from the oncoming train just as it smashed into the helpless vehicle. Shaken to his core, Reynolds got up soaking wet. The impact drove the car in mid-air and several hundred feet down the tracks. The train roared past into the night.

As Reynolds raced to the wreck to see if anyone could have survived, the storm abruptly faded and the night cleared! Before his very eyes, the wrecked car also faded—as if in a dream—it slowly disappeared!

"Wh-what's happening?" he muttered, out of breath. "The wreck—it's disappearing!" By the time he reached the site, the moon shone bright and the stars were twinkling once again. All traces of the wreck were gone! Reynolds stood there for quite some time, trembling, and his mind in turmoil.

"Was I dreaming? Was it an hallucination? Can it be real? I know what I saw, I know it happened! No sign of an accident. The ground isn't even wet!"

At last, Reynolds climbed shakily into his car and drove on. "There's got to be an explanation. Maybe I fell asleep at the wheel and dreamed the whole thing. Maybe I was hypnotized by this winding, narrow road. There's got to be an answer."

Reynolds finally arrived at his host's home without further mishap. After a short greeting he excused himself and went to the guest room, exhausted and fell asleep shortly thereafter.

Next morning his friend Barry Williams had breakfast ready and introduced him to his other overnight guests.

"Morning Barry," said Reynolds still driving sleep from his eyes.

"Hi Charles. Sorry you were so late last night. I didn't get a chance to introduce you to our other guests."

Reynolds noticed a well-dressed couple with their backs to him filling their plates at the buffet table. When the two came over to meet him, Reynolds suffered a severe shock. They were the two people from the car wreck!

"Charles," said his friend Barry with a broad grin, "I want you to meet Tom and Wilma Lovell. They're old friends of mine, on their way home from their honeymoon."

The first shadow of anxiety touched Charles Reynolds before he could say anything he glanced from one to the other of them and paled. His face turned a ghastly white!

"Hey!" remarked Barry, "What's wrong?"

"I-I-it's nothing. I-I thought I knew them, that's all." He seemed to whither as he watched the couple walking towards him.

"You looked more like you'd seen a ghost!" observed Barry, his expression changing to one of puzzlement.

"Sorry," said a distracted Reynolds. "Awfully glad to meet you two."

"Hi," said Wilma. She had soft skin, flowing black hair, and a charming demeanor, "Let me pour you a cup of coffee."

The weekend passed in pleasantries and normal conversations, but Charles brooded over the strange happenings of the past couple of nights. He kept wincing, agonizing over it, "There must be a rational explanation," he kept thinking, "There must be. It's got to be an omen, that's it, a premonition!"

Sunday, Reynolds went out to put his suitcase in his car when he suffered another jolt. The Lovell's car was the very same one that was in the wreck! "I've got to tell them, warn them somehow—without sounding like a stark raving lunatic."

Sheepishly, Reynolds took the Lovells to one side and expressed concern about their safety on the trip back.

"I realize how silly this must sound, but please don't take Grissom Road. I know the other road is longer, but it's safer."

"Don't let it worry you, Charles," said a condescending Mr. Lovell, "We'll be all right."

"We're not superstitious," exclaimed Wilma, "Let's forget the whole thing."

But Charles Reynolds insisted, "No, please, just do me this favor. Don't take Grissom Road. The other way, like I said, is a little longer but I'll feel a lot better, if you take it."

The young couple looked at each other and smiled. "Okay," said Mr. Lovell, "If it'll make you happy, we'll take the longer route. But I still think we're being silly about the whole affair."

Reynolds bid them a safe trip, said goodbye to Barry, hopped in his car and drove off. Ten minutes later Wilma and Tom Lovell were speeding towards the fork in the road at the opposite end of Grissom Road. Soon it began to grow darker, rain clouds had suddenly gathered. The sky opened in a torrential downpour, unexpectedly, just like that Friday evening. Beneath the darkening clouds it became impossible to see clearly. Vivid flashes of lightning lit up the sky, followed by deep, rolling thunder. A howling wind sprang up. As the couple approached the fork, Tom couldn't possible see the small street sign pointing the way in the direction from Grissom Road. He missed the turn off completely and sped down the very road he was trying to avoid. The storm grew in intensity as the couple drove down Grissom Road, unaware of their mistake. Speeding along, they actually passed Reynolds on the road.

"This is almost worse than Friday night," thought Reynolds when he noticed the Lovell's car speeding past him. Not long afterward he came up to the car stalled out over the railroad tracks, just as it happened Friday night. The events took on the same pattern. In the distance a train was hurtling towards them. Reynolds screeched to a halt, leaped from his car into the driving rain and ran toward the doomed couple. Too late. He stumbled as the train smashed into the Lovell's car. Reynolds knew, this time the wreck wouldn't just disappear. And he was right. He walked slowly to the crushed vehicle. It was still there, and there was nothing more he could do.

Silver Lining

Whitepine, Montana was a lazy town at the close of the nineteenth century. It lay between the Cabinet Mountains and the Bitterroot Range along the Bull River. It was ordinary, as ordinary western towns go. Once thriving because of its silver deposits, now, mostly a run-of-the-mill farming and ranching community.

Sally Hawkins saw nothing wrong in an evening walk, despite the warning against it. There had been rumors of a werewolf on the prowl. But people around those parts said it was a wolf, maybe a mountain lion, not a werewolf. But the cold bitterness welling up in her throat made a believer in her. There a few yards away was a monstrous figure, standing six feet tall and on two legs. With piercing yellow eyes and a mournful howl the creature came closer. A shrill cry from Sally Hawkins broke across the ravine. It was over quickly.

The Sheriff, deputy, the coroner and many townspeople gathered around Sally's body that morning. "I can't figure it doc," said the grim-faced Sheriff. "The third murder this month. Looks like she's been hacked to death by some sort of…" His words were cut short by the voice of an outsider, "Werewolf, Sheriff Trask? For it is a werewolf attacking your community, Sir. And you are a fool if you can't see it.

"Pitt! Said Sheriff Trask, disapprovingly, "I told you to get outta here with that malarkey, or…" A townsman interrupted, "No. Let him speak."

"Thank you, friend," said Pitt. "My partner, Mr. Wyle and I have tried to warn you against this menacing werewolf and have made our considerable experience available to you all."

His partner, Mr. Wyle continued, "And all we ask you, good people, is a small payment and access to all the silver you possess. As you are all aware, the only way to destroy a werewolf is with silver bullets, a silver staff…whatever weapons we can forge. We'll rid the town of this nightmare once and for all."

"Silver!" cried a rancher in the crowd, "Mister, you just said the wrong thing. Ain't been any silver in this town since the load was mined out back in '75." Another citizen spoke up, "Only silver we got is our family heirlooms and some other jewelry, and we'd never part with those!"

"Do you hear them Mr. Wyle?" said a frowning Mr. Pitt, "They value their petty silver more than the lives of their loved ones and their own town."

"I hear them, Mr. Pitt," replied Wyle, "I just can't believe them."

"The decision is yours, friends," continued Mr. Pitt, "Either let us fashion your silver into weapons to fight the creature…"

"Or," Mr. Wyle said finishing the thought, "this community of yours will become a ghost town in fact as well as in name."

That night the beast struck again killing one of the Sheriff's own deputies. The people were moved to action. They lined up with all their silver and deposited it on a table set up by Pitt and Wyle. "Step right up, citizens. Have your silver weighed and recorded. The same weight, minus a small commission will be returned to you after the werewolf has been killed," said Mr. Pitt.

The Sheriff, leaning against a post opposite the gathering was mulling over the situation, eyeing the two men and listening intently. *"Maybe I'm just gettin' superstitious in my old age,"* thought Sheriff Trask, *"but I don't know if I trust these fellers. After all, they showed up the day after the first murder. And they seem a might too anxious to holler—uh—wolf!"*

His thoughts were racing, *"'Sides, ain't werewolves supposed to come out only when there's a full moon? Pshaw, first full moon this month is tonight. Yeah, might be that a little investigation is called for…subtle-like. Yeah, like that Sherlock Holmes feller in those British magazines."*

After Pitt and Wyle collected all the townsfolk's silver, they bagged it and headed toward the wharf at the Bull River crossing. "He's following us Mr. Pitt, just like you predicted," smiled Mr. Wyle.

"So nice to know my talents are appreciated, Mr. Wyle." A grin crossed Pitt's face, peering over his shoulder.

Sheriff Trask was trailing the two toward the outskirts of the little town and waited near the ferry house. "Looks like they're makin' camp for the night. Gives me a chance to snoop some." He pawed through their belongings, opened a trunk, "Lots of interesting stuff. Hel-lo!" He found a costume of a wolf claws and all, "Mighty peculiar long underwear even for them two. I bet this ain't just rust on these claws…huh!"

A sharp blow came down on the Sheriff's head, momentarily dazing him. For a few moments the Sheriff lay semi-conscious on the pier. Standing ten feet away were Pitt and Wyle. "Ah, back with us Sheriff?" said Mr. Pitt, "Just in time, I'm afraid, to meet your death!"

"There…there never was any werewolf. It was all a con job," said a groggy Sheriff Trask, "A con job to get what little silver those poor folks had left!" He swallowed, his throat jerking.

"Perceptive, Sheriff," said a gloating Mr. Pitt as he pulled out his revolver. Wyle had hog-tied the Sheriff as Pitt continued his tirade, "A little too late. Mr. Wyle and me met in a saloon some weeks ago, and decided to pool our resources when neither one of us could swindle the other. It was Wyle's idea to collect all the silver in town and murder the unsuspecting townspeople. It worked like a charm."

He paused a moment, "Check the chains, Mr. Wyle."

"Okay, Mr. Pitt," said Wyle as he finished binding the Sheriff. "I really regret this Sheriff, but it's time to part company. And the same goes for you Mr. Wyle!"

Pitt shot Wyle square in his back. Wyle fell to the pier.

"Yuh just shot your own partner!" cried the Sheriff.

"Business, Sheriff Trask. I admit his plan was quite clever, imitating a werewolf. But I'm a greedy pig. I'd never share that loot with anyone." He raised his revolver and pointed it at the Sheriff. "And now, Sheriff your time has come." Pitt shot him several times. With a low moan, the Sheriff fell backwards against the pier, dead.

"Now," thought Mr. Pitt, "to dispose of all my equipment and the evidence, of course, in the river. I'll vanish with the silver and…" Pitt stopped in his tracks as he heard a growl from behind. As he turned his face went white, his body limp. "Oh no—no, it can't be!"

"But it can Mr. Pitt."

Mr. Wyle had changed, changed indeed, into a werewolf; the bright August moon was shining full and bright! He lunged at Mr. Pitt, "You were so impressed by my plan; you never stopped to think I might have another reason for depriving the town of all its silver. That silver no one will ever see again." Wyle kicked the bags of silver into the river as he ripped into Mr. Pitt. Soon after, he turned his hungry eyes toward the town, knowing nothing would interfere with his feasting for many nights to come!

Fireballer!

When I was pitching in the New York—Penn League in the States, the Yankee scouts tabbed me as "Strong-armed with plenty of control." They were right because I won my first game in the Major Leagues when I was brought up in August of 1950 for a try-out.

Then, my baseball career was shelved, another team called me up—the U.S. Army and I was pitching for the infantry in Korea by July of 1951. But I wasn't throwing baseballs, and the penalty if I missed was a lot worse than a base hit. My life was on the line like the rest of the players on my team. My name is Todd Handley and this is my story.

They taught me about accuracy on the rifle range, like the rest of the guys in basic. I was thoroughly trained in small-arms handling. Even though I could throw a grenade farther than anyone and with plenty of control. When I hefted a grenade it was always on target!

We were shipped out as soon as basic was completed.

In Korea we took the place of a battered company in the front line. I saw walking dead men, the lucky ones, I know were wounded and got to go home quick! My platoon took a position at the top of a hill just on the outskirts of a town named Taegu. Mortar shells and small arms fire pinned us down.

"Hold tight, you guys," said Sergeant Crosby, "This is just to feel us out. It's not an attack in force."

"This one'll do," said a shaken private,

"I ain't complain' Sarge." We returned fire.

I never figured myself to be short on courage, but I was plenty shook by the time that first "little" attack was over. And the next day the Commies threw the book at us! A whole regiment was advancing up a far hill.

"They're over beyond the ridge," said a scout. "They're down where our bullets can't reach them." The Sgt. asked me to go forward and toss a couple of grenades over the ridge. It so happens a medic was tending to a wounded soldier when several of the enemy were advancing. My toss landed right in the midst of several enemy soldiers and took them out of action.

"Nice pitching, Todd," said the Sergeant, "Stay close to me." I felt good, just like I broke a curve ball. Best throw I ever made. "Okay, Sarge. Y'know if I wasn't in the army, I'll bet I wouda had a good year!"

We had rifle grenades, mortars, but the Sarge said none of them could put a grenade in just the right place like a GI with accuracy. We beat off the first assault and the North Koreans retreated. After a while we were held up in some bombed out ruins. The Sergeant noticed a group of enemy soldiers inside a building with a huge blast hole in it.

"See the hole in the wall of that building?" remarked the Sergeant pointing in that direction. "The Reds fire through there at our guys and move back in after a few bursts."

"From this angle, I'll have to either toss it so it bounces off the side wall into the hole, or curve it, like a hard slider," I said, holding a grenade, ready to pull the pin. I pitched it right into the hole. "Let's go, I really curved that one in there Sarge." There was an explosion, then silence.

The Reds kept falling back as we advanced. They took shelter in an abandoned brick hut. It gave them adequate protection as they rained down a constant barrage at us. I saw an opportunity to toss one right through an open window, but it was a great distance, maybe a hundred feet or more. It was becoming a real pressure cooker for our guys, so I took action, sprang up from behind a wall and hurled the grenade. It sailed right through the center of the open window exploding on impact.

That was my first week. I was throwing grenades all the time, showing off at first. One guy remarked, "Todd can do more with a grenade than I could with a tank. He never misses."

But the inevitable happened. Because of my intense throwing, I snapped and tore some muscles in my shoulder. My arm went numb and pain shot through my shoulder. My tosses went off the mark. I had no more control or distance.

"What happened pitcher?" asked one of my buddies, "Somethin' wrong?"

"Arm's gone." I said grimacing in pain and holding my shoulder. "I tore something in the shoulder."

"Never mind the pitchin' arm, Todd," interrupted Sgt. Blake, "Hate tuh' mention it, but we still got a war on."

"It's gone for good, I'll bet," I said holding my shoulder tightly, "But if I take good care of it, nurse the shoulder real careful, there's a chance…"

"Come on," ordered the Sgt.

I didn't throw anymore grenades. The injury wasn't the kind you can take to the medics when you're in the infantry in wartime. So I used my M1 and disregarded the other guys when, “Hey kid, there’s a bunch of Commies down behind the brush,” shouted the Sgt. As he handed me a grenade, “You can nail ‘em.”

“Not me Sarge. Can’t do it.”

“I know you got a sore arm and yer savin it for the World Series, well, this is our World Series. If that bunch hidin’ in them bushes smacks us, we’ll all be losers. How about it?”

“Yeah!” I said in anger, “You don’t give a damn if my arm falls off!”

The Sergeant put his face two inches from mine, “Half the guys in the Company are casualties and you’re worried about that stupid arm? We’re worried about our skins, son. You gotta do somethin’.”

“I’ll try,” I said as the Sgt. thrust the grenade in my hand. “I’ll try, but my shoulder’s really bad. I probably won’t do so good. How many have we got.”

“Three,” answered the Sergeant, “So don’t miss.”

I didn’t reach on the first throw and I felt like a knife went through my shoulder.

“Todd missed twice,” said one soldier, “Make this one count,” shouted another.

I tried to forget the muscle tear, and pretended it wasn’t a war and this was a baseball and all I had to do was have control this time. I tossed it. I didn’t have to look, I knew it was right on the money.

“Yuh did it kid,” cried the Sgt. “They won’t wipe us out now. They’re all dead.”

I fell to the ground holding my shoulder. I never regretted doing it. Now, I had a scar that didn't show—all my life I'd be the guy who could've made the majors if—and I'd live with that the rest of my life.

We Attack at Dawn!

Private James Miller was just an average G.I. He obeyed orders and did his duty. Beyond that nothing distinguished him until the Army suddenly realized he possessed a rare gift...a gift which was destined to save many lives once it was recognized!

Somewhere on the German border, 1945, nearing open farmland...

"Joe, crawl down the line and tell the guys we're going to break off! Our mission is accomplished," said the grubby, stubble-bearded sergeant.

"Okay Sarge!" answered the Corporal as he headed away from the squad down a ditch. The platoon was still engaging the enemy with small arms fire. As the Corporal spread the word, the platoon withdrew, and twenty minutes later...

"This beats me!" said a perplexed Sergeant Blare Davis as he was stooping down looking at an unfolded map. "The fork in the road isn't marked on the map!"

"We better know which road to take Sarge!" replied a concerned soldier standing nearby, "One of these forks can lead right into a Krout position!"

Pvt. Miller approached the Sergeant, he was a tall figure, slim, blonde hair, light colored eyes, also with a stubble from days in the trenches, "I don't want to butt in Sarge, but the LEFT fork is the one that leads back to our position," he said with confidence.

The Sergeant was credulous about that, “It can’t be, Jimmy! This road was on our right when we moved toward our objective. It’d got to be the RIGHT fork!”

Sgt. Blare Davis was boss, and the platoon moved up the right fork as ordered…”Yeah,” thought a worried Sgt. Davis, “We’re on the right track now! Seems to me I remember this section of terrain.”

It was a desolate area, the moon was shining so the platoon could clearly see the surrounding countryside. Mostly it was in rubble from artillery bombardment and many weeks of battle.

Suddenly, they were under fire! “Take cover! Taylor! Simkovich! Set up a rear guard fire party, so we can withdraw,” cried a startled Sgt. Davis. The platoon scattered. “Heads down and keep dispersed,” ordered the Sgt.

Ten minutes had passed when the platoon found itself out of harms way. “Guess Jimmy Miller was right!” said a confused Sgt. Davis, “We take the LEFT fork. Where’s Jimmy?”

“Bringing up the rear as usual,” shouted one of the soldiers.

“Jim, how did you know about that left fork? It isn’t on the map!” asked a curious Sgt. Davis.

“I dunno!” answered a rather grim-faced Jim Miller, “I remember seeing a stone wall on our left bordering the road when we came in. I figured it would have to be there when we came back.”

“You’ve got some memory, Jim.” The sergeant continued, “I wish I had taken your advice in the first place.”

"Oh, it wasn't anything special. I just remembered, that's all!" They walked together with their weapons slung.

When they reached base, they were de-briefed on their mission. "Then your recon mission was just routine, Sergeant?" question the Colonel. "Yessir!," answered a tired Sgt. Davis, "Nothing unusual. There were more infantry troops than usual passing along that road. The Krout trucks looked sort of new, but that's about all."

Pvt Miller, interrupted, "Funny thing about those troops. They had two jagged marks on the side of their helmets."

"What's that?' asked the Colonel, "Do you say two jagged streaks?"

"Yes sir!" replied Miller, "Two streaks, sort of like lightning bolts."

A spark ignited in the Colonel's next remark, "Those jagged marks are the insignia of SS troops! This information can change the course of the entire allied plan in this sector!"

The Colonel put his fingers to his chin to think on it some more. "The presence of SS troops in this sector signifies weakness in the Nazi forces! The regular troops of the Wehrmacht are being stiffened by die-hard SS thugs!"

"I'll rush this information straight through to division." Said the adjutant as he jotted down some notes on his clip board.

The group of soldiers left the tent, "My eyes were open," said a thoughtful Sgt. Davis, "but I never saw those marks you mentioned Jim."

"I just happened to notice it!" said Miller rather meekly, "I thought it was a pretty queer insignia."

Meanwhile some miles ahead at the front, General Gallagher was peering through his binoculars, “Somewhere out there a Krout observation post is calling signals on us…and the artillery fire is pretty accurate!”

“We have our direction finders working to locate the OP, sir.” Said Captain Forrester.

A runner approached the general, saluting and handing him a dispatch, “Signal Corps report on the enemy observation post, sir. I think they’ve pinpointed it.”

“Good,” commented Gen. Gallagher, “We’ll have a photo recon plane get some shots of the area.”

The following morning, at headquarters…the photos were developed and the Colonel was briefing Sgt. Davis on what action to take. “Now, right there is the abandoned silo the enemy is using to radio artillery information from. Take a good look at these shots. Your mission will be to destroy the silo.” Jim Miller was standing nearby also browsing over the photos.

Beacon Green Platoon moved cautiously toward their objective, and a few hours later they reached the outskirts of the farm, the Sgt, peering intently through his binoculars. “That’s it!” he said, “Take a good look at it Jim.”

“Must be it,” said the Pvt., “It’s the only one around and that’s the approximate spot the detectors pinned down.”

“How does it look?” continued the Sgt.

“It’s a silo, but I don’t know. I’m not sure.” Jim was looking through the binoculars when he answered the Sgt.

"What do you mean you don't know?" said the Sgt. In a frustrated, strained voice, "That's the place. Let's get ready to jump off!"

But Jim Miller wasn't so confident. He was rubbing his chin, deep in thought, when he continued to object to the Sgt. "Something about that silo, Sarge. I can't pin it down yet, but I'm still not sure."

Sgt. Davis prepared to attack. Everybody was ready except Private Jim Miller.

"Get set to jump off!" shouted Sgt. Davis, then he turned to Miller, "What's eating you, Miller?"

Miller took his helmet off, and like a flash of light he suddenly realized what was bothering him about that silo. "I got a hunch about that silo!" he said as he adjusted the straps in his helmet, "I got a feeling that's NOT our objective."

Then he paused reflecting on what he had said, "Listen, Sarge... give me a chance to make sure. Let's scout this area once more. It will only take an hour or so."

The Sgt. sighed, "I'm crazy to even listen to you, Jim. I'll go along for one hour, but when it's up, we attack!"

For one solid hour the men of Beacon Green Platoon probed the area carefully, observing, feeling, checking, and searching.

"Are you satisfied now, Jim, that silo is our objective?"

"NO WAIT!" said an excited Jim Miller, "Look at these fresh wheel marks. Heavy stuff has been dragged to that silo from the woods. Let's check." He pointed ahead.

Ten minutes later, Miller led the platoon to another silo and pointed at it, "There's the silo we're after. The other one is a dummy, set up to throw us off track!"

"You're right, Jim" admitted the Sgt., "We ought to flush something out of that nest."

From dispersed positions, Sgt. Davis led the attack. "CUT LOOSE!" He cried. Screaming, he led the attack through the flimsy boards of the silo, as the attack increased in intensity.

"They're firing back!" yelled Miller, "Does that prove we're hitting the real thing?"

"It sure does," responded the Sgt., firing his machine gun in short bursts.

"Belton, DiMatto, Farrell, get around to the rear. Let's hit 'em men." The Sgt. ordered as they ran toward the foot of the structure.

Another ten minutes passed, the Nazi defenders surrendered. "Farrell, take a couple of men and check inside an' see if we got 'em all."

On the road back, the Sgt. asked Miller, "Jim, how did you notice the difference between the two silos?"

"I wasn't sure at first," Miller began, "But then I remembered those black and white photos. The film showed up the CAMOUFLAGE in shades of gray." He paused, turned and then continued, "The real silo had camouflage markings which gave it away on film!"

The Sgt., impressed, shook his head, "Jim, the army is going to make use of your talents from now on. I'll see to it personally."

Milk Run

Johnny Wexler was a seaman aboard a submarine based on an island south of the Philippines. In four months they hadn't done anything except skulk off the Japanese occupied islands at night doing all the chores which enable a guerrilla force to operate behind enemy lines. Johnny didn't like the monotony, but he liked it even less when the doldrums were shattered one dark night by a long, screaming burst from a Jap MTB.

Wexler was on a rubber raft returning from one of his missions when the Jap PT boat opened up on him. The deck gun of the American sub returned fire and seriously damaged the PT boat which turned away. Wexler was hauled aboard the sub, shirtless and exhausted.

"Come on, come on," said a crewman as they helped Wexler aboard, "Let's get below sir."

"The PT boat's gone," said another officer, "The skipper's on the bridge and wants to talk to you."

Wexler was tall, muscular, lean. A navy frogman for several years and extremely fit. Pushing back a heavy quaff of his blonde hair, he approached the Captain.

The Captain looked at Wexler up and down, his eyes resting a moment on Wexler's untidy hair and then on his shirtless chest. "Quite a shock to have 'em open up on you, eh, Johnny," said the Captain, placing his hand on Wexler's shoulder, "Did you find Espinoza in there as scheduled?"

"Yessir!" Wexler replied, slightly out of breath, "He gave me a message for you." He reached into his waterproof pouch, "Got it right here..." He blinked hard and fumbled through the pouch, "It. It's gone, skipper! Must have dropped out of my pouch when I went over the side."

The exec interrupted, "Jose Espinoza is Naval Intelligence. He's our top operative. Whatever was on that paper was important."

Wexler stood motionless, confused and wretched. The Captain didn't say a word.

The sub submerged in a deep cove, and just in time. The enemy torpedo boat had radioed news of the American sub as it was limping away.

"I'll have to send a detail back ashore, Johnny," said the Captain as he was peering through the boat's periscope at the incoming destroyers, "Think you can find Espinoza's rendezvous again?"

"By myself, skipper," Wexler responded, "More than one would be spotted right off. I ain't no hero but I'd better go alone." The Captain agreed.

Later that evening, after a brief rest, Wexler swam ashore out if an escape hatch while the sub was still submerged.

Once ashore, Wexler pulled out his rifle and side arm and other equipment he had and proceeded inland.

From behind him, a voice, "Japanee?" Wexler fell to the ground and turned to see a Filipino guerrilla pointing a carbine at him.

"No Jap," said Wexler, careful not to shout, but loud enough to be understood.

The insurgent lowered his weapon and said with his thick Philippino accent, "You no Jap! You Yankee sailor. You look for Espinoza? You want heem, I take you."

They marched off through the thick brush careful not to run into any Japanese patrols. Two hours later, deep in a Mindanao swamp—Espinoza was sitting under a tree smoking a cigar. He was a rough-looking character, with chiseled features, a well trimmed mustache, thick black hair with gray at the temples. He was in uniform with a Colonel's insignia of rank in his shoulder flap. He looked up at Wexler.

"So, the message went to the bottom? Bueno, you come back. I'll give you another message John. I've learned more since you left—it is better this way."

Both men entered the command hut and sat at a wooden table. The colonel gave Wexler some hot coffee as he brought him up to date on the latest intelligence.

"You know," began Espinoza, "We're fighting the Japanese all the time. Constantly ambushing them. Maybe thousands get shot over the past three years. The invasion by Mac Arthur will come soon. We know this. Now you Americans are back to help us win the war." He was writing another message for Wexler to take back. The colonel finished and sealed it in an envelope.

The colonel asked Wexler to join him on a raid that night as he handed him the dispatch.

"Here," said Espinoza, his wide unflinching eyes gazed at Wexler, "We're going to raid a Jap port tonight. Come with us."

“Okay,” said Wexler, rather puzzled, thinking he should be off immediately with the dispatch. “I guess you know what you’re doing.”

The colonel showed vigor and courage as he led the raid. The former fishing port, now a Jap military base, was the target. The detail reached the base by midnight.

Their surprise attack worked. Suddenly the port was ablaze and the gas storage tanks an inferno. As the guerrillas rushed in for the kill, Espinoza pointed off the docks and told Wexler to take a row boat and join the sub.

Minutes passed and Wexler was aboard again, this time with the message.

The captain’s eyes widened as he read the coded message.

“Good God! Espinoza says Layte’s the place to invade. I’d been figurin’ on Mindanao. Johnny, you sure earned your pay for the week this time!” The Captain looked up at him curiously. “You still think this is a milk run?”

Wexler smiled, “If it was any more excitin’ my heart couldn’t stand it skipper.”

“...toughen ‘em up!”

In the Fall of 1942, General Douglas MacArthur's forces began attacking the Japanese troops in New Guinea. The Japs had everything, air superiority, artillery and tanks. The U.S. service men who began the attack were inexperienced draftees who'd never been in action before. Career soldiers like Sergeant Larry Turk, knew the best way to lead them in an unequal fight was to "...toughen 'em up!'

Third squad was embroiled in hand-to-hand fighting near a Japanese outpost deep in the jungle.

Sgt. Turk was yelling at one of the raw recruits when the boy hesitated..."Either ya fight them, rookie, or me! Make up yer mind!" The Sgt. grabbed him by the collar.

The tough N.C.O. drove his squad hard...he tried to make them mad...mad enough to forget their fear of the enemy.

“The Japs will call out durin’ the night! They’ll say they’re G.I.s and they’re hurt. They’ll plead for help! They’re great little actors. Don’t fall for it...if you creeps leave yer foxholes, you’re dead men, ‘cause, if the Nips don’t get ya...I sure will!”

Night was the worst for these young, untried soldiers, who’d been thrown into battle after minimal training.

Sure enough, the cries in the night began. Very convincing, but Sgt. Turk kept the men in line. He’d toss a grenade at the Japanese pretending to be wounded Americans.

"How could he be so sure it was a Jap?" asked one of the men. The Sgt. turned to him with a scowl on his face.

The squad leader hammered at them, bullied them, and tried to keep them alive until they learned the ropes.

One of the recruits was sent to take out a machine gun nest.

"Just keep runnin' Sonny," advised the Sgt. "No matter what happens...don't stop! We'll give you cover fire!" A tap on the back, "Now—GO!"

Sonny ran a short distance, then fell on his belly. The concerned Sgt. Turk knew he'd be riddled with bullets if he didn't get him out of there. He turned to Cpl. Allen..."If I get knocked off, corporal, you're in charge!"

Then he ran toward Sonny, but to the flank of the machine gun nest. While the Nips had Sonny pinned down, the Sgt. had time to sneak up on their flank and toss a grenade. Both Japanese soldiers were killed and the gun destroyed. But as luck would have it, a Japanese officer pulled his pistol and captured Sgt. Turk!

Their squad leader was now a prisoner of war, and Cpl. Allen, held the squad in the same position until Lt. Haze clued them in.

"Losing Larry Turk was a tough break for this squad! Now... stay awake. The Nips have tanks. If they try to break through, use bazookas!" he turned to Cpl. Allen..."Who's your bazooka man?"

"Floyd, Sir," replied Cpl. Allen, "But we haven't been using it so far."

The Lt. continued, "The field hospital and ammo dump are right behind us! If the Jap tanks break through, the division may get wiped out! You've got to stop them."

"Y-yes, Sir!" Allen stammered. The Lt. left to attend to Baker Company. Moments later, the squad could hear Jap tank engines roaring through the jungle, and the clatter as they came nearer.

"Listen," said Floyd, holding the loaded bazooka on his shoulder, "There's a tank close by Tom."

"Remember…the field hospital and ammo dump…don't miss," came the warning from Tom.

The lead tank crushed its way through the brush and smashed its way into the clearing in front of Pfc. Floyd.

"Pull the trigger, Floyd!" commanded Allen.

"I—I can't!" exclaimed Floyd.

Shirtless and chained, spread-eagle, on the front of the lead Jap tank was Sgt. Turk!

"Shoot Floyd! That's an order!" shouted Sgt. Turk.

"B-but the Sarge'll be killed!"

Floyd took aim. His shot went right over the head of the Japanese tank commander standing in the turret hatch, driving him back into the tank. Floyd immediately dropped the bazooka and ran to the side of the oncoming tank, climbed aboard, and before the officer could close the hatch, he dropped a grenade through the turret. The explosion killed the tank crew and the machine came to a halt.

The rest of the squad rushed the tank and unchained Sgt. Turk.

The Sgt. commended Floyd, “That was pretty smart, firin’ close to the tank to bluff the Japs. I still think you should’ve aimed right at the tank!”

“Gee, Sarge! I DID aim at the Tank!” said Floyd, “You don’t think I’d disobey a direct order, do you?”

A slight grin crossed Floyd’s lips, as Sergeant Turk wiped sweat from off his brow!

I Married a Werewolf

"I froze with fright at the sight of it as it came closer, closer! I couldn't scream...my throat was paralyzed!"

Ellen Mayfield was a strikingly beautiful woman, tall, bright red hair, delicate features, slim. One moonlit night, walking home, she felt uneasy, as if stalked by an unseen animal—and she was!

In one agonizing moment I felt his breath on my face...his sharp claws came up slowly, and his long, white fangs came near to my throat! It took all my strength to turn and run. I ran until I thought my lungs would burst, along the deserted streets...and all the time I could hear his footsteps behind me!

I fell from sheer exhaustion...I couldn't go on!

A hand grasped me by my shoulder...

"Please...have mercy! Why me?" I pleaded. But as I looked up...I saw a rather handsome gentleman, dressed in a business suit, striped tie, and neatly combed brown hair, bright, light brown eyes.

"Well, what's this all about?" he said softly as he helped me to my feet. "I heard you yell for help several blocks back!" He smiled in reassurance.

"Ohh!...then it was you who was running after me. I thought it was that hideous werewolf!"

The stranger gave me a long, hard look. "I can see you don't believe me!" I said rather perturbed at the whole affair. I noticed the streets around me were not empty anymore. There were a scant few people curiously looking on. I hesitated saying the next words and looked about me to make sure no one was in earshot, "There was a werewolf…but he vanished!"

"Young lady, it's a long walk back to my car, but you'd better come with me. I'll drive you home." he smiled. His name was Mark Sheldon.

I had forgotten about the werewolf by the time we reached his car—a sporty Karmann Ghia—"A pretty girl like you shouldn't be out so late."

"I went to a party, Mark. I love parties! Why, they're my life's blood, as a matter of fact!"

My house was on the outskirts of the city, an old nineteenth century Victorian. By the time we reached my house, I realized that Mark Sheldon was the kind of person I was very attracted towards.

"You know, Ellen," Mark said with a romantic gleam in his eye, "Im not sure I blame that werewolf. You're really a beautiful woman!"

"Don't joke about it please…the thought of being eaten alive is enough to drain the blood out of me!"

"I want to be around to protect you. If you don't mind, I'd like to call on you soon!" I nodded in agreement and really looked forward to seeing him again. I said goodnight and he drove away.

Mark took me out regularly after that. He told me that he loved me, and I was extremely happy. But he always seemed worried, pensive, and ill at ease. Over a candlelight dinner, one evening, I asked him about it.

"Ellen, you know I love you and want you to marry me, but, there's something I must tell you…"

"Nothing could possibly make any difference, dearest," I reassured him.

"Ellen, I know that, indeed, a werewolf was after you the night we met…because I WAS THAT WEREWOLF!" His eyes narrowed and his face turned dark, as his lips tightened, expecting a horrifying reaction from me.

"I don't believe you. That's impossible Mark!" I said with a bit of trepidation.

"Why do you think I've never kept you out past midnight?" he continued, "That's when this awful curse effects me. That's when I change…then towards dawn, I become myself again!"

"Oh, Mark…it was towards dawn when you caught up with me!"

I was frightened…but I still cared enough for him…more than I could say.

"Ellen, I'm sure we can work it out somehow." We left the restaurant.

"Please, Mark…I've got to think! Maybe mother and dad could help us figure a way out of this terrible dilemma."

My folks were very understanding…and as dad made a suggestion, our hearts swelled with new hope!

Ellen's father was a distinguished looking gentleman. Although balding, he was very austere, with a full mustache. He was dressed in a smoking jacket and bowtie the evening Ellen and Mark approached them. Her mother was a very attractive elderly lady, charming, gracious and stately in appearance. She was as tall as Ellen, with speckled gray hair she wore up. Both Ellen's parents were highly educated, articulate and well mannered. They sat on the living room sofa as the four discussed the situation.

I've heard of a Doctor Morris Vallencourt," said father to Mark, "He has performed wonders with cases such as yours Mark. If you agree to undergo treatment, I see no reason why you and Ellen shouldn't marry."

To Mark, it seemed incredibly too easy! Not many parents would have consented to such an arrangement after discovering this terrible secret!

"I'd do anything to rid myself of this curse, Mr. Mayfield." Said a hopeful Mark Sheldon.

Mark and I were happy again. We talked about the future, and forgot about the time of day! Then Mark turned to me in horror…

"Five minutes! For heaven's sake, lock me away somewhere! I'm starting to turn into that hideous creature!"

"Quickly," said father, "Follow me…"

It was a long way to our cellar, and even as we went down I could hear Mark pant with his wolf-like desire for human flesh!

We raced toward the fruit cellar, opened the heavy oak door and Mark ran into the room. The walls were solid stone, no outlet, no windows other than a small one on the oak door. There were three iron bars running vertically through this small window.

"Hurry!" cried Mark, as father led the way. I felt anguish, fear and pity all at the same time.

Mark ran into the far end of the room as father bolted the door shut. The three of us watched the transition take place.

I fell into mother's arms, "There, there dear, everything will be all right." My mother told me in solace.

A morbid fascination forced me to watch Mark change…an agonizing growl came from deep in his throat! I was overcome with revulsion at the sight of a man, the man I loved, turning into a savage beast!

Mark's eyes turned red, his face and hands were slowly covered with dark, bristly hairs! His nose and mouth protruded more and more and took on the shape of a snout! He became a snarling, drooling werewolf, enraged with hunger!

He rushed towards the door with a crash—growling, howling, pounding the stout wood…grabbing at the iron bars. But they held—we backed off instinctually, even though there was no chance of him escaping.

My father grabbed me, "You shouldn't be seeing this Ellen! Come on upstairs…" We turned and went back up the stairs to the parlor.

None of us could sleep that night. And when dawn broke, mother, dad and I went down to release poor Mark. Later, that evening, we went to see Dr. Vallencourt.

After an extensive examination…

"Is there any hope doctor? Mark asked anxiously.

The doctor was a balding, elderly man, wearing heavy horn-rimmed eye glasses. He had white hair around the temple, was heavy-set and donned a white surgical tunic. He had a wise and noble visage about him, which showed how well he carried his years. There were many plaques and framed degrees hung on his office walls.

"I have cured many of lycanthropic disease…it takes time, but in the end you will be a normal, healthy man, Mr. Sheldon."

Treatment started that same evening…injections, blood transfusions, and electric shock therapy.

Slowly, over the next several weeks, an improvement could be seen. We planned our wedding and in three months we got married. It was the happiest moment of my life! And I'll be even happier after the final stages of the cure have passed. We moved into my parent's house so we could monitor the treatments better.

Every night while Mark was undergoing treatment, we locked him in the fruit cellar. We saw a gradual improvement over the next several weeks.

Those long, dreary months finally passed, and one evening, Mark came home to our house very excited! He ran up to all of us.

"Honey, honey, the doctor says I'm completely cured!"

"Are you sure, darling?" I asked hopefully.

"There's one way to find out," dad said casually from his easy chair. "Let's all go down to the cellar."

Dear dad…he always thought of everything! He locked Mark in his cell for one last time, and that last quarter-hour barely seemed to pass.

"…thirty seconds more." Said father as he studied his wristwatch and looked at Mark through the window bars.

Midnight came…and it was true! Mark WAS cured. Mother, dad and I were ecstatic! We unlocked the door. My husband was the picture of health…his cheeks had a warm, pink glow…his jugular vein pulsated with excitement!

"See that," Mark beamed, "A hundred percent cured. I'm human flesh and blood again!"

What a thrill, just to hear that word, BLOOD!

Mark stood staring at father and mother as I approached him. For what he saw was an incredible transformation taking place!

"We've waited so long for you Mark!" I said as I drew nearer to him, "So very long—now you can really join our family—not as a werewolf—but…"

We came towards him, our eyes aflame, and our fangs dripping…

"Vampires!" he shouted, "Y-you're all vampires!"

Crime Wave!

There had been one man crime waves before! But the law swiftly obtained a full description of the wanted criminal. This time it was different. There was a baffling twist—the hood never looked the same twice! The law enforcement officials were desperate in an effort to learn the crook's true identity.

It was March 14, 1952, Yonkers Raceway, an unhappy gambler, Barry Stevens, a television actor, was losing his shirt. He played the soaps and lately played tough-guy roles on a TV series. Although famous, he passed unnoticed in the large crowd at the track. He was walking away, gloomy, dejected.

"I—I can't believe it! I really went in over my head this time." Stevens brooded, as he walked to the parking lot.

He was a tall, handsome man in his thirties. A perfect face and voice for an accomplished actor.

"That blasted tipster—he said 'Prince Boy' was a sure thing in the third race. Now I owe a pile to that bookie—and I'd better get it up. These guys play rough." His thoughts agonized him.

But, by eight o'clock, Barry Stevens had put aside his worries and concentrated on his role of the heavy this week. He played the part to the hilt. The crew and cast applauded him. Afterwards, in his dressing room:

"Hey Barry," said a fellow actor, "Aren't you going to take off the makeup now?"

"Sure," he answered, "Sure, you go right ahead—I'm—er—I'm a bit tired."

When the others had left, the hapless actor's troubles settled in on him like a weighty pall.

"I've got to raise some money! But how, how?" He thought, holding his head…then…*"Mmm…"* he was staring at himself in the dressing room mirror. Holding his prop gun and sporting a fancy mustache, *"I could walk into some place wearing this disguise, hold it up and nobody'd ever recognize me! I wouldn't even have to wear a mask!"*

The actor, still wearing his makeup slipped out through the side entrance and worked his way to a local gas station.

"Reach, you guys, and keep 'em up!" The two attendants did what they were ordered, while Stevens emptied the cash register. The two men got a real good look at the thief—twenty minutes later the cops came to get the description.

"The burglar had brown hair, a reddish brown mustache, and he wore a light blue shirt, under a tweed jacket."

Barry was back at the studio, busily destroying the evidence.

"This is perfect—perfect," he laughed.

"The cops'll spend forever looking for the crook that pulled the job tonight! This is perfect!"

In three weeks, Barry Stevens had paid off his bookie, but the germ of easy money and the thrill of real-life action had now taken root and on an April 3rd telecast of his Thrill Theatre show, he went on his crime spree.

This time a half hour after the show, at a roadside restaurant…

"Don't say a word lady, just hand the cash over!"

"Don't shoot mister, here, take it all!" said the terrified cashier. Moments later, Stevens ditched his outfit and went home.

"Yes officer," said the woman he had just robbed, "He was about five feet, ten inches tall, rather dark, beetle-browed, and wore a blue shirt, black bow tie, fedora and double-breasted suit jacket."

At 11:30 the next morning, Lieutenant of Detectives, Mark Carmichael, and police Captain Roy Benson met in the Captain's office.

"Usually, Captain, a sudden outbreak of Lone Wolf burglaries and hold-ups signifies the work of one man," said Carmichael.

"There's only one thing wrong with that theory Mark," the Captain rose from his desk and went over to a board hung on his wall with illustrations of each of the men described in the crimes committed.

"These are police artist's drawings made from the descriptions of eyewitnesses to the various crimes. But they're all different! The only common denominator is that in each case the criminal wore a blue shirt!"

Barry Stevens' disguises were working like a charm and in the weeks that followed, he struck again and again. He was smart enough not to use the same makeup and character impersonation he just played. He mixed it up, carefully changing each personality so they couldn't connect him to any of the crimes!

On May 19th, Detective Carmichael sought relief from the perplexing case with a quiet evening at home. He and his wife and children were watching Thrill Theatre.

"You were once on television too, weren't you daddy?" asked one of the kids.

"Sure, but not as an actor—I was a guest on a panel show."

Moments later as the TV crime play reached his climax…

"Oooh! He's a bad man, isn't he daddy?"

"Don't be afraid, honey! He's only an actor—Barry Stevens, and he's only a bad man on television!"

"He looks ugly, doesn't he dear?" commented Mark's wife.

"All hoods look ugly, my dear."

As the show ended, "I have to say, Barry Stevens wasn't half as mean tonight as he was on the studio's show two Saturday's ago," said Mrs. Carmichael.

"It beats me how you remember all those TV programs."

The phone rings.

"Oh, no—if that's headquarters…" said his wife.

"Don't say it, sweetheart," as Mark answered the phone.

"Hello…"

"It's Sims, Lieutenant. Another hold up tonight—the eleventh Lone Wolf holdup in two months—on Columbus Avenue."

"Any description of the hood, Sims?"

"Yes, Lieutenant—a pretty good one! He had black hair, wore a blue shirt and dark, pin-stripped suit."

Carmichael repeated the description—"Black hair, a dark suit and a BLUE SHIRT, did you say? Mmm…"

He mulled over the blue shirt—then said to Sims, "I've got it! Contact studio WMCA at once. I want to see the head of the casting department. And tell Captain Benson I'll meet him at headquarters in half an hour!"

Later, at precinct headquarters…

"This case is going to your head Mark," exclaimed Captain Benson, "You mean, just because that hood tonight had black hair and wore a blue shirt, you think…?"

"I'm sure of it Captain, but we've got to catch him red-handed! Now listen…" Mark began to unfold his plan.

The case neared its end when, on the evening of May 29th, Barry Stevens completed one of his usual tough-guy roles on stage…Nice black banded fedora, pencil mustache, checkered jacket and dark bow tie. The actor moved cross-town to East 57th Street and slipped into the cellar of a nightclub where…

"Don't make a false move, Mister, and you won't get hurt!" Stevens demanded as he pointed the gun at the owner in his man's private office.

Just then…"Don't make a false move either Mr. Stevens, and YOU won't get hurt!" Lt. Mark Carmichael had the drop on him.

"HUH?" said the stunned actor, "You followed me here? You knew! But how? I had a fool-proof gimmick!"

"Yes you did," replied Carmichael, as the officers disarmed and handcuffed Stevens, "Wearing a different get-up for every job, the identical ones you wore on your TV shows! Except for one thing Barry—that blue shirt you wore on every caper you pulled."

He paused a moment to let that fact sink into Barry's thoughts. The Lt. continued, "You see, I played a guest shot on TV myself once and I suddenly remembered what the director told me—to wear a blue shirt, because white causes dark shadows on the screen! And when I checked with the casting department of your studio and found out that your TV appearances coincided with the dates of the hold-ups, I was sure it was you!"

"Okay, okay, you've got me," Barry muttered as he was lead away, "Let's get it over with."

Barry Stevens was found guilty and was sentenced to a twelve year stretch up the river.

Amanda's Watchful Eye

Donald Cosgrove considered it a genuine act of mercy—to himself. For longer than he cared to remember, his wife, Amanda Cosgrove, had been an overwhelming force in his life. She needled him, bossed him around; judged him harshly and constantly. In other words, she was a tyrant who made his life a living hell. And so, on that fateful day when Amanda told him—for the thousandth time—to shine his shoes, straighten his tie, and adjust his jacket, Mr. Cosgrove helped his wife down the stairs—with a lusty push! There could be no doubt that he had done an excellent job. Amanda was very, very dead.

The next problem was to dispose of the evidence in such a way that he would be able to enjoy his new-found freedom. The train ticket which he had previously purchased for Amanda's visit to a mythical cousin was, he thought, good sound thinking. So was the forged exchange of letters announcing that Amanda was fed up and had no intention of returning home. Now there was only the matter of arranging for the final disposition of Amanda herself.

The living room fireplace, he decided, was the most appropriate spot for what he had in mind. Mr. Cosgrove neatly stowed the body of Amanda in the repository he had selected. It was the work of almost the entire day to brick up the front of the fireplace and seal forever the secret. When he finished, Cosgrove stepped back…it was a job well done.

The following morning he turned instinctively for a survey of his previous day's efforts. A bit of apprehension seized him when he saw that all of the bricks he had so painstakingly tamped into place were unquestionably wobbly. Almost, he thought, with a shudder, as if someone, or something, had kicked them loose from the inside! A momentary wave of panic gave way to grim resolve to learn from his past error. Whistling a sprightly tune, Cosgrove went to work again. He stepped back, test-kicked a few spots and, pleased with the result, went on his way to the office.

Returning home that evening, he checked his morning's project: the fireplace bricks were as firmly in place as when he had left earlier in the day. With a broad grin and a snap of the fingers, he proceeded to the telephone and, in a surge of excitement, invited several friends to join him that very night.

One half-hour before his guests were scheduled to arrive, Cosgrove decided upon a bold course of action. With a snicker much louder than Amanda would ever have permitted, he went to great lengths to make certain that his shoes would be smudged, his tie crooked and his jacket adjusted in such a way that it closely resembled a gunny sack. Then, with a final snap of his fingers and click of his heels, he went down stairs.

He glanced around the living room to make doubly sure that everything was in a disheveled condition. The ash trays, he noted with pleasure, were piled high with butts, the cushions totally unplumped and—final note of triumph—his oldest pair of boots rested atop the cocktail table.

He turned to the fireplace, and his gasp was extremely audible. There, as if etched clearly on the bricks of the secret crypt, was the face of Amanda Cosgrove!

Dangerous Deception

I hadn't meant to deceive William of course. He was the last person in the world I wanted to trick. After all, I'd soon be his wife. But that realization still didn't stop me from worrying about how to make ends meet. You see, I wasn't what you might call a rich girl—or even one who had her savings put away in some bank. I took care of my Mother and my younger brother and everything I earned seemed to melt away like butter.

William, on the other hand, was very rich. That is, his family was. And all his friends and the places we went to personified the enormous wealth he has at his command. Then one would think I could easily have asked for a loan, but I wasn't like that. My pride wouldn't let me. I would either marry him on my own resources or I wouldn't marry him at all! There was my trousseau to be bought, my various clothes, a hundred-and-one detailed odds-and-ends to be acquired and arranged before I could walk down the aisle of a very fashionable chapel with William.

Then too, from the way William talked, I didn't dare shatter his ideals about me. To him I was a girl different from the rest. I wasn't after his money, and I was completely independent of any financial problem. How could I say otherwise? I couldn't! And I didn't want to, frankly, even though Mother and Tony, my brother, called me a fool for not explaining my peculiar situation to William.

I was a model and saleslady at Arnold Constable in Manhattan. William met me there a year ago and soon asked me out. Now, we were all set to be married. William was what you might call—somewhat stiff. Yes, a real stuffed shirt. He was all manners and propriety—a man removed from the relentless toil of everyday life. He conducted his romance with me like a broker buying or selling stocks at the exchange. But he was young and very distinguished; had a good name—and he was wealthy. That's all that mattered I told myself. And it was enough! But now I had to find some spare-time work for the next three months until the wedding day—so that I could finance my own small arrangements without bothering William.

I got a job after hours as a lap dancer at a swank Murray Street night club. Fantastic? Yes—but I was desperate, and the dancing job paid the best! The nights I danced in front of the high-society crowd weren't without their pleasant moments. Neither William, nor my family knew anything about it—obviously—and I was saving for my coming marriage.

Everything would have turned out as I planned if it weren't for Vic Evans. He was a young man whom I met at the nightclub. He'd always be watching me, talking to me, walking me to the subway. He'd accompany me almost every night, sort of a bodyguard to see me safely home. I got to know him over time and became rather fond of him. He was a file clerk at Met Life, on his way up the ladder.

Then one night he kissed me in the park—and I knew I'd never marry William. My dream of wealth and position were ended with Vic's kiss—and I resented it. We fought terribly. I told him off one night and ran to the subway. I was determined that my marriage to William would come off, and that following night I danced seductively to the strains of the saxophone for the last time, content with my thoughts, supposedly.

Then I saw William's shocked face watching me from the crowd! His high-society clique was with him. He berated me, accused me, shouted at me and left me humiliated and ashamed. Then Vic broke in grinning unpleasantly at William. It was Vic that tipped off William and brought his crowd to the nightclub. He wanted me to see William as he really was. I was convinced.

As Vic's lips found mine afterwards, I realized that the false lure of position couldn't compare to the bright promise of true romance. Though my short career as a lap dancer came to an end, it was funny, but no real surprise that a saleslady and file clerk would be wonderfully happy. This one detail I had overlooked with William. A detail that had changed me into the kind of girl I should have been long ago—a girl in love!

Tale of the Salted Lake

Clear Lake was like a flat blue mirror, placid, unruffled, reflecting the broiling sun overhead. The lake was surrounded by dense woods and high mountains. There in the calm waters the red painted hull of an overturned canoe made a stark smudge against the cobalt water!

Lonny Harris, a young State trooper was at the scene with an older man, Patrick Gray, another Trooper. They stood in the bow of the police boat and watched as men righted the canoe and towed it to the near shore. A man, Charles Jenkins, was also pulled from the water. An accident? A simple drowning? Lonny had to be sure. He was placed in charge of the case.

"Poor guy," said Pat Gray, rather dryly, as he was motioning to the stern of the police boat where the dead Jenkins lay under a tarpaulin. "Guess he was fishing or something and his canoe tipped over. Canoes are tricky. I got dunked myself once when I was a kid. It's really lonely around here too. Not a soul to help you if you get in trouble."

"Maybe," said Lonny. They headed for a tiny dock at the far end of the lake, around a bend, where there was a general store. On the way they passed the lonely cabin where the dead man had been staying. Wisps of smoke were still curling lazily from the stone chimney.

"Must have had a pretty good fire going," commented Pat, "Still smoking. Probably ate his breakfast early, looking forward to a day on the lake. He was on vacation, wasn't he? Poor guy." Lonny nodded.

As they approached the dock, Lonny said, "doesn't it strike you sort of funny, Pat, that a fellow like Jenkins would drown in a lake as calm as a mill pond? We don't know too much about him yet, of course, but look at the facts. This isn't a tourist spot. Except for the general store, and Jenkin's cabin, there are no other folks around. This is a place that experienced hunters and fishermen, real woodsmen would pick. And men like that can usually swim! Or, even if they couldn't swim, they'd have enough sense to hang onto the canoe and paddle to land. This guy Jenkins was no green kid!"

Pat gave the young trooper a searching look. "Better take it easy kid. You go off half cocked, start spouting lot of theories about murder, and you're going to get laughed at. It looks like a plain and simple accident to me. You're forgetting that knock on Jenkin's head?"

"That bothers me too," said Lonny, "That lump is right at the top of his head, right in the middle of his crown. How'd he manage to strike his head that way?"

After the body was taken away, and Pat left also, Lonny stayed behind to talk to old Mr. Hanley, owner of the general store. Hanley was stooped, with graying hair. He peered over his rimless glasses at Lonny. "Terrible thing," he said, "Terrible! Going to hit Mr. Maddox awful hard I'm afraid. They were such good friends, shared that cabin and all. Came here every year about this time. Just shows you, though. You never know! In here yesterday, they was, both of them. Laughing and joking, as happy as you'd want."

"Tell me about Maddox," asked Lonny. The old man continued with evident relish. "Name was Bartholomew Maddox. He and poor Mr. Jenkins was partners in some business, I think. A big garage or something. Way they worked it was one of them would come up here for a spell, while the other one watched over the business. Except some weekends, when they'd both be at the cabin together."

"This is the middle of the week," Lonny said, "What was Maddox doing here yesterday if Jenkins was already here?"

The shopkeeper shook his head. "You don't understand son. Mr. Maddox drove Mr. Jenkins up yesterday, but he didn't stay. He went back last night. I know because I was here when they came in to buy their salt. Jenkins put the salt in his canoe and went back to the cabin, while Maddox drove away toward the city. I remember them joking about making Mr. Jenkins carry all that salt."

Lonny was bewildered. "Not so fast, old timer. Tell me about the salt. Why did they need a lot of salt?"

The old man snorted, "They didn't! Least ways not a hundred pounds. But Mr. Jenkins was that kind hearted—he liked to put salt around the cabin for deer, or any other animals that came around. So I sold it to him, naturally."

Lonny considered a moment, then asked,"You're positive that Maddox drove away? He didn't go back to the cabin with Jenkins?"

Anger quavered in Mr. Hanley's voice. "I still got good eyes, young feller. Jenkins went back alone with the salt, like I said. And I see what you're getting at, too. That maybe Mr. Maddox killed his friend! But he didn't—he couldn't. I know!"

"How do you know?"

Hanley held up one skinny finger. "One—because I got trout lines down around the bend, close to that cabin, and I tend them every morning real early. I tended them this morning and there was smoke coming from the chimney. But no car. So I reckon Jenkins was there and Maddox wasn't. Anyways, the road passes the store and I'd hear any car that went up there."

The old man continued, holding up two fingers, "Two—there wasn't no canoe or body floating in the lake when I was around that way this morning! I was all over the lake and I'd seen it sure. No—poor Mr. Jenkins was in the cabin, fixin' his breakfast like I say. He must have come out later, after I got back here to the store. Then when I went down to the dock I saw the canoe floating upside down and called you fellers! That enough for you, young man?"

Lonny grinned. "Maybe it is, old timer. Maybe it is!"

Lonny took the police boat back down the lake to the cabin. The door was still ajar, and Lonny entered quietly, feeling almost like an interloper. Rapidly he went over the interior of the cabin. A few embers still glowed in the fireplace and he stirred them with a stick, saw that Jenkins had been burning boxes or crates of some sort, as well as the logs that were stacked against the wall. As he bent toward the fire a strong, oily odor struck his nostrils. He was familiar with the smell, but at the moment he could not identify it. He shrugged and went on with his search. A half hour later he emerged from the cabin, knowing now that his suspicions had been justified.

No salt! Lonny frowned. The old storekeeper had said Jenkins had carried home a hundred pounds of salt the night before, yet all the salt in the cabin now was in the shaker. Remembering, he searched the vicinity of the cabin. He found the salt holders, where the deer were given the stuff, but they were all empty! Very odd! He wondered if the salt had been ordinary table salt, or the rock variety. You usually gave animals the latter.

Later, when Mr. Hanley said it had been rock salt he'd sold to the men, Lonny thought he knew. He also knew that he would have a tough time proving what he knew! Very tough—unless he could set a trap. He ordered more salt from the storekeeper, only twenty-five pounds this time, and left the man staring after him. Lonny went to get Pat Gray. He needed help in baiting his trap. He also talked to the police surgeon.

It was late that afternoon when the two troopers reached the lake again. This time they had Mr. Bart Maddox with them. Maddox was a tall man, well over six feet, with a tiny brown mustache over a weak, pursed mouth. He was also considerably agitated.

"I don't understand this," he grumbled, "Pulling me away from my business on a fool's errand. You've got no right! Charles was my partner and my friend, and I'm sorry as can be, but what can I do? I don't know anything about the way he drowned. The way you act, you'd think I had something to do with it."

"Just routine," explained Lonny. He winked at Pat Gray.

"The boat ready, Pat? I just want to show Mr. Maddox where his friend died. Maybe he can give us some idea how it happened!"

Lonny helped Maddox into the police boat with a firm grip. A moment later, they were speeding toward the spot where the red-bottom canoe had floated that morning. Maddox went a little white beneath his heavy tan. "I—I don't like this," he complained, "It's ghoulish! I demand to be taken back."

"In just a few minutes," said Lonny. He slowed the boat. They drifted slowly over the spot where Jenkins body had been fished from the water that morning. In the west the sun was sinking, a red ball of flame splintering on the now dark water. A little breeze sprang up, moaning eerily in the willows lining the bank. The boat glided quietly. The three men were quiet also. Lonny sneaked a glance at Maddox, saw the man's mouth working convulsively. Lonny turned back to stare at the water. Shouldn't be long now!

Suddenly, just beside them, the water began to boil. It swirled in a miniature whirlpool. Something white bobbed to the surface, went under again, came back! The object floated, staring at them. The dead face of Charles Jenkins!

Maddox began to scream, little piercing yells of agony and fear. Listening, the two troopers shuddered as the man cried out his story of murder and confession.

Later when Maddox was in a cell, Lonny explained to Pat Gray:

"He did it with the rock salt, Pat. Yesterday he left, but circled around and came back on foot. He killed Jenkins with a blow on the head, and then sunk the body and the canoe in the lake. He weighed them with the hundred pounds of rock salt, knowing it would be about twelve hours before the salt dissolved and the canoe and body came up. He put a candle on a box in the fireplace in the cabin, let it burn down and started a fire later so it would look like Jenkins was home. I found the tallow. Old man Hanley almost gave him a perfect alibi, because the body hadn't come up yet when he made his rounds. But I couldn't find the salt and when the surgeon said Jenkins had salt all over him, I got suspicious enough to set the trap. And now we know that Maddox had been stealing money from the partnership and was afraid Jenkins would find out."

Pat shivered. "It was a good trap, Lonny, but count me out from now on. A death mask, a dummy, and twenty-five pounds of salt can almost scare a fellow to death!"

Hit and Run

The country road was unpaved, made of hardened gravel and dirt, and the night was moonless, pitch-black. Mr. Williams, driving his 1949 Nash, was speeding over the bumpy surface. Suddenly, unexpectedly, a man crossed the road right in his path, from out of the dense woods.

"That man! I'm gonna hit him."

Williams did. Smashed him square on with a bone cracking thud. The victim disappeared under William's hood.

"I won't stop!" Williams thought, "He must be dead. No one saw me…I'll just keep driving."

He began to sweat and reasoned with himself. He kept looking in his rear-view mirror, but it was too dark to see anything. "Why should I stop and get mixed up with the police? It was an accident anyway. It wasn't my fault. I didn't mean to hit him."

He was battling with his thoughts and his conscience. "But what if he was still alive? What if he needs help?"

Another long pause as he continued driving along the deserted roadway. He kept staring in his rear-view mirror. Still, nothing but darkness, pitch-black cold darkness.

"Nah! It ain't my worry! Someone else will pass by and help take care of him. If he's still alive! Besides, what do I care. He's a stranger. I don't even know him."

He drove about a mile when he noticed a sign just ahead. A town called Lookout Mountain was no more than a half a mile away. He was on the outskirts. At last! He'll be able to get a hotel room and some shut-eye.

He laughed to himself. A nervous laugh. "Lookout Mountain, heh! A real hick town I bet. I hope they got a hotel."

It was about ten o'clock when he drove into the town and passed several men sitting out in front of the general store. He drove slowly by thinking:

"What a bunch of deadbeats staring at me. I guess they aren't used to strangers driving through their hick town."

Williams drove a short distance passed these men when he noticed the hotel. He parked in front.

There were perhaps six or more townsfolk on the steps of the hotel glaring at him and approaching his car. The men he passed at the general store were also closing in from behind!

"I guess this is some sort of welcoming committee," he thought. As they grew nearer, he could see they were carrying clubs and a thick rope. The townsmen surrounded his car, opened his car door and dragged him out. All their faces were grim and angry.

"What are you doing?" Williams shouted as they hog-tied him with the heavy rope.

"Knock it off. Let me go. I didn't do anything. Are you people crazy?" he cried as they tightened the knot.

One of the men spoke, "You didn't do anything?"

They hauled Mr. Williams to his feet and lead him to the front of his car. Williams looked on in horror.

"No, stranger. We ain't crazy!" another man said as they showed Williams the body of the man he had struck in the road. The dead body was wedged between the grill and bumper for all to see!

The Showdown

His reputation as a gunfighter rode into Silver City ahead of him. Brad Carlisle was tall, gaunt, with chiseled features, clean-shaven, dark flowing hair under a wide brim, black cowboy hat. He was well dressed with maroon colored shirt and a fancy, paisley vest, and heavy shod Mexican boots and spurs. He was a man in his mid thirties, riding slowly into town, straight up in his saddle! His gun, a colt .45, was hand crafted to his personal specifications, with an ivory handle. There were no notches on this gun; it was much too precious to mark up! He carried a Winchester but seldom used it. He strode into Silver City and went right to the local saloon. Word got out immediately… "Brad Carlisle, the fastest gun alive, was in town!"

Sheriff Billings, on the other hand, enjoyed a reputation as an affable, warm-hearted, capable and honorable man, well liked by the people of Silver City and respected by outlaws and troublemakers as well. He was in his early forties, about 6', jet-black hair with just a touch of gray at the temples. His face was weather-beaten, and pock-marked, but still retained a certain comeliness. He commanded attention wherever he was. His presence was felt the minute he entered a room. He had been sheriff of Silver City the past eight years.

Both men had been through the Indian Wars in 1876 and were hardened and somewhat volatile!

Carlisle never said a word to anyone until he entered The Sagebrush Saloon, sat down at a corner table, with his back to the wall. After he ordered a bottle of whiskey he told Mitch, the bartender, to deliver a message to the sheriff.

Mitch went right over to the jail, a short walk down the street. "Sheriff Billings, sir," said a shaken and white-faced Mitch, obviously hesitant to relate the message, "It's Brad Carlisle, you know…the gunfighter! He's over at the Sagebrush."

"Yeah, so?" said Billings.

Mitch paused a moment, looking at the sheriff and his deputy. "He told me that he'll meet you in the street in two hours!"

"No explanation?" asked Billings.

"None! Just…a showdown in the street. That's all."

Clay Billings looked at Mitch and got the words out, "All right Mitch. Go back to the bar; I'll be over in a few minutes."

Deputy Cort Evers was standing near the sheriff when Mitch told his story. "Clay," asked Evers, "What do you make of this?"

"Dunno Cort, but I'm gonna find out. Stay here. I'm going over to have a chat with our friend."

"Clay," interrupted Cort, "You know Carlisle is the fastest draw in these parts—or anywhere for that matter! No one knows for sure how many men he's gunned down—must be at least thirty-five from what I hear!"

"I heard tell over fifty!" said Mitch as he headed out the door.

"Clay," continued the deputy, "You're no match for this killer." The sheriff, grim-faced, looked up at Cort as he was bucking his gun belt, "Maybe so. Let me see what's going on first. Stay here Cort, and out of trouble. I don't want both of us barging in on him and goad him into doing something rash. Let me deal with this in my own way. Stay put, will ya?"

Billings walked out of his office testing the weight of his six-gun. He took a loaded Winchester off the gun rack just to be certain the gunslinger wouldn't get the drop on him.

The bar was crowded. Everyone of drinking age seemed to be there, from curious citizens to hotheads and the usual drunks. But it was strangely quiet, subdued, the atmosphere tense, charged with anxious, expectant men. No one dare look at Brad Carlisle, who sat quietly drinking his whiskey.

The owner of the saloon was a rather stunning, middle-aged lady, Kate Murphy, who had acquired the place three years ago. A strawberry blonde, she had soft milky-white skin, pure Irish through and through, a short-tempered woman, but stately and never loud or vulgar. She was well respected and close friends with the sheriff. Kate approached Billings as soon as he entered through the swinging doors.

"Hello Clay," said Kate solemnly, "I heard about this calling out. What's it all about?"

"That's what I'm here to find out," said Billings, spotting Carlisle at the far table. Clay glanced quickly at Kate then moved slowly toward the gunfighter.

"Your name Carlisle?" asked Billings with a hard, cold stare.

"That's right, Sheriff!" Carlisle gulped another shot of whiskey and laid the shot glass down gently on the wooden table. He looked up at Billings. "You got my message?"

"I got your message, sure enough! What's this all about?"

"I mean just what I said," Carlisle checked his timepiece chained to his vest pocket, "At exactly four o'clock I'll see you in the street." He looked up at Billings squarely in the eye, unflinching, not blinking once.

"Why? It's the obvious question."

All eyes and ears were turned on the two men. There was complete silence. No one took a breath, no one dare move!

"It's a nice day to die, Sheriff!" came Carlisle's answer.

"That's no answer. No reason!" said a perturbed Billings.

"That's all the answer and reason you'll get," Carlisle said pointedly. He poured another glass of liquor and gulped it down.

The sheriff raised his Winchester and threatened to arrest him.

"What's the charge, sheriff?" It was a sarcastic question.

"Threatening a peace officer. We'll start with that."

"You know that won't stick. Besides, look around you. Take a good look. The townsfolk hereabouts wouldn't cotton to a cowardly peace officer, now would they? Not only would you bring down every bushwhacker and hired gun from these parts, but you'll be voted out of office next election." He took a long, hard look at Billings. "No, Sheriff, you won't arrest me. You're going to meet me in the street in two hours."

The sheriff didn't move a muscle. He thought about it, and then lowered his rifle, turned and walked out of the saloon, Carlisle staring after him.

Kate signaled the piano player to pound out a lively tune. It certainly relieved the tension. She then followed Billings out of the bar and they both headed back to the jail.

At the sheriff's office, Kate, Clay and deputy Evers sat down and after a brief silence, Kate began the conversation.

"I saw that gunfighter two years ago in Deadwood. He's a cold-blooded, vicious killer. And he's got nerves of steel!" She paused and looked at the two men square in the eyes, "He gunned down three men he faced together! They were all dead before they hit the ground. All three! Carlisle had his gun back in his holster before any of them could reach for their gun. It was incredible. He's the fastest we'll ever see!"

"Sheriff, what will we do?" asked a very concerned Cort Evers.

"What can I do?" Billings took off his hat and sank deep in the hardwood chair.

All three looked grim, yet unbowed. An hour passed when Cort got up and said, "I'll make the rounds sheriff. Kate, please stay with Clay till I get back."

"Sure thing," she replied.

Cort stepped out of the jail, but he didn't make any 'rounds.' He headed straight for the Sagebrush.

Evers walked defiantly into the bar right up to the table where Carlisle sat, calmly drinking. His bottle was half empty by now, but he showed no outward signs of being drunk. Carlisle ignored the young deputy at first. Cort was young all right, early twenties, slight build, lanky almost, sandy colored hair, thin lips and handsome features.

"Carlisle? Get on your feet and face me!" demanded Evers, as he swallowed hard. Carlisle yawned and looked up at the deputy. A slight grin crossed his lips. "Don't, son. I know why you're here. There's nothin' you can do about this. My business is with Sheriff Billings, no one else. This is none of your concern."

"It is my concern. Why are you doing this?"

Carlisle didn't answer. He poured himself another drink. "Son, go home. I don't want to kill you. But I will if you force the issue. I admire your courage, defending your sheriff, but I'll put three bullets in you before you could reach for your gun. And that's a fact."

Mitch, the bartender, saw what was happening and quickly went over and grabbed Cort by the arm. "Come on Cort. Don't mess with this gunslinger." He tugged harder, almost dragging him away. "Come on, please, come on." Cort backed off and left the bar.

Back at the jail…

"You can't do it, Sheriff," pleaded Cort.

"What choice do I have, Cort?" Kate sat silently. She couldn't speak.

"It's almost four. Let me get a posse together and run him out of town." Suggested Cort.

"No, Cort, no! I'll take my chances."

"You haven't got a prayer, and you know it Clay," said Kate, choking back a tear. "You know it!" No more words were said.

Billings checked his revolver one last time and headed for the saloon. Carlisle checked his watch. He slowly rose, put on his hat and walked out of the saloon into the street. There were hundreds of people lining both sides of the dirt road. Looked like the entire town had turned out—young folks, old folks, ladies and gentlemen, riffraff and every child age six and up. All were watching, waiting, whispering softly. Then, not a sound.

Carlisle was first to plant himself squarely in the center of the street, facing the direction of the oncoming Sheriff Billings.

The men were no more than sixty feet from each other. Carlisle looked up at the clear blue sky. He extended his right hand in front of himself. It was his gun hand. He looked at it. It was steady as a rock!

He looked at Billings and said in a firm, clear voice, "It's a nice day to die, Sheriff."

Carlisle drew his pistol, clearly beating Billings to the draw. He aimed and pulled the trigger. It clicked three times. He then twirled the gun around his trigger finger and dropped it back into his holster, just as Billings cleared his own holster and fired a single shot.

The bullet went square into Carlisle's chest. He fell to the ground, alive, but mortally wounded. Billings hurried over to him and knelt by his dying body. Kate, Cort and half the townspeople surrounded the fallen gunfighter.

"Why didn't you fire?" asked a puzzled Billings.

Gasping for breath, Carlisle explained, "They were coming at me, calling me out, day after day. Most were just boys, just young foolish boys. I couldn't kill them any more, just couldn't, Sheriff."

He gasped for air, blood dripping from his mouth as he coughed. Kate and Evers looked at each other in a surprised, almost downcast way. The sheriff cradled Carlisle's head in his arms.

"I came here to die. I knew by challenging a lawman with your reputation, no one would come after you and it would finally end. I'd finally have peace."

His eyes closed and he died.

Sheriff Billings looked up at Kate and Cort with a painful, sorrowful expression. He gently laid Carlisle's head on the bare dirt. Then he stood up, staring down at the dead gunfighter.

Everyone stood there looking down at Brad Carlisle, the fastest gun in the West. They all looked on with their heads bowed. There was a long silence as the wind stirred and some horses neighed in the distance.

The Inventor

It was the first day of summer vacation from school, the year, 1894. Young Terry Haynes sat at supper in his home in Ottumwa, Iowa. He had eaten his ham and biscuits; finished his applesauce and was impatient to play a couple of innings of back-yard baseball before dark. But it didn't look as if supper would ever end, now that his father and the boarder, Mr. Hewitt, were in a heated argument about "progress" again.

To a school boy like Terry "progress" didn't matter. But to grown-ups it did indeed. For the past fifty years invention had followed invention. Steam engines crossed the continent from sea to sea. Gas and oil, the food for the machines, had been discovered and refined. Electricity shot through wires and carried messages. Mr. Hewitt was full of interesting information about all these things. He knew about machinery, too; how engines worked and what made pistons go up and down and how this turned wheels round and round. He understood how electricity ran along a piece of wire and about gas light, since that was the reason for his being in town.

Mr. Hewitt had come to Ottumwa to lay a pipe line so that the citizens of the town could cook with natural gas and light the streets and houses. During each day he rode out into the countryside, supervising the laying of the pipeline. At night he returned to his room and tinkered with his inventions. Mr. Hewitt was always getting parts sent by express mail or asking Terry to stop at Mr. Tate's blacksmith shop for a roll of wire or a piece of iron rod. Hewitt's room was always littered with unfinished contraptions.

"And they're likely to stay unfinished," Terry's father had been heard to remark. He said there were limits to the ingenuity of man. It stood to reason. He would rattle off the new inventions that had come into use just in the last century—railroads, gas and electric lights, the telegraph, talking machines and telephones! "And that's all," Terry's father would say. "We've gone far enough. There can't be anymore changes after today!"

But the disapproval and limited vision of Terry's father had not kept Mr. Hewitt from tinkering anyway in his spare time. He was trying to make a self-propelling buggy. He traveled all over the country and his horse was always worn out. "A vehicle that can go without being pulled by a horse is what I really need," he was saying at the supper table.

A horseless carriage! The very idea annoyed Mr. Haynes. "It can't be done," he snorted, "and even if it could be made, it would be perfectly useless. What are horses and railroads for? They've already tried this new fangled contraption in England. It was so noisy that a man had to walk ahead with a red flag to warn drivers to keep a tight hold of their horses."

"That was a steam vehicle," said Mr. Hewitt mildly. "I'm not working on a steam engine," he added. "I had thought of it, but a steam engine is too heavy, and it would have to stop every mile or so to stoke the fire and keep the steam up. I thought of using electric batteries too. I once saw an electric carriage on the streets of New York, but it couldn't compete with steam engines."

Terry hoped that Mr. Hewitt wouldn't go into details. It was getting dark and if supper went on any longer he wouldn't be able to play baseball.

"I've ordered a gasoline motor from an engine company in Michigan," continued Mr. Hewitt. "A single-horse-power gasoline engine."

At that very instant Terry's mind made a connection with Mr. Hewitt's talk and what Mr. Hollingsworth, the stationmaster, had said one morning. Terry leaned forward and entered into the conversation. "Mr. Hewitt, your engine's come. It's down at the depot. Mr. Hollingsworth said it was so big you'd have to fetch it in a dray!"

When the motor came to the house the next morning, there was no room for it. It weighed over one hundred and eighty pounds, and taking it up to Mr. Hewitt's room was out of the question. "The kitchen is big enough to handle it," Terry ventured to suggest, timidly.

"I always did want to see how these inventions came about," Terry's mother said. "I'd be glad to have Mr. Hewitt put his engine in my kitchen where I could keep an eye on it." So she made room for the strange looking machine in one corner.

Mr. Hewitt wanted to test the gears and traction. So he got Terry to fasten his bicycle by a rope to the rear of the buggy and tow it up Maple Street. And when Mr. Tate came out of his blacksmith's shop, they made the test all over again.

Each time Terry passed by Mr. Tate's for the next few days, he'd see him working on something for Mr. Hewitt's machine. When Terry went to the depot to meet the trains, people would ask him "How's the invention?" Everyone in town was interested; everyone, that is, except Terry's father.

Mr. Hewitt pulled his buggy to the back yard outside the kitchen door and Mr. Hollingsworth came by to help him. They lifted the motor into the frame and fastened the gears and levers next to the hand brake. Terry stood around and watched, fascinated.

Mr. Hewitt got all dressed up in his striped pants and stiff straw hat with a brown and purple hatband. Terry followed him out to the yard where the buggy was standing. Mr. Hollingsworth was also the deputy constable as well as the station agent. He stepped up and pulled out his badge and Terry heard him say, "You can't take that contraption on the streets of Ottumwa!"

"The streets are free, aren't they?" Mr. Hewitt retorted. "There's the railroad," Mr. Hollingsworth said.

"The railroad is fine for where it goes. One road west; one east; another south to Keokuk and north to Humboldt. But what about going somewhere the railroad doesn't go?"

Mr. Hollingsworth looked very uncomfortable as he wiped perspiration off his forehead. "I tell you what," he said, "I can't let you start to drive a horseless vehicle on the streets of town, because there've been objections, but you could pull the buggy out of town where I have no authority. Then if you happened to come back again, I don't see how I could stop you—not if the engine does what you say it can."

"I could hitch the horse to the buggy, but how would I get the horse home?" Mr. Hewitt asked.

"How about the Haynes boy? Couldn't he bring the horse back?" queried Mr. Hollingsworth.

That was how it happened that Terry Haynes set out with Mr. Hewitt for the crossroads three miles out in the country. Away they went in a buggy with a gasoline engine fastened under it, all ready to run by itself!

At the crossroads, both Mr. Hewitt and Terry did not talk. They unhitched the horse and buckled on the saddle. Next they pulled the shafts of the high-wheeled buggy. They poured a can of gasoline into the tank underneath the seat. The horseless carriage looked so small against the tall cornfield.

Mr. Hewitt swallowed hard. He jumped into the buggy and set the levers for starting. Then he climbed down and pulled out the crank handle, fitted it into that part of the engine that was set between the iron wheels and gave it a quick twirl.

There came a sputter and a cough and a great chugging. A trail of smoke came out at the back of the vehicle. Then the noise stopped. The buggy stood helpless in the road between the cornfields.

Mr. Hewitt twirled the crank again. There came another sputter and chug. This time he jumped into the leather seat, grabbed the steering stick, and fed gas to the motor before it could stop again.

The Fourth of July barbeque was well underway in town. Terry's father was scheduled to give a speech outside the courthouse. Meantime, the buggy lurched forward. "Better hold the horse," he called out to Terry as the wheels began turning. "Come down to the barbeque. I'll stop there." The rest of Mr. Hewitt's words were lost in the sudden tumult. Down the road trailing a column of dust went this amazing vehicle, with nothing to propel it along except some machinery that was fastened under the seat and somehow attached to the wheels!

Terry rode the horse at a gallop, but he didn't catch sight of Mr. Hewitt again until he arrived at the picnic grounds in a field behind the courthouse. There in the center of an awe-struck crowd was the horseless buggy, dust-covered and smoky. "What kind of contraption is this?" somebody asked the inventor. "It's incredible that it didn't tear up the street. It must have been going ten miles an hour!"

Terry's mother came forward and said, "The engine stayed in my kitchen." She looked very stylish in her starched white shirtwaist dress. She took great pride in her boarder's accomplishment. Terry looked at his father, still on the speaker's stand. Everyone had lost interest in his speech, which he never finished!

Mr. Hewitt waved to Terry's father, the ever-skeptical Mr. Haynes. "If it hadn't been for Mr. And Mrs. Haynes, I couldn't have built it," said Mr. Hewitt. "I'd be honored if Mr. Haynes would take a short ride around town with me. And there's room for Terry and his mom."

Terry's father folded up his speech. He climbed into the buggy and clutched the sides firmly. Terry and his mother squeezed between the gentlemen.

Mr. Hewitt got out, the crank was turned, the spark caught and the explosion echoed off the buildings. Hewitt leaped nimbly into the driver's seat again and grabbed hold of the steering stick. They stared down Main Street, with a shouting, checring crowd following along behind.

Mr. Hollingsworth was just about to intervene and stop the vehicle as it neared the train station, but Mr. Haynes called out, "It's all right Mr. Hollingsworth, I've changed my mind about this gas contraption. If it is going to be invented anyway, Ottumwa might as well get the credit!"

After they had traveled a little further, Mr. Haynes spoke again, rather slowly and thoughtfully, "I guess we must get used to the idea. Inventors like Mr. Hewitt will always be thinking of something new."

A Ghostly Visitation

He had a comfortable, roomy one bedroom apartment in Upper Manhattan. It was a typical bachelor apartment, if a one bedroom is typical. It was stately, spacious, modestly furnished with high ceilings and ornate molding. Carved, wooden pillars accented the entranceway to the foyer. There was an arch leading to a hallway which connected the bathroom. Here were marbled, mosaic floors with a huge tub that had the old style lion's paws for feet, besides a deep white porcelain sink. The large, multi-paneled windows faced the courtyard and the front street. It was cheerful, bright, airy. It was his home for the past nine years.

On a typical, uneventful weeknight, early in an uneventful, routine week, he came home from work, exhausted. After a hasty dinner he decided to go to bed early so he'd be refreshed for work the following morning. He fell fast asleep.

It was around one o'clock in the morning when something nudged him as he slept. At first it was a gentle tap, a subtle push, ending in a shove. He swore to himself that someone was in bed with him. Lying on his side, he brushed his arm back instinctively, trying to stop whatever it was. Groggy, he woke up gradually, still elbowing thin air! Naturally he was dreaming, he reasoned, or maybe it was his cat Oliver in one of his playful moods. "Get lost you pest," he muttered, weary and only half awake. There was no one there. He shrugged off the whole thing and soon was asleep again.

It wasn't too long afterwards that he was awakened again. There was a buzz in his ear, an imperceptible whisper. At first, it seemed far off and faint, then a heavy breath trying to form words, but only managing to confound him…"Psst, psst, psst," and more unintelligible gibberish, but just loud enough to be annoying. He opened his eyes and lay there trying to make some sense out of this formless breath which was more dreamlike than real! He couldn't tell. But, he noticed there was also a trace of a perfume, a fragrance familiar, yet he couldn't quite identify. He was wide awake now, the scent gone and the whispering had stopped. "Go to sleep you fool," admonishing himself.

More time passed. A couple of hours perhaps. By this time he was a little more than disturbed and couldn't fall back to sleep as easily as he had done earlier. "Please, no more hallucinations," he scolded himself. Trying to sort things out in his mind, there came the beginnings of a headache, from sleep deprivation he thought. He desperately tried to reassure himself that everything was all right. But he still felt uneasy, on edge, like something pricking at his skin, irritating. He just couldn't settle down.

He then turned to some soft music on his CD. It was soothing and helped him relax somewhat. It's the sort of thing you do to try and fill an empty void, where music becomes a substitute companion. He was sound asleep again. Later the CD turned off by itself. The room was quiet again.

It was around four-thirty a.m. when the bed became a deep-freeze. It was like icy fingers poking him with the atmosphere becoming heavy and oppressive. His breath was steamy. He wondered how the weather could have changed so drastically. It was autumn! He began to shiver, teeth chattering. The blankets weren't enough, obviously. "What the devil is going on here?" he said aloud.

There was an eerie, yellowish light flooding the room. Perhaps it was moonlight filtering through half-opened Venetian blinds. No, the blinds were closed tight. The mystery deepened. He was desperate for answers. Many people have experienced a premonition, a feeling of dread, that something bad was about to happen. It can be very disquieting to say the least. He had a premonition. Fear suddenly gripped him. The cold became unbearable and he sprang to his feet tossing off the covers in anger. Apprehensive, his heart was pounding, racing.

Turning towards the entrance to the bedroom, there was someone standing in the doorway, motionless! It was a shadowy yet distinct figure. Solid. Yes, it was definitely solid, not a silhouette. This figure had depth, weight. Although its features weren't discernable, when it turned slightly, the outline of a man could be determined. He was tall, maybe six feet, heavy set, with short cropped hair, a pot belly and a rather Romanesque aquiline nose. It was a man for sure, with limbs, a shape, standing there, menacingly.

Startled, our unnerved hero instinctively backed away toward the wall, frantically searching for a weapon of any sort, a broomstick, a heavy ashtray, even a shoe, anything to give him a little courage. He was completely overcome with fear. It must be a burglar or worse, some lunatic who had broken into his apartment. His thoughts were racing. He began to panic.

He was trapped. The only way out was through this intruder. "What do ya want!" he shouted. He didn't expect an answer, and was hoping this maniac wouldn't talk at all, just go away. He kept thinking to himself, how did this character manage to break in? There were two locks on the front door, one a deadbolt! Still no sound, no movement, not a peep out of the intruder. Paralyzed with fear, our scared roomer couldn't move either. He shouted again, "Get outta here or I'll brain ya!" No reply, no movement. He strained his eyes to get a better look at him. It was then he spotted the paperweight, grabbed for it and hurled it directly at the intruder's head. It passed right through him! It smashed against the parquet floor in the other room. Suddenly the figure turned and floated, yes floated, into the adjoining woodwork. He disappeared!

Rubbing his eyes in disbelief, he said aloud, "Get a grip on yourself." He couldn't move for many moments. He was dazed, shaken to the core, utterly bewildered.

Finally, after a long pause, silence. He figured it was safe to approach the doorway. The burglar must be lurking around the corner of the next room. He must be. He just couldn't have vanished into the molding. When he reached the threshold and peered cautiously around the corner, he prayed he wouldn't meet up with this character. Nothing. Not a trace. He breathed a long sigh of relief.

He tried to steady himself, his hands trembling badly. He could hardly catch his breath, taking a seat in a dining room chair, panting. It was then he noticed, or rather felt, the temperature in the apartment had returned to normal. Normal for this time of year. He wasn't shivering anymore; rather his trembling was from a bad set of nerves. The feeling of being in an icy morgue was lifted. That strange yellowish light was also gone. "Turn on the lights you idiot." Funny how he didn't think of doing it before.

He wasn't about to let down his guard just yet. Getting to his feet, he searched everywhere, under tables, his bed, behind the shower curtains, inside the two closets. He checked the locks on the door. All was in place. No one had come in through the front door. All the windows were drawn and locked. It was his habit since he lived in a ground floor apartment. No. No one could have slithered in through the windows either! How, by all that's holy, did he get in? He turned slowly, scanning the room, expecting someone to leap out at him at any moment. All was quiet, except for an occasional noise from the street outside.

He reached for a cigarette and poured himself a triple shot of bourbon. Sitting down again, he tried to gain his composure. His head ached right behind the eyes, which were bloodshot and weary. The night was nearly gone, and dawn was about to take its place. He just sat there against the table-top resting his head in one hand, dumbfounded, taking long drags on the cigarette. What had happened? Could there be a logical explanation? He didn't think so. He turned on the radio, once again looking for company. Company?

Wait a moment! Where was Oliver? Curiously he remembered his cat would hide whenever there was an unexpected visitor, like the super come to fix a leak.

As he got to his feet to look for him, there he was, crawling out from behind a table at the far end of the bedroom. He was whining loudly, hugging close to the floor, actually dragging himself across the room. The sound he was making was an awful shrill, almost like the wail of a baby crying from hunger. The animal was scared. He then darted toward his favorite corner in a pitiful state of nerves. "You saw it too, didn't you?" That clinched it for him. He hadn't imagined any of it. It was real. But what to make of it? He couldn't rightly say. He poured another glass and drank it quickly.

Thankfully the dawn came. He opened the blinds to let in the daylight. Daylight drives off all demons, even the ghostly kind, which our friend concluded to be what visited him last night. Nothing else added up. Yet he was the consummate skeptic, and wasn't the type to believe in ghosts. Not at all.

Then, as if a spark erupted in his mind, he recognized that apparition at the bedroom door. Of course! The height, the weight, the unmistakable shape, a potbelly, short hair, distinctive nose, even the perfume scent which was a special brand of cologne! It was the image of his own father! His dad had passed away some two months ago. Why wasn't all this clear to him before? He shuddered. He glanced at the cat almost expecting him to say he knew who it was all along. Shaking his head in disbelief, he lit up another cigarette and polished off another shot. His father!

He knew he was in no condition to go to work that day. It was fast approaching eight o'clock. He dialed the office using a raspy, sickly voice and with an exaggerated anguished tone. He told the receptionist that he had a fever and couldn't come to work today and pass the message on to his boss. Fine. That was done. He hopped back into bed, turned down the volume on the radio a bit, feeling a trifle worse for wear! He began to doze off into peaceful sleep.

His headache was slowly disappearing, even with all the steady drinking he had done. So, he was partially awake. It was a little after nine a.m. when the news blared off the radio. The World Trade Center had been attacked. Today was Tuesday, September 11, 2001. Now, he was fully awake, and stunned. How many of his co-workers had gone to the office today, the 96th floor of the North Tower? How many? He sank down to the floor and pounded it hard, weeping along with the rest of New York.

The Magic Fountain Pen

It was a cold, moonless December evening when Franklin Cable decided to take a shortcut down Crescent Lane, a narrow cobblestone street. It was deserted, not a soul around. Franklin was headed home to his Brownstone apartment on Greenwich Street in lower Manhattan. The bishop crook lampposts dimly lit the alley way as he walked fast, his shoulders huddled under his heavy topcoat; hat fit snug on his head. It was a bitterly cold night, ten below. The piercing cold made it difficult to see, but he hurried down the block nonetheless. As he walked, something nearly tripped him up. He stumbled a bit and as he regained his balance, he squinted down at the sidewalk. A fountain pen lay at his feet. It was a beauty—deep purple, with a gold embossed insignia of some sort—looked like a pelican. It had a fancy trim all around, and a gilt-etched engraving along its length. He picked it up, put it in his jacket breast pocket, and continued on his way. "Lucky find," he thought.

It wasn't long afterwards that he arrived at his apartment. One flight up the wooden stairway and he was in the warmth of his parlor. "A fire would do nicely," he considered. Taking off his topcoat and suit jacket he gathered some logs for the fireplace and lit them.

Franklin was a bachelor, thirty, tall and quite good looking, but a rather shady businessman, who would stoop to break a rule or two. He had a bright future at the investment firm and knew the tricks of how to be ruthless to get to the top. He had just come from a late night meeting with some board members to decide the best way to get their client to underwrite their latest investment scheme. As he began to open his leather briefcase, he groped for a pen. He remembered the beauty he found on the sidewalk.

Unscrewing the cap, the pen point flickered brilliantly, like a silver gem. He noticed there was no way to refill the pen! No suction clip. Odd, he thought, but, no matter, he gave it a once over. There was an inscription etched near the design. The language was, curiously enough, in Latin. He read it aloud, slowly, trying to pronounce the words, "Infinitus est numerus stultorum." These words were familiar but his Latin, being rusty, couldn't quite translate it. The letters were beautifully inscribed, twirling, tilting to the right in a stylized script. It was deeply etched and glittering.

As he began to write some marginal notes on his document, he noticed how smoothly the tip flowed over the paper—the jet black ink spreading evenly and unbroken. It was quite a fine writing instrument.

One note he jotted down was a declarative statement—'Marcus [his client] must approve this figure.' After a few more cursory notes, he poured himself a nightcap and went to bed.

The pale morning light crept through the blinds and Franklin Cable arose to a new day. It wasn't long before he was at his office desk and soon summoned to that all important meeting.

Practically before any of the details of the document were discussed, Franklin's client agreed to the figures set down in the statement, unequivocally! Everyone in the conference room was startled and impressed. Cable's boss, at first, had a keen, contemptuous gaze, but it softened after what he heard.

Days passed after this remarkable incident. Franklin realized that each time he wrote down a need, want or wish with this fountain pen—it came to pass! It was more than coincidence. This Latin phrase engraved into the stock of the pen intrigued him more and more.

Stopping by a local church he visited with the Parish Priest. Entering the Rectory he approached the Monsignor.

"Hello Father. I need a quick favor if you would. I have a pen which has some Latin words etched into it. Could you translate it for me?" The priest was cordial enough. They sat down in the study and he reached for the pen, glancing along its length, he muttered to himself the words in the inscription—"Infinitus est numerus stultorum."

"This is rather amusing," chuckled the Monsignor. "What you have here is Latin in the vulgate. It reads—'Infinite is the number of fools.'"

"Father—what did you say?" An inexplicable frozen look came over Franklin as he heard those words. The Father repeated the translation…"But it is more than just a simple Latin phrase," he continued, "It is a passage right out of scripture—Ecclesiastes Chapter one, Verse Fifteen, to be precise."

"But what does it mean? Why would someone have it inscribed on a fountain pen?"

"Where did you get this?" the priest inquired.

"I found it Monsignor, in an alleyway not too long ago."

"Curious. I've never seen a pen quite like this. Fine workmanship. I suppose its previous owner was a scholar of sorts. But why that particular phrase? Perhaps it was meant to remind him to be prudent and not do stupid things. What its true meaning might be, I haven't a clue, young man."

"Well, thank you for your time Father." They exchanged some casual pleasantries and Franklin went home.

He couldn't restrain his anxiety. In an amazingly short space of time, his entire life was changing.

"I wish I had a yacht."
"I wish I had a million dollars, no, five million."
"I wish for a Rolls Royce with a private chauffeur."
"I wish I be granted unlimited wishes."
"I wish for a beautiful woman that won't quit."

On and on, day after day. Each time he wrote a line, it came true. His every whim, every fantasy, every need was fulfilled. It was magic, it was a miracle.

Several weeks passed and he became more and more obsessed. Every desire was satisfied, his health was guaranteed. He simply had to wish for a long and fruitful life and it was his. All this changed him. He became bored, callous, petty, and short tempered, arrogant and even more ruthless and vindictive than he ever had been. He ruined people's lives for the fun of it. He amused himself with crass and profane pleasures. Still this wasn't enough. He needed more and more excitement. More stimulation. Good turned to bad. There was more excitement, he reasoned, in evildoing. It became intoxicating, like a narcotic. There was no stopping him. He had an irreversible power, no one else possessed. He could be master of the world if he wanted!

With clear-cut clarity, he began his campaign of robberies, vendettas and an assortment of other atrocities. The pen seemed to posses him; corrupt his very soul, with the same elusive need driving him into crime and worse.

One day, while reading a local newspaper report, there was to be a shipment of precious jewels, rare coins and other amounts of precious stones to be stored in the underground vault in London, where there was a massive hoard of incredible wealth. Also in this sealed vault were the Crown Jewels of the Monarchy. It was a vast hoard of treasure gathered into one deposit and placed, securely sealed in a tomb of steel and rock. Franklin couldn't resist this opportunity of making fools of the aristocracy and everyone associated with them. And he wanted this hoard all for himself, to satisfy his uncontrollable lust and greed. These cravings were getting stronger with every wish he made. He had to see this treasure trove for himself in its natural surroundings.

He wished himself directly into the vault. His heart leapt with excitement. All around him—the cache of coins, gems, jewelry. A storehouse of wealth beyond anyone's dreams. This vault was impregnable, one entrance, time-locked, a combination of stone and steel. It was airtight, hermetically sealed. Airless, for the most part. But Franklin wouldn't stay long, just long enough to gloat.

Glancing all around, he amused himself with what would be the robbery of the century. All he need do now was to transfer himself and every ounce of gold and precious gems to a place of his own choosing. "What a mystery these men would have to solve…where did all this disappear to? Ha," he chuckled, "They'll never suspect, never know it was Franklin Cable—master thief."

The air was stale and getting worse. There wasn't much oxygen to breathe down there, so he decided it was time to leave.

Reaching into his suit pocket, he pulled out his writing pad and the pen. He unscrewed the cap and began to write his instructions on the paper that would transport him and this entire hoard back to his mansion in New York, when horror gripped him.

As if an invisible hand had a strangle hold round his throat, his eyes bulged wide and his whole body trembled in panic.

The fountain pen had run dry!

The Tower

She took a step forward up the curved stairs, her footsteps echoed off the steel, her hazel eyes shifting, looking up, 'round and 'round the spiral staircase—chattering nonstop; sniffling and blubbering talking to herself—

"Hell's bells await…my twenty-third year; I never make mistakes like this…I'm more responsible than that…"just a climb—to the top of the stone tower.

"I like fine wine, I'm not insane."

"Anybody who knows me can tell you—I'm not crazy!" She was searching for a medically descriptive term, but she had none of the symptoms—

More sniffling and blubbering, her hair was unbrushed, sticking straight up!

"So," she said, as if a single word was a finished thought.

Her jaw tightened, her lips pursed, her soulful eyes remembered; her thoughts were hemorrhaging again!

She blinked, and climbed, slowly up the tower. She was tall, with a face of sculptured cheekbones and that stubborn jaw—right now it was thin and straight when she blinked again. Her gaze narrowed—looking up the tower.

There were so many stairs to climb. A slight smile, then more mutterings—"Got to get to the top of the stairs," she said covering her mouth laughing as she continued the ascent. She grinned, glanced around as sunshine faded at the top of the tower. She shrugged, and moved upward. The smugness returned, "I'm sane, I'm coherent."

She had adored him. Raising her dark eyebrows, she thought upon it. "I had lunch with my brother Reid the very day he died."

"I had lunch with my brother." She paused upon the stair. She laughed. "He was only nine."

And what of her husband? He was thirty-nine, now dead these past four years. She continued to climb. "I need to do this on my own.' "Penny," she whispered to herself, for that was her name, "Penny, go up, go up."

"Can't bring back the dead."

"It must be a mistake—pretty much. That's it, a terrible mistake. They're not dead." She brushed her hair off her forehead, rising upward—up, up toward the tower's great height.

And what of her own son—lost at sea? "Henry—my sweet Henry—I said a farewell from the cobblestone courtyard—you, a stable boy gone to sea!" Henry was eleven, and gone to sea. He grumbled about the weather. He was no sailor. He was a stable boy. It was raining, pellets of rain falling against the stone tower. It was only a brief distraction, for her thoughts returned. "Henry was good at shodding horses, you know." He was so very young. Only eleven, you know. It was a sickening realization. Penny would never see her son again! How many times she played with him in the parlor, in the yard, going on shopping errands on Front Street. Unhappy memories now. "Must forget, must not think too much on it. That's right. I'm fine, you know. Very well indeed, you know."

She was well out of the driving rain. The top of the tower would be well scrubbed.

She wondered how Henry died, "Drowned? Scurvy? Some dreadful disease perhaps?"

She smiled, "He was buried at sea, so I've been told."

She was wearing her best gown. It was molded around her buxom frame. Full-figured, her body passed the next level—up—up! She smiled again, surreptitiously, coyly smiling. It was a soft velvet, some lavender blue shades—a spirited gown with emerald-green threads, silky, intricately designed gold leaves. Frills and other fine lace adorned her dress.

She was half way up the tower when something appeared at the bottom of the steps. It was Mathilde with Father Grayson—they too were dead, as dead as dead could be.

Peggy glanced, shrugged and struggled upward, "Too late to change my clothes," she uttered moving up the cold steel staircase. Mathilde was her mother, Father Grayson, her uncle. They were country villagers caught in a landslide one day—buried alive!

"Oh, and what about David—my cousin, killed in the war?"

"Soldiers don't die in sin, you know."

Her mind conjured up these images, while smiling that smile, then she sighed. It was damp, bone chilling damp, slightly frosty as she mounted the steps, slowly upward. She remembered the priest's patient eyes, her mother's warm smile. She remembered her brother's handsome features and playful ways, his boyish grin and tiny build. Her journey up the tower progressed. Along the way there were more gasps and exclamations, more dismay, more laughter and mirth that flushed her cheeks.

There was a sudden rush of light at the top of the tower. Her slim lips and buxom frame swaying with every step. The wind moaned.

She thought how her husband might have been killed by a scoundrel. She trembled. Outside, rain lashed against the wall. Only a few steps further and she neared the top. There was a faint scent of lavender as her eyes became alive with tears. In the heat of a blush she found a moment. A moment to catch her breath. After all, it was over a hundred and twenty foot climb.

At the top at last—there was no sky here. Her heart was swooped upward, the brisk breeze slapping against her face. With arms outstretched she hugged the chill wind—then—ignoring the rain, the chill, and the wind, she spoke, “My name is Peggy Woods.”

Her own breathing echoed in her ears. Like racing to a demon, her cheeks glowed an eerie red, her gaze drew downward. The rush did not wane, the tears did not cease, just a slight throbbing of the lips. Leaning forward from the top steps, she threw herself down the hundred feet or more, the undercurrents of her voice rose as she wailed her final agonies.

They were waiting for her at the bottom of those steps. All of them—there—in that cobblestone courtyard at the floor of the tower.

Twelve Years

Would you sacrifice twelve years of your life for enough wealth to put you on easy street for the rest of your life? I did.

It all began on a lonely, deserted street in Lower Manhattan twelve years ago. I had been working very late one evening, and left the office after 2:00 am! It was a dark, moonless night with a chill in the air. Like some dim pearls, the cast iron street lamps were shedding pale light on the cobblestone streets. The steady drizzle and haze made it extremely difficult to see. I was hungry and tired and could hardly keep my eyes open as I drove cross-town in my four-door sedan.

Without warning a shadowy figure of a man dashed into the street right in the path of my car. I struck him with a bone-crushing thud. There was no time to react but I slammed on my brakes and skidded to a stop. He was still some fifty feet in front of my car. The impact had thrown him quite a distance. Dazed and trembling I ran to see if I could help. Too late! The man was dead. I could barely make out his features in the dark. He was clutching an attaché case.

My eyes darted around, praying no one witnessed this accident. The street was mostly warehouses, empty lots and a few closed shops. I breathed a sigh of relieve by then. I knelt by the body for what seemed like minutes before deciding to haul him back to my car and throw him into the trunk. I wrested the black leather case from his closed fist and placed it on the seat beside me. Although he was well dressed in a gray colored business suit, curiously I found no ID or wallet in any of his pockets.

Panic suddenly overwhelmed me. I drove a couple of blocks and pulled into a dead-end alley. My thoughts were racing, considering the consequences of a hit and run, so my next task was to dispose of the body. I was tense, gripping the steering wheel with both hands, my eyes closed tight! I realized I was talking to myself out-loud, "I can't report this, the law'll crucify me." My attention turned to the black leather attaché case on the seat besides me. Maybe it was the impact, but it wasn't locked.

When I opened it, I could feel my eyeballs bulging—it was filled with all kinds of precious stones, there seemed to be hundreds—diamonds, rubies, pearls, and a number of others, some set in silver rings or bracelets, some loose and neatly arranged in foam rubber mats or in clear glass boxes. It was a jeweler's case for sure! I found a caliper gauge, loupe, polishing cloth, silver and gold mountings and other paraphernalia there among the gemstones. I could only imagine what the total value could be—but I knew this much, it was a king's ransom I had in my hands!

I sat in the car stunned. I kept searching the street for any signs of people passing by or peering out of their windows from the four story apartment buildings bracketing the alleyway. "This guy was either a jeweler or a thief. Maybe both."

"There's a fortune in that bag. I could live on easy street for the rest of my life."

I was just an under-paid and overworked shipping clerk. I had a wife, a kid and a mortgaged shack. I was less than the average Joe. I had to make up my mind—run away from the drudgery and rut of dead-end life or take a chance at freedom and the 'good life.' I knew enough to understand that I couldn't cash in on this. It had to be fenced—but I didn't know any crooks. I had no choice but to wait until these missing stones couldn't be traced to me. I was struggling with my conscience. It was a dubious battle; I was losing. *"Should I go to the local precinct and report all this?"* Then I thought of the stagnant life I made for myself and what this would bring. The guilt, the shock the discovery of the gems all took hold of me. The coherence in my life was suddenly thrust between doing what was right and taking advantage of this once in a lifetime opportunity.

Before I realized it I found myself heading north out of the city on the Bronx River Parkway. *"I'll go to some other town and get a job. Can't fence these gems, they're too hot. I'll sit on them for five, maybe ten years until it's safe to cash them in. Then I'll be set for the rest of my life."* I smiled briefly, and then remembered I had a stiff in the trunk!

Hours passed as I drove up the Thruway and turned west toward Buffalo. While I was passing Lake Erie I got an idea.

"This is a good place to ditch the car and the corpse. Besides, my wife'll be putting a missing person's report out pretty soon, so I have to get rid of this heap. It'll be too easy to trace." I heard my own voice quivering as I was conversing with myself.

I found a perfect spot to roll the heavy sedan into the lake. I watched as the car slowly sunk under the water till it was completely submerged. I was standing there holding the attaché case and with only the clothes on my back and a hundred dollars in my pocket. *"That's the end of my old life, and this black case is the beginning of my new life!"* The decision was made, and suddenly I felt elated, excited and in some way, happy!

But my new life turned into a nightmare! I became suspicious of everybody and everything. I kept on the move from city to city, from town to town, always running, always hiding, always carrying that attaché case. Shadows haunted me. Every policeman I saw, or person on the street might some day identify me. I'm sure my wife had sent a photo of me to the police department in town. Maybe it got into the papers. I felt a terrible remorse for running out on my wife and kid. But I kept focused, knowing my future was assured.

Three years passed; three years of running and hiding, but I still had those jewels. Nine years dragged by. Everywhere I went I looked over my shoulder. I couldn't rest. I had no peace. I kept seeing signs in jewelry store windows exhorting customers: *Take those jewels out of hiding! Trade them in for cash now!* The irony was all too real for me. "But it's not time to cash in those jewels yet. I have to be sure. I have to wait rather than take a chance of something going wrong."

Twelve years of hiding in flop houses and cheap hotels, renting tenement apartments. Twelve years of working at menial jobs for low pay and living like a pauper. My health was failing as well and so I just couldn't wait any longer. *"I can't stand it. The time is now! It's time to cash them in. Time for me to start living like a human being again."*

Next morning, I cleaned up a bit, grasped my attaché case and headed for a local jeweler to have them appraised. Walking down the street, suddenly everything went black. I had fallen to the pavement, unconscious. I had been struck in the back of the head. I awakened in an alleyway behind a garbage dumpster. I had been robbed. My pockets were empty and my attaché case was gone. My gut did a flip-flop. My heart banged inside my chest. I began to shake and sweat; my vision blurred. All this hiding, running, living like a rat—all for nothing! I wanted to die right then and there.

'Well Lieutenant, that's my story. I'm ready to sign a confession and admit everything. But it was a cruel joke, this whole thing. I lost a fortune just when I was ready to cash it in."

"You didn't lose any fortune Mr. Williams. We apprehended that thief hours after you came into Headquarters. Turns out those gems were paste, just costume jewelry. They were phony. The whole package was worth, maybe two to three hundred dollars. Must have been a prop for some play or movie production. No, Mr. Williams, the joke is even crueler than you could have imagined."

The Bullwhip

Marshal Wade Bannister spotted the tawny puma as it soared from the rock and battered the Cayuse to the ground! The Marshal was stunned but managed to raise his gun from his holster and fired. Thunder rolled across the canyon. He never saw the mate of the mountain lion which attacked him from the rear. His first shots brought down the male. Mountain lions are notoriously lightening fast, powerful and swift to kill. Marshal Bannister almost came to 'the end of the trail,' in that deserted canyon. His gun was knocked from his grip when the male mountain lion fell on his hand, dead. The mate was closing in for the kill. The Marshal always carried a bullwhip, strung to his gun belt. It was a handsome rawhide bullwhacker, unique, even. He grabbed the handle and flailed the whip at the charging beast. It snapped and its crack echoed off the canyon walls. In very quick succession he cracked it again, driving off the lion. But, not after he sustained serious mauls from the animal. His horse was dead. The puma's paw broke the horse's neck like a piece of straw. *"Got no choice now but to turn around and go back to Silver Ridge."* It was a ten mile hike! There were three men in town gunning for him, and he knew they'd take him on when they saw what condition he was in. He washed his cuts free of dirt in a nearby stream, and then bandaged them using a torn undershirt. Then, he buttoned a clean shirt on over the bandaged wounds.

The Marshal was a tall man, straight blonde hair, light blue eyes, clean shaven. He holstered his colt across the left front of his gun belt not the traditional right side, so he could reach across with his right hand for an easy draw. He carried a hunting knife as well as his bullwhip. But his thoughts turned to his injuries. *"If someone slaps me on the back,"* he thought, *"I'll cave in! I can't even shake hands, my fingers were almost torn off...I can hardly button my shirt!"*

He continued deep in thought, *"Those three bandits swore to gun me down. I'll have to act unfriendly so nobody will dare come near me...try to live long enough by bluffing...till I can heal up these wounds, then if someone starts trouble, I'll have a fightin' chance!"* It was a wearisome walk back to town. He was tired and hungry by the time he reached the outskirts. It was nightfall.

Luck wasn't with him at all. That morning the next cowpoke he saw was a gentleman gambler named Tucker Webb. Webb spotted the Marshal near the stable. "Bannister!" yelled Webb with a cold, hard stare. "Yuh gunned me in Tuscon last year, remember? But yuh was lucky then. Go on and make yore move!"

"Webb!" said a startled Bannister.

"That's right Marshal," Webb continued, "I swore to gun yuh some day...this is the day!" Although the Marshal wasn't sure if Webb knew of his condition, but he never flinched and tried to hide his constant pain caused by those deep gashes of the puma. "Somethin' yuh didn't know, Webb," ventured Bannister in his slow Texas drawl, "Cost six dollars tuh kill a man in Silver Ridge. Six dollars!"

"Huh!" said Webb, completely bewildered and caught off guard by such an unrelated remark. "That's right," continued Bannister, in a steady, determined voice, "Six dollars—an' I'm not agonna gun y'all down less yuh got six dollars cash in yore pocket! I'm tired of payin' for buryin' out of my own pocket!"

Bannister gave him a long, hard, serious stare. Webb put a finger to his lips to mull over what he just heard. Tucker felt there was something odd in the way Bannister moved...stiff-shouldered...but Webb's mind wasn't functioning now, fear had driven off his ability to reason straight.

"Dunno what yer talkin' about!" spoke Webb, "I'm ridin' out, an' don't you dare try an' stop me!"

"Go on—ride, Webb! Silver Ridge got enough yella coyotes here already, 'thout addin' you to the list." The bluff worked. The Marshal had talked his way out of this one! However, the local hardcases, the "yella coyotes," heard Bannister was injured…they fummed and threatened…and just simmered. Hank Pawley was scruffy and every bit a tinhorn bushwacker. He's speaking with his sidekick Lance Tompkins. "I'll show that babyface punk of a Marshal who's runnin' this town."

"Go ahead," replied Lance, "I'll watch an' see there's fair play. Then I'll shoot him in the back." He laughed and got excited at the prospect! Hank poured himself another whiskey as he sat at the table in the saloon. "That little sidewinder's been gettin' by on his reputation, that's what. Any of yuh ever see him do anythin' but talk big? If he was here now, I'd tie him in a knot and bounce him off the walls."

Just after uttering those words, Bannister was seen standing through the swinging doors of the saloon. A startled Hank Pawley turned in dismay! "Lessee now…yore name is Hank Pawley! Yuh're a real bad man, a desparado Pawley! Robbed a rancher's widow in the Green River last year, I've been told! Shot up Pete Barlett's store too…" Bannister said, in his usual cold and steady voice. He walked toward Pawley.

"Yeah, yeah…real tough one you are! Pulled a gun on a tenderfoot too, I recall. You're not just a bad man, Hank…" he reached for his bullwhip as he distracted Pawley with his palavering, "…you're rotten clean through. You're a skunk, a stink-in-the-nose of all honest men." He sideswiped Hank's arm with the whip, a snap which tore the fabric of his plaid shirt and bloodied his forearm. Hank staggered back and fell over a chair. He landed square on his back, totally stunned.

Bannister continued, "Get outta this town…the Sheriff couldn't prove any of this, but you gonna ride outa town and stay away." Hank's pal was standing near the bar and reached for his gun. Wade side-armed him too and cracked the whip across his gun hand. It was a hard snap that gashed his hand and the gun fell to the floor. Bannister turned to the other men in the room. "Nobody want tuh try me out? One at a time or all of yuh…if yuh won't try now, don't bad-mouth me in the future, or you'll all be six feet under. I won't use a bullwhip next time." They backed off.

Later, at the hotel, Wade Bannister asked the clerk for the local doctor to come up to his room. The clerk passed a remark about Wade's hand being hurt, since the Marshal's gloves were still bloodied." My hands are just fine, Mr. Phelps." He grabbed Phelps by the nose, squeezing it till his head leaned to one side. "Think the hands are all right now?"

"Y-yessir!" cried the clerk in pain.

Even the Marshal thought these bluffs were a little too blatant! Too easily seen through, as he sat in his room applying salve to his lacerated hands and chest. He wondered how long it would be before those hard cases banded together and came for him.

The discussions ran heated in the saloon. Hank Pawley was speaking to another cowhand who had a run-in with the Marshal years ago. Phelps was in the bar getting a drink before going home. They asked him about Bannister…"…about a doc! I seen him holdin' his hand and I asked about it. Thought he'd twist my head right off my shoulders! Nothin' wrong with his hands!" said Mr. Phelps as he drained his glass of beer.

Another man spoke up, "I owe the Marshal a bullet. He downed me two years ago comin' out of the Cullock Bank. If he's hurt now, I an't gonna miss the chance tuh finish him off."

Back in his hotel room, Wade was putting on his shirt after the doctor treated his wounds. The Marshal had seen mobs created before. He knew how men drew courage from one another, and from a bottle of whiskey…how it took time for them to steam each other up! The day after Bannister arrived in town, his wounds became infected. No one saw him on the streets at all the next day…and the outlaws began to regain their shattered nerves! The doctor, Justin Reese, went up to the Marshal's room to toward the afternoon to check on his condition again. He went up the back way.

"Figured you were hurt Marshal, when you called me yesterday," commented Justin in a sympathetic tone, "Here…drink this. It'll put you to sleep, break the fever…I'll put new bandages on your cuts!"

For five days, Silver Ridge was teeming with indecision and halted violence…men anxious to kill, were uncertain! The doc assured

Wade, “There are five or six of us Wade, you nor the others will see us until the gunplay starts. We’ll protect your back.” The Marshal knew he couldn’t use his revolver…”My hand burns, just holdin’ the gun… can’t grasp the trigger…”

He thanked the sawbones and told him he was ready to go down to meet the outlaws. He twirled up the bullwhip, tested his grip in the handle just below the knot…he was confident. He walked slowly toward the saloon where five of the desperados had gathered. “Hear tell yuh wanta see me, mister! You and the others! Well here I am,” said Bannister defiantly, “You still wanna see me?”

The men were lined up outside the saloon looking down on Bannister from the steps above on the wooden walkway. In a flash the Marshal pulled his whip and striped one hat off the head of Hank Pawley and in a quick motion snapped it overhead across the chest of another man. He did this with his left hand, keeping his gun hand free. The men were fooled again.

They backed off—mounted their horses and rode out of town. The doc came out from behind one of the nearby sheds, with several other townsfolk. “Marshal,” he said with a huge smile, “looks like you cleaned up the town with two snaps of your bullwhip! Thanks, thanks from all of us.”

Dreamer?

Gene Cass was standing besides the church steps. A newsboy strolled by as Cass turned to go inside. The service was in progress, sonorous voices intoning all familiar words, organ music somberly swelling, and every color shined through the stained glass windows. Gray masses of stone within reflected myriad textures of black. There was a shuffle of feet and the faint far off voice of the priest. Boots squeaked, someone coughed. Footsteps echoed off the hard, high-heel shoes of the ladies. It was all very real. Even the smell of incense and wax candles germinated the still air inside the cathedral.

A man of tall stature was immediately in front of Cass, close to the doorway. "Did you see that, Mr. Cass?" whispered the man. There was an odd dignity to the fellow, this man stranding in the doorway. There was a coolness and confidence about him. He was lean, quite smartly dressed. His wry, intelligent face was lined with weariness framed with locks of brown hair neatly combed.

"See what?" replied Cass quietly.

The man's face was impassive. "Did you see the monk?" asked the man with a slight movement of his head in the direction of the apse. "He's an intruder," the man continued. Cass stared in that direction but could only see the parishioners, no one else.

"His name is Basil," the man snapped, his voice hard in spite of its very quietness.

"I don't see him, whoever he is." Cass replied, annoyed at this whole affair.

"Look harder. You'll see him eventually." Cass opened his mouth then closed it again.

The mysterious stranger was gone!

Cass went out into the street. It was raining. It hadn't been raining a moment ago, and the sky had been cloudless, clear, and dry. He walked down the sidewalk, rain drifting in the lamplight and glistening on the pavement. "Good Lord," Cass said with a dry throat, the sound robbed of its force by his tongue sticking to the roof of his mouth. "It was morning a moment ago. Now it's pitch black!" He hastened his steps into the darkness. "Preposterous." He felt fraught with personal danger. He was beset with a succession of emotions chased away by fear!

Cass found his apartment and went straight to bed. At first he lay awake staring at the ceiling puzzled by the day's events. He slept fitfully and awoke confused and heavy-headed, wondering what was wrong.

It was a sharp, glittering day just above freezing but Cass was feeling far colder because he knew it was summertime, not winter. He was certain of it. He winced. His judgment and intelligence must be impaired, he pondered. Somewhere there must be an explanation for all this, he reasoned.

Cass looked out his draped window peering through the half-opened Venetian blinds. Gulls wheeled overhead, flashing white wings against the sky. The incoming tide splashed and slurped against the wood piers and wet stones of the steps leading up to his apartment house. From his fourth floor bedroom he could see the river was busy this morning. Everywhere he looked there were men at work, lifting, pushing, wheeling large sacks and bales. Their shouts were carried by the wind then blown away. Further into the city there was only a pale wisp of smoke rising from two smoke stacks of the manufacturing plant.

"But all this isn't right," Cass said dourly, "My apartment house isn't on the wharf, it's in midtown." He shook his head and rubbed his eyes, "I must be dreaming. Or maybe I've had some bad liquor."

Somewhere down the pier there was a roar of laughter and someone shouted, pointing at Cass's window. In the clear air he could see as far as the river bends and the crowd, all pointing in his direction, laughing and pointing.

He turned away, wide eyed and trembling. Hopefully he'll wake up from this nightmare. He'll wake up and the day will start over.

A sudden knock at the door and he was brought back from hysteria. "W-Who's there?" he shouted. No answer, just another loud rap at the door. He hesitated, the sweat running down his back in spite of the chilling cold. "Who is it?" he demanded. No answer still. Just another couple of hard knocks. He approached the door. It was locked. He put his ear cautiously against the metal, listening, wondering. Summoning up his courage he pulled the door open and jerked back. He had seen a shadow against the door lintel. He snapped his head sideways down the corridor. His face froze. There was no one there. Not a soul, living or dead.

Cass jumped back into his dimly lit apartment, shut the door and turned to look around the room. He stood with his back to the door jam. It was bitterly cold in there, so cold his fingers were dead and his feet were growing numb. He felt the dampness everywhere. There was a sudden reek of mud and an effluent, sweet smell of rot. Everything began sagging, dripping, full of imperceptible creaking sounds, sounds of rats feet scurrying about, soft treads of human feet, more creaking, like a shifting of weight. The stench became overpowering.

His thoughts clamored loudly, wondering what was really happening to him as he ran from the room, down the building's marble stairway, out into the street. Running past the wharf he became accustomed to the dampness in the air and the smell of the tide, the movement and constant sound of the water. The light was different than before. It was sharper, clearer and full of angles and reflections. He ran down an icy street, looking above him toward the dense rooftops of an unfamiliar city! He ran past polished surfaces of brick and stone, past gardens of tall trees with flashes of pink and primrose. No one on the street seem to notice him. No one cared to look. He ran outside of the pavement, guiding his stride along a slippery cobblestone street, across corners, dodging the traffic and crossing sweeper. Turning one corner he stopped in his tracks, not out of breath, but aghast at what he saw—gas lamplights, hansom cabs, men in top hats, ladies dressed in flowing dresses down past the ankles. It was the age of copper and pewter plates, post horns and steam railroads. It was several seconds before he grasped the meaning and his hand flew to his mouth to stifle a shriek.

The heavy clop of the horse's hooves made him well aware of the predicament he found himself. His face grew grim and anxious, and turned pink, his hair poking in wild angles. His heart sank although he could think of nothing specific that he feared. "What has happened?" He said aloud.

This is the stuff dreams are made of. He could hardly imagine otherwise. But how could it be a dream? His thoughts of reality came flooding back to him. His face puckered with confusion. He stared around with anguished eyes. His breath became heavy and labored. Panting, he began to walk again, turning his head from time to time with disbelieving pall. Cass was struggling for his sanity. When he traveled a short distance, he went into a building on a street called Grimwade. He went upstairs and it seemed strange, as if reliving something already known to him. He got to the top of the third landing and hesitated at the door he found there. He knocked. No answer, yet he swung it open easily and went on in. The room was airless and unnaturally silent. Immediately upon entering, he turned up the gas jet to flood the room with a dim light, just enough to reveal a mirror in the foyer.

Cass turned to see his reflection. He was a tallish young man. The high color of his cheeks pushed upwards even to his forehead where it scattered itself in a few formless patches of pale red; and on his hairless face there scintillated restlessly the polished lenses and bright gilt rims of the glasses which screened his delicate yet weary eyes. His glossy black hair was parted in the middle and brushed along in a wide curve behind his ears where it curled slightly. He was transfixed there for a moment—not sure if that image was really true. It certainly fit the times he found himself in, but it wasn't who he thought he was. Not for a moment.

Once past the foyer the drawing room came into view. He went through the doorway out of the narrow passage, glancing around to see the wall hung with portraits and other framed pictures. Advancing further, he observed the parlor with floral patterned red carpet, and papered walls. Rich tapestry adorned the windows. The fireplace mantle was richly ornate and decorated with many marble carvings. In one of the soft, brown armchairs was a shawl carefully folded over the arm, with needle and thread nearby. A thimble and scissors lay in a basket aside the chair.

The place was well furnished with a low mahogany coffee table well polished, near the front of a cloth-covered sofa. Upon the table was a tray of tea cups and what appeared to be a steamy pot of brewed tea ready to be served.

Cass heard a soft whisper behind him, and as he turned there was a woman sitting in the brown chair sewing the shawl. She looked up at him. She was somewhere in her mid forties, dark-haired with a mass of freckles. She had a long, rather lugubrious face, and no one could call her pretty. Far from it. But she seemed intelligent to

Cass with a certain charm. He nonetheless was startled to find her suddenly appearing out of thin air! She shrugged, pursing her lips. She kept knitting as she asked him, "Would you care for some tea Mr. Cass?" The mere fact that she knew his name jerked him out of his daydreaming thoughts. She had a broad smile on her face as she looked up at him.

He was beginning to feel cold and a little shivery, even faint. "Ma'am, how do you know my name?" he said, half expecting to wake up any minute. "Come, come, Mr. Cass. You always have your tea at this time of day."

It was growing dusk already, even though it was mid-afternoon, and he couldn't be sure of that either. He shivered. He moved backwards out the way he came, never taking his eyes off her. The gas light grew dimmer and the room was indistinguishable and became a dark blur.

He stepped out into the street again, keeping his balance on the wet stone with some difficulty. He found himself on an embankment as he walked past into the nearest street looking around. He could not afford the time to explore; he needed to ask someone what was going on. Where was he? What year? What town? Where in heaven's name was he doing here? For several minutes he moved along in silence except for the water and far away sounds of foghorns. He realized he was by the river again. There were boats in the water answering to each other. Schooners, barges, skiffs, fishing boats and larger steamers. But it was too dark to see clearly. He could only see shadowy outlines against a bleak, dark sky. The water gurgled around a nearby pier as if something had washed up against it passing in the gloom. Whatever it was it sloshed against the stakes and the wood creaked and sagged sideways.

Mr. Cass sighed. He had had just about enough. He backed away, turned and picked up the pace as he fled down a narrow alleyway between what appeared to be two factory buildings. There was a gust of wind through the narrow street and the blustery darkness was lit only by a few gas lamps. He maneuvered through the alley with skill, making headway down to the other end.

He felt a fool, his mind in turmoil, and his emotions raw. He had to thread this needle to find out what was going on. He felt as if he were in a bad dream, a dream that would never end. He wanted the truth, and something definite to do. As he emerged from the alley into a broad street, he past ironmonger's shops, ships' chandlers, sail makers and general stores. He made note of other public houses not far from dockside. The streets seemed deserted, almost ghostly in its silence. He strained his ears to listen for any sign of life.

Farther down the street was a funeral parlor. Cass shivered and shot a sour glance toward the window. As if his feet were stuck to the pavement, he tried to press ahead to get a better look. Repeating over and over again in his thoughts, *"None of this seems real anymore. None of it."* Cass' face lost its momentary look of fear as he slowly approached the doorway to the funeral home. But that changed very shortly, as he once again became fearful. What might he find inside? He felt oddly drawn to the place, compelled to go in—almost seized with an uncontrollable urge. As he entered he glanced around, rather fretfully, straining his eyes, looking up to see a molded ceiling. He frowned ruefully as he scanned the waiting room. No one was there. The lush furniture decorated in scrolls and curlicues of gilt, upholstered in velvet and gilt edged. But not a soul around. "Hello! Anyone in?" he said in a shaky voice.

His ears caught a faint sound which grew louder—weeping! He heard weeping. Cass' eyebrows rose as he neared an entranceway with a dark blue curtain hung across the threshold. The surrounding wallpaper was pink and embossed in gold. He drew a deep breath and pushed the curtain aside to see a dimly lit room with an open coffin at the far end, surrounded by bouquets of flowers. He wondered for a frantic moment where the weeping was coming from and whose body lay in the coffin. The weeping and moaning continued, along with the sound of muffled voices.

He blew his breath out sharply, his cheeks flushed and growing pinker. He glanced sideways almost expecting to see someone sitting in the neatly lined rows of chairs facing the coffin. But the room was empty of people. The air was oppressive, filled with the all too familiar scent of flowers. It was a sickeningly sweet smell. His body tensed as he approached the open coffin. It soon became clear to him; the figure laying in repose was he! Cass screwed up his face, his lips curled, shifting his weight, he leaned against the edge of the coffin, turning his head downward to see his own body—white, cold, and dead. The weeping of the invisible mourners was steady, but as he fell upon the kneeler aside the coffin, the weeping faded. It faded very slowly, drifting off, and then there was silence.

Cass froze in terror, letting out a low moan. The brocaded curtains he had passed through moments earlier were becoming engulfed in a bright, blinding light. The light tore away the curtains from their frame. The light grew ever brighter stinging his eyes as he turned to look. Suddenly his sorrowful and fearful mood melted away and a smile crossed his lips—one of peace, ease—almost one of comfort and relief. He drew another deep breath and let it out slowly. Now he was no longer confused or frightened.

The bright white light flooded the room—he moved towards the threshold. Yes he was dead. He knew it. And all this made sense at last—the dreamscape was his last grasp for reality. But this was his reality now. He headed into the light to his eternal rest beyond.

The Mission

He had been chosen for a special mission, a mission to mankind. But no one would believe him. No one!

The rumbling of the trains sent exhilaration through George's body! It was new to him as he hurried along the ramp toward the station waiting room. It was the Grand Central Station waiting room, as he looked at the hundreds of people moving ahead of him…bustling, hurrying New Yorkers, scurrying in every direction! People, who seemed anxious to rush from the station into the busy streets outside, hurrying home. George laughed to himself as he discovered that, unthinkingly, he quickened his pace too, and he hardly felt the weight of his over packed suitcase as he stepped into this tremendous station.

On a brief vacation from upstate New York, he had overtones of a jolly conversation buzzing inside his head:

"New York…I'm finally here…and this is going to be the most exciting week of my life!" George was thinking as he half-ran into the street.

George had planned on a vacation in New York for months and was so excited about the planning; he found it difficult to concentrate on his work in the office. But now he was in the great city, and he whistled as he walked along the streets gazing up at the tall buildings along Forty-Second Street and Vanderbilt Avenue.

When he finally reached the Hotel Biltmore, where he had made reservations, he felt quite the man-about-town, as a red-coated bellhop took his suitcase and walked ahead of him to the sunny room on the eighteenth floor. He tipped the bellhop and began to unpack and made himself feel right at home.

He showered, changed into a smart three-piece suit, classy fedora, key chain, wingtip shoes, the works! He was ready and anxious to see more of New York City as soon as possible. Within an hour, he had joined one of the Sightseeing Tour groups, and chatted enthusiastically with his seat partner as the glass-topped bus wound its way through Times Square heading for Chinatown on Canal Street.

Two hours passed swiftly, and George was even more excited than before. He felt particularly good as the ferry took him across to Liberty Island to see the Statue of Liberty looming up before him!

Night was drawing close, but not the slightest bit tired, George stepped out of the elevator onto the observation deck of the Empire State Building. The air he breathed was electrifying. He walked to the rail and looked down. The sight from the eighty-sixth floor was dazzling! He blinked his eyes.

"It…it's like some magic land…a thousand lights blinking, little specks, automobiles moving so snake-like along the streets…and noises…it…it sounds like they're coming from hundreds of miles below us." George shivered. He was so enthusiastic that he felt he had to share his enthusiasm with someone else. He softly tapped the shoulder of a man who stood next to him.

"Uh…pardon me, sir…but I couldn't help…Excuse me, I…"

George saw that the man didn't hear him. He stared at the stranger and when he realized what was wrong, he gasped!

"Good grief…he's…HE'S MOTIONLESS…AS IF HE…HE WERE FROZEN SOLID!"

George Rogers turned swiftly, his face wrinkled with horror when he saw that all the others stood silent, statue-like, as if simultaneously stricken with a baffling plague. He looked over the rail again, and covered his mouth to stifle a scream. The entire metropolis, which had been animated with the brilliant city lights and noises, was now dark…and silent!

He regained some composure in a few minutes and then he tore himself away, and ran to the elevators. But they were still, frozen like everyone around him. His heart pounded madly as he headed for the staircase, and went down, down, closer to the street. He had to get away.

When he rushed out into the street, his heart pounded even more furiously. Where was he? Nothing around him looked familiar. What was happening?

He looked about him. This was not the city he had been standing above moments before! This city was new…it was filled with broad streets, ultra-modern buildings that shone in the bright sunlight, people moving about leisurely, smiling, cheerful.

He looked above him, and could hardly believe what he saw. Space-type vehicles flew noiselessly above the city, carrying passengers from one sky-station to the next…some people along the street didn't walk…they were carried along effortlessly by moving sidewalks.

George was amazed! The people all looked so friendly, and yet he hesitated to ask one of them what was going on. But when a man waved to him and approached him quickly, George felt relieved. Now he would know.

"Hello Rogers…you're looking well…but then, aren't we all?" The man laughed.

"Hm? That's a strange thing to say," George said, noting that it was true…everyone looked healthy, fit and happy. Then he continued, "Say, how do you know my name? Who are you? And where in the world am I? I'm awfully confused."

"Well, George," the man said, "We have known you would come to join us for a brief time. Apparently you've been chosen to be projected into your own future to see what life is like here and to bring the message back to your own times. Your future holds peace and prosperity."

"My…FUTURE? Why, then this…all this that I see is actually TOMORROW? But tomorrow doesn't exist yet. It should be a blank… NOTHING SHOULD EXIST HERE!" George exclaimed, dazed.

"There are many possibilities, many avenues that can be reality," the man answered, "Yes, this is how you and your ancestors are destined to live, IF you and they can succeed in abolishing wars… there are no police, no military. Law enforcement is unnecessary. This is a world at peace with itself. But this is only one possibility. There are countless others—all very unpleasant. Here, people strive not for passion or personal gain, but to fulfill individual goals in whatever fields of endeavor they want to pursue—the arts, philosophy, and the sciences, all the humanities. We all benefit. Poverty, insanity, famine, sickness have been wiped out!"

"UTOPIA?" George exclaimed.

"You may call it that, but it goes deeper. We have overcome our violent past. We have attained true enlightenment. Crime is not an option because people here want for nothing. No one faces the dire evils that were prevalent in the past. No ego rises above another—no conquest of wills. No domination."

"But how can this be?" George said incredulously.

"Pass the word among your people. Like a subtle suggestion, it will grow into an absolute truth. We're counting on you. You must succeed or all this will not exist."

"How can you expect me to do that? No one will believe me. NO ONE. They'd throw me in a booby-hatch!"

Just as George was about to ask more questions, he began to feel dizzy. He held his hand to his eyes, and everything began to swim.

"G-got to get back…tell the people…g-got to get…"

The sun had disappeared and it was night again.

In a moment he was again on the observation roof of the Empire State Building gazing down once more at the flickering lights below, hearing again the murmur of voices of the people that stood nearby. George Rogers knew what he had to do, and turned to face the people who stood talking and pointing to the sights below.

"LISTEN!" he shouted, frantically, "I've seen what the future holds! Ahead lies peace and contentment, if only we will work for it…"

One woman turned to him, snickered, "That man's gone mad…it must be the height!"

George's mission could prove difficult. He rushed to the elevators and when he stepped into a waiting car, he grasped a man by his arm and shouted, "TOMORROW…I'VE SEEN TOMORROW."

He heard the man mutter, "What a nut! Go away or I'll call a cop. Get outta here."

"No. No…I've seen it…highways above the ground, streets that carry people along on belts…" The man ran out of the elevator back onto the observation deck.

George rode the elevator and when it reached the ground floor, he was determined to make the people believe him. He spied a group of men waiting for a bus and they were reading newspapers that had large ominous-looking headlines.

"YOU'VE GOT TO BELIEVE ME!" he screamed, shaking the arms of the astounded men, "THE FUTURE HOLDS NO FEAR OF WAR…OF DEPRESSION…GIVE OURSELVES A CHANCE, AND WE CAN ENJOY THE MAGNIFICENT TOMORROW THAT SCIENCE WILL BUILD FOR US!"

When one man looked at George as if he were mad, he shook his grasp loose and boarded the bus. The other men backed away, pointed and laughed.

The whole scene around George began to fade…he felt dizzy again. His vision blurred and he felt a restraint on both arms—as if they were being twisted like a pretzel. He couldn't move his arms.

* *

"Get the straight jacket on him Bob. He's going off his rocker again!" A man in a white uniform said as he held George down.

George found himself surrounded by several husky men, all in white suits, just finishing strapping on the restraining jacket.

"This loony is going to harm somebody one day," said another attendant.

"Yea. He's been here ten years already and its been one lunatic tale after another. Now it's something about the future. Two weeks ago he was squawking about having breakfast with the President in the White House! They outta put him back in Ward Thirty-three. Hurry, call the doc!"

George Rogers was restrained for the moment. His home is Bellevue Hospital Psychiatric Ward. George muttered, tears welling up in his eyes:

"…they m-must hear me…b-before it…before it's TOO LATE!"

Stand Your Ground!

In World War II, Terry Lockhart was a G.I. in a sad sack outfit that got clobbered by a crack German Division. Terry lasted about eight days before he got lucky and caught a shell fragment in the tail! After he came home, he finished college and wound up, when the Korean 'police action' began, with a news syndicate and was assigned to a Marine battalion to cover the war. Sgt. Nick Siguiera was given the unhappy chore of babysitting the reporter, and it wasn't easy.

Note: *The Chinese divisions had crossed the Yalu River in October 1950 driving back the U.N. forces. This offensive was halted by Jan. 1951 along a front just below the 38th Parallel.*

On a hill, somewhere near Ch'ongson below the 38th Parallel, Lockhart and his adopted battalion were caught in a massed assault by the Chinese communists (called Chicoms). Terry was a tall, distinguished looking man with a bushy brown mustache, heavy eyebrows and scruffy face. Sgt. Siguiera was a hard-nosed, unflinching veteran born in Spanish Harlem, NYC. He's been with the outfit since they landed at Pusan in '50 and his division was instrumental in driving back the North Koreans.

The Sergeant and Terry were behind a dirt wall, the Sgt. firing rapidly as the Chinese came wave after wave up the hill!

"Siguiera, are you crazy? Your platoon can't stop the Chicom attack!" said Terry as he hugged the ground and covered his head.

"Stay put Lockhart," was the Sergeant's gruff reply. "The whole outfit might bug out if they saw us run and they'd get chopped up. We're stayin'…and so are you!"

"You marines are no supermen," pleaded Lockhart, "Get out while you can." His face was filled with horror as he watched what seemed like an inexhaustible supply of Chinese coming up the hill! A MIG was staffing the US troops at the crest. A soldier rose to his feet and fired at the jet with a machinegun he unhooked from its tripod!

Terry turned to one of the soldiers in the Sgt's platoon, "He's off his rocker! He'll never hit the MIG that way!"

"Don't bet on it, Lockhart," came the private's retort.

The private must have caught the gas tank because the MIG exploded about three hundred feet above them!

Terry was shocked and muttered, "I just don't believe it!"

The first assault had been stopped. The men regrouped behind some rubble and a bombed out house. A medic was attending to the soldier's wounded leg.

"This'll buy yuh a ticket to base hospital, then R and R in Tokyo, Bob!" said the medic.

"Sound's great doc…but don't put in the papers till tomorrow… those Chicoms'll hit us heavy again tonight!"

Terry overheard the conversation, "I want your name buddy…I'm going to file a story on the way you M.G.'d that MIG 17."

Bob Peters was his name. As he lit a cigarette and propped himself up against a wall and he spoke to Terry, "You write me up an' my old man reads it, he'll bust me in half when I get home! Last thing he told me before I shipped out…was 'be a good Marine, but don't try to be a hero!'"

Lockhart had been with the U.S. Eighth Army for a time and he knew the G.I.'s in Korea were good, tough soldiers, but these Marines, he couldn't believe!

Lockhart came over to Sergeant Siguiera to let him know the latest news. "Intelligence reports indicate at least a full division is across the valley ready to attack! Charlie Company can't stop a whole division!"

Siguiera slowly turned, "We can slow 'em down a lot, writer… long enough for reserves to be sent up to help hold the ground!"

There was an uneasy quiet all night. The men strained and peered into the darkness listening, watching, and waiting!

A soldier approached the Sgt., "The skipper just got creamed Nick! And our platoon leader got busted up this morning."

"Senior officer in the company'll take command, I guess." The Sgt. answered.

"No officers left Nick! What'll we do?"

"If the skipper was here, I'd say sweat out the Chicom attack… but he ain't. Get on the horn and tell battalion artillery…give us star shells 100 yards down the slope! Stand by for a barrage!"

Battalion artillery got the word.

At the moment the first shells rained down on enemy positions, the attack was mounted! They came by the thousands, all bunched together. The Sgt. called for continued bombardment. He ordered his men to use rifle grenades…and machine gunners to shoot into the clusters of enemy soldiers, while he kept directing artillery fire.

Ten thousand Chinese were trying to overrun the positions. They were so closely packed that every artillery shell found at least two or three victims!

The battle raged, reinforcements for the beleaguered Americans were promised. Lockhart questioned the wisdom of staying on the hill any longer. He wanted to fall back.

"Don't bother me writer…" the Sgt yelled.

Cries for medics, exploding shells, screaming men in the heat of battle, there was no time to bicker!

Third squad on the left flank was being overrun, but the line stayed intact…a few men from other squads slipped out of their foxholes and met the Chicoms as they loomed above the battered Marines of the first squad!

"Barney, get the flame-thrower up here," shouted the Sgt.

The flame-thrower, usually used when cleaning out bunkers and caves, suddenly turned the night into a blazing hell!

Lockhart was jotting notes:

Tonight, I observed a platoon of Marines, less than forty men in all, drive a division of Chinese infantry off! I witnessed a Russian-built MIG shot down by a light machine gun fired by a Marine who held the blistering metal in his bare hands!

The Sgt. kept directing artillery, "Raise the artillery barrage to 200 yards north of this position…"

The Chinese were mounting another assault when the Sergeant ordered a counterattack!

Back at the base…
"How's Charlie Company doin' up there Captain?" the General inquired.

"Captain Ross answered the commander, "All the officers have been hit…a squad leader from the third squad's running things."

Terry Lockhart became a believer that night! He went down the hill with what was left of the platoon. He was with them as they machine-gunned and grenaded the fleeing Chinese Communists into panicked flight!

"Okay, writer…you can bug out if you want before they counterattack us." Sgt. Siguiera said to Lockhart, under fire. But Terry was busy jotting down notes!

What was to be a carefully timed Chinese attack on a remote Korean hilltop, turned into an incredible victory for the U.S. Marines! A Marine Sergeant named Nick from Spanish Harlem in Manhattan, New York who took command and then:
Terry turned to the Sgt., "You guys RETREAT? I didn't know you knew how to give ground!"

"We're here to kill enemy troops, writer. Now, the Chicoms will reorganize…they'll come blastin' up the hill again in an hour or so…" he paused to fire his weapon, then continued, "…and they're gonna run into more firepower than they knew existed! The reinforcements are here…we can take a breather while you phone in your story."

There was quiet now. A brief moment of peace, calm and rest. The Sergeant lay asleep near one of the bunkers back at base.

Terry Lockhart was resting too—after he phoned in his report and ended with a footnote:

Now, Sgt. Siguiera is asleep on the bare ground, he doesn't think he did anything special when assigned to this outfit, I was saying "A Marine is only only a man!" I changed that slightly, they held their ground, and say a Marine is all man!

"Hey, Joe!"

Every night it was the same...from the stinking, steaming jungle around him he heard the moans...the cries for help. How much could he take? It was the same plea for help.

You knew about the barrages of mortar shells the Japanese would throw at you. You were warned about the Banzai charges and the wicked hand-to-hand fighting! You wore Corporal stripes, Joe Rumsford, and you did your job! But you never got used to that terror in the night.

Joe Rumsford lay in his foxhole, close to the bottom as possible. Alone in the pit of night, the oppressive heat rising all around him while he heard distinct cries for help. Alone, in the Guadalcanal jungle.

"Help me Joe, I'm hurt."

"Hey, Joe, over here, I need a medic!"

"Joe, please, get a Corpseman. Help me Joe!"

Rumsford was warned about the tricks the Japanese would pull to lure soldiers out of the safety of their foxholes, or pinpoint their positions when the GI would answer their phony call for help! The pleas seem to come from all directions.

"They're all around me! I've got to get out of here." Rumsford thought to himself.

Suddenly, a voice was heard in the distance:

"Hold your fire Rumsford, I'm coming in!"

"There's another one!" Rumsford muttered, "I've got to get this clip loaded and let him have it!" He pushed the clip into his rifle and took aim.

"I'LL FIX 'EM...I'LL GET 'EM ALL!" he shouted as the shadowy figure approached.

You heard the whisper Rumsford…you heard the man use your name! Yet, when you had the clip in, you turned, half blind with fear.

The voice in the distance shouted back, "Keep down Rumsford! You'll…" Rumsford emptied his clip. "Stop it you fool…it's me, Sergeant Carey!"

Carey ran up just in time to wrestle the rifle from Rumsford's grasp.

"C-Carey! It…it is you!" A shaken Rumsford said.

"Take a good look Corporal! Next time don't fire till you know it's a Jap."

Rumsford sat back into the foxhole, "They moan and call for medics…I went out twice and each time it was a Jap."

"I know kid," answered Master Sergeant Carey, "I heard them calling to you all night. They wear you down after a while."

"I don't mind fightin' 'em—but I can't stand it when they come in the darkness, whispering, sneaking around they way they do! I can't take it, Sergeant."

You said the words, Joe Rumsford…even to you in your condition, they sounded horrible…because you must take it…you've got to fight the way your buddies fight, no matter how rough it gets.

"I'm sorry, Sergeant." Rumsford said contritely, "I'll be all right, now, honest."

"You'd better be all right Joe. This island is crawlin' with Japs. Keep your eyes peeled for a Bonzai attack in this sector. The Major said he's expecting a counter-attack! I've got to get back to the C.P."

You heard the whispers again as soon as Master Sergeant Carey was gone. The American words, the piteous moans of men begging for a doctor!

"Help me…water, please!"

"Corpseman, help me."

"Joe, help me. I'm hurt real bad."

Rumsford fell for it again! He crawled out of his hole shouting into the darkness…"WHAT'S YOUR NAME AND OUTFIT? SHOW YOURSELF SO I CAN SEE YOU."

You know better Rumsford—the others who've been in combat a long time warned you about the whispers! Still, they fooled you! You left your foxhole.

"I'm over here Joe," came the faint voice, sounding like a man in agony, "My name's Smith...Joe Smith."

Three Japanese soldiers lay in ambush. They jumped Rumsford as he took refuge behind a palm tree.

"RUMSFORD! YOU HEAR ME? HIT THE DIRT WHEN THE FLARE GOES UP!' It was M/Sgt. Carey.

The flare flickered out a second later as Sgt. Carey blasted down the enemy soldiers.

"Come on in Rumsford. I'll cover you."

Rumsford crawled back to his foxhole; lucky to escape with is life.

Daylight came at last...you thought it never would, didn't you Joe Rumsford?

"Hey, Joe, you almost goofed out there again last night," said one of his buddies.

"Yeah—they've fooled me every night since I joined the outfit! I can't help it—I get to thinking one of our guys is out there hurt, needing help, and I have to go out and see!" Rumsford explained.

At the Command Post, Master Sergeant Carey reported the incident to Major Schmidt. The Major was already aware of Rumsford's problem.

"Joe Rumsford's okay Sir, but he almost shot me in the dark!" Said M/Sgt Carey.

"He'll be all right, Sergeant. Look—we just received new orders..." said the Major, pointing to a map pinned to the Command Post wall. "We've got to move across the top of this ridge ahead, then swing across to a stream ahead a half mile and to the west! Division promised some air support—the rest will be up to us."

You got the word, Joe Rumsford...you saw the planes come over at 07:30! There were six of them...only six.

"All right men," said M/Sgt. Carey, "We move out when the last plane comes into bomb and strafe."

The jungle terrain was choked with underbrush and tall trees. Many of the trees were toppled or had their tops blown off. The planes soften up the concentration of Japanese troops that lay ahead entrenched in the hillsides.

It's daylight now, Rumsford! The bullets slam past your ear, the mortars flail the jungle around you…but there are no whispers, no imagined dangers present!

The battle raged on. The Division was slowly making headway knocking the Japanese out of their entrenched positions. There were heavy casualties that day, and no let-up in the fighting! At nightfall the attack ceased and the Division dug in.

"Hey, Rumsford," said one of his buddies, "You're not drillin' for oil. How deep are you gonna go?" referring to Joe's feverish digging efforts at a new foxhole.

"As deep as I can. After dark I'll wish it was an oil well," Rumsford yelled over.

The M/Sgt gave Rumsford some more sound advice, "Listen, Corporal, the sun's going down. Try to keep your head tonight. Don't pay attention to anything you hear."

"I'll try Sarge…" Rumsford promised.

The tension began to build in you as the sun dropped below the trees, Joe Rumsford! You felt the vice of fear begin to tighten…and then the deep dusk gave way to the jungle night. And you heard them.

"Hey, Joe, over here, I hurt real bad!"

"Help me Joe. Get a medic."

Rumsford covered both ears with his hands, "They've got to stop. I know what I'll do." He muttered to himself.

You left your foxhole, Rumsford, against orders…but you didn't care anymore!

"Hey, Joe, please help me!"

"Corpseman, someone, help me!"

Rumsford inched his way to the enemy position, beat them off and blasted them down, "That's four that won't whisper again!"

Two American soldiers heard gunfire:

"Who's out there Smitty?" asked one man.

"I think it's Rumsford. I heard several shots."

You were in the middle of a squad of Japanese—all around you! This time they weren't worrying you. You were after them!

Hand-to-hand, more gunfire. Piercing screams of dying men.

"Rumsford's got 'em shook up!" said M/Sgt Carey to his men. "The Major said to move up if we got the chance! THIS IS IT! Come on!"

The flares went up…your buddies grimly moved forward and the whisperers turned tail and ran for the darkness!

They found Rumsford, "What happened Rumsford? How come you turned into a night fighter all of a sudden?' asked M/Sgt. Carey.

"They scared me once too often, Sarge! I figured I'd attack for a change instead of hiding in my hole waiting for, 'Hey, Joe!'"

The next morning they counted eight dead enemy soldiers.

Range War

They were the great cattle barons of the Old West and carried a tradition of getting things done in the most direct way possible...even if it meant a range war! On the Texas panhandle...

The Ranger, Chad Lowery, rode to the pass to cut off Big Mike Perry and his boys from Bar-Z. Perry was a large man, with steady gray eyes and a high forehead that lost itself in the shiny baldness of his pate. Now in his early forties, he had wandered by devious and sundry ways over a dozen states and territories, finally ending here in Texas where he had hundreds of acres breeding cattle. The Ranger, Chad, was tall and wiry. He joined the Rangers when he was seventeen. That was seven years ago. He's a veteran now. Alone, with two guns strapped to his sides, with traditional Chaps over his pants, he confronted Big Mike Perry and his men. Perry was about to stop a rival from crossing the boundaries of his property.

"Hold up there Perry," shouted Chad.

"It's the Ranger!" cried one of Perry's men, reigning in his mare.

"Get outa my way Chad! This is my property and I'm handlin' things MY way, see! We don't want the law in on this," Perry said in anger.

"But the law IS in on it!" countered Chad, his hat now strung behind his head.

"Then I'm getting' it right OUT again!" Perry raised his rifle.

The Ranger grabbed the reins of his horse and spoke to the animal, "Show him how wrong his is Whitey!"

A flurry of horse hooves…

He then circled Big Mike and kicked up a great deal of dust and dirt that choked the old man. The blinded and irate cattle king yelled at Chad while rubbing his eyes.

"Oooooph! What kinda way is that for a man to fight?"

"It's a way of stoppin' yuh from makin' a fool of yoreself! It's not healthy to cross the law."

He stopped and forced Big Mike again, then continued, "You're an old-timer, Big Mike! You were tough when tough men were needed here in the West. But there are peaceful ways of settlin' arguments now…courts of law."

Perry rubbed the dirt from his eyes, "I chased every outlaw in this county outta here before you were born! And when my neighbor cuts through my fences to let his cattle into my water hole, I'm agonna put a stop to it!"

Chad reached for his tobacco pouch and rolled himself a smoke, "Even if it means a range war on the panhandle, Big Mike?"

"Yup! And when it's over, I'll still be the boss man in these parts."

Off in the distance, down the arroyo, Todd Hunter and his men rode through. Big Mike brushed aside Chad and rode down the slope to meet Hunter and his men. Hunter was an ornery old coot, long gray hair and a huge mustache, polka-dot bandanna around his neck and a huge ten gallon, wide brim hat.

"Here comes, Big Mike, mad as a mountain goat! And shootin'!" cried one of Hunter's men.

"There's only one way to talk back…with our own guns! Let 'em have it boys!" cried Hunter, blasting away with his revolver.

Back on the hill Chad was helpless. He stood there frozen to his saddle, thinking, "There, it begins…and it'll spread through the panhandle, unless I can do something to stop it!"

In a matter of days, every ranch in the panhandle became an armed camp, as the men took sides in the dispute between Big Mike Perry and Todd Hunter. The very air exploded with trouble—and war swept from ranch to ranch.

Chad had to act…and he would! He had a plan!

"Big Mike and Todd both claim they're rugged individuals, used to handlin' things in their own way, so…" Chad rode into the Perry ranch unannounced and unseen. At gunpoint he got the drop on one of Perry's men, knocked him cold then entered Perry's bedroom.

"Don't move, Big Mike!" said Chad, holding his six gun to Perry's temple.

"Chad! Yuh workin' for that sidewinder Hunter?"

As Chad tied up and gagged Perry, he explained, "I'm workin' for the law, Big Mike! I've gotta make sure yuh don't squawk none while I take yuh with me!"

A short time later, Chad was stealing into the home of Todd Hunter, got the drop on him, tied him up and hauled him away too! It was a busy night for the Ranger.

After safely stashing the two old men, Chad rode back to each ranch. He approached the foreman of each party. "Hey! Todd wants to see all the men who are on his side in the range war over at the hollow for a showdown!"

Then at Big Mike's ranch, "That's right!" shouted Chad to the hands, "Big Mike says for all his boys to meet him at the hollow!"

At dawn…

Todd's men and Big Mike's outfit showed up in force at the hollow. The Ranger was in between the warring parties.

"Hold it boys!" Like I said, Todd and Big Mike are here and they're gonna settle this range war…in their own way."

"That's good enough for us!" said one of the hands.

Chad brought both sides into the Hollow and then addressed them. "They were strong men once, and that's why you follow 'em now, right?"

"Right," said Todd's foreman, "They're the Old West, those men! But where are they?"

Chad walked behind a boulder and brought out Todd, ungagged him and cut him loose. Then he brought out Big Mike.

"And here's Big Mike!" said Chad untying him. "Now let's see how tough they are when they fight it out man to man, the way they used to do in the old days!"

Chad untied the old enemies and they rushed at each other like two bulls! They hurled insults at one another as they closed in. But the glorious charge was a sad sight to behold as the old foes floundered, puffed, missed and grunted!

This sparing went on for twenty minutes till both fell from sheer exhaustion. Men from both sides began laughing.

Chad pointed to the two sluggers…"There yuh are gents! They TALK big, but their day is past! There's another day come now, and time for NEW ways to settle arguments."

"Haw! Haw!" laughed one of the men in the crowd, "You're right, Chad. Them old coots talk louder'n they can act!"

Puffing away, Big Mike approached Todd, turned to Chad, "Okay, Chad you made your point. We know when we're licked. What d'ya say Todd?"

Todd was also embarrassed, sweating and completely humiliated.

"Let's call it even, Big Mike," said Todd, desperate to save face, "And the next time we got an argument, we go to court."

Chad smiled, so did everyone else!

Lenny's Leap!

The cloud-covered, moonless night shrouded the Victorian mansion in pitch-blackness. After locking up, Mr. Calloway sent his servants to bed and retired into the library to have a nightcap and read before going to bed. He settled into his comfortable leather chair by the fireplace and relaxed with a good book.

Lenny Carbone and Pete Tedusco entered through a side window after jimmying the lock. No alarms went off. They were pros, well-dressed pros. They always wore suits and ties and an occasional fedora. It went along with their aspirations, burglarizing only wealthy estates. And these hoods were dressed to kill!

Mr. Calloway was dozing off by this time, when the pair grabbed him and Lenny placed his hand over Calloway's mouth so he couldn't make a noise. He was dragged over to the wall safe above the fireplace mantle. Where else would it be but behind a family portrait! These crooks had cased the place weeks before.

"N-no! You mustn't take my savings. I-I won't let you…I…" Calloway didn't have a chance to finish his eloquent plea…" Arrrgghh!" Lenny cracked him in the head with the butt end of his automatic. Calloway fell lifeless to the floor with a thud.

"Ya killed him Lenny! Why did you have to kill 'im?" Pete nervously whispered.

"I only tapped him," Lenny said with a satisfied smile, "It ain't my fault if he's got a tissue paper skull."

"You're always killin', Lenny! Every time we go out on a job, you've gotta dirty things up!"

"Stop beefin' ya jerk…an' get busy on that safe! One more peep outa you, and you'll keep the old geezer company!"

Pete knew the threat was real. He knew Lenny was psychotic and unpredictable, but the best second-story man around. A silence fell between them, broken only by a soft rasp of metal as Pete placed his burglar tool against the metal of the wall safe. He was a well-seasoned safe cracker, with a golden touch. But this caper took a little longer than usual. Ten minutes passed.

"Stop draggin' it out! An' quit shakin'! The way you're goin' at it, we'll be here for a month!"

"It's giving way Lenny! I'm almost on the last tumbler now! One more turn…I'm through!" A piercing alarm sounded.

"What did I…?" Pete said as he jerked backward, startled.

"Hold it, stupid. The door's wired!"

"L-let's go, Lenny. That alarm'll wake up the dead! We'll get caught."

"And leave this stuff behind?" snorted Lenny, "Get out to the car and get the motor going. We'll blow as soon as I load up! Now get goin'."

Minutes later their powerful sports car leaped for the open road with a throaty roar. The servants had come running downstairs just as the crooks made their get away.

"Head north, egghead," commanded Lenny, "and don't take your foot off the pedal! Our only chance is to hit the main artery an' get lost in traffic!"

"I never dreamed the tin can was wired, Lenny…honest…"

"Shut up an' lemme think! I heard the old man's servants come barrelin' down the stairs. If they haven't called the cops, the wired safe must have been linked to the station house."

And as though in answer to Lenny's thoughts…

"Sirens! It's coppers Lenny! They'll get us. We'll fry for murder!"

"If you slow down now, I'll blow your head off."

Three shots echoed from the squad car…shattering the frosty air!

"They got the tires!" shouted Pete, "I-I'm losing control! We're heading into that ditch!"

But within the wreckage, the pair escaped unhurt.

"C'mon. On your feet! If they catch us penned up this way, we're dead pigeons! Our only chance now is out in the open!"

"Y-you're right Lenny! I-I'm comin'."

Lenny held on to the briefcase he stuffed with the Calloway loot and they ran up the road.

"Up ahead!" said Lenny pointing, "It's a foot bridge! That gives me an idea. We can beat 'em! C'mon!"

"Huh? I don't get it."

“That’s no surprise!” Lenny panted as they ran toward the bridge, “Now get those legs goin’.”

“Sure, Lenny! Whatever you say.”

Quickly they raced out to the center of the narrow span and then Lenny came to a halt. He turned to Pete.

“The minute they don’t find us in that wreck, they’ll be heading this way! We’ll never make it on foot, so that leaves only one choice…the river below! We’ll have to jump an’ swim our way out!”

“J-jump?” Pete hesitated, “N-no! I won’t jump. I can’t swim!”

“Then it’s your funeral, ‘cause you’re jumpin’ all the same! I don’t care if you go down like a stone, but I’m not leavin’ ya here to squeal to the cops!”

“You can’t make me jump. You can’t make me!”

Pete turned away, running to the far end of the bridge.

“I’m getting’ outa here! Ya can’t make me…arghhh!”

Lenny blasted Pete twice in the back!

Staring down at the corpse, “So long, sucker! I never intended splittin’ the loot with you anyway! You’ve made it easy for me pal… real easy!” He holstered his gun.

Then, as the police charged up, one of the officers shouted…” Halt…or I’ll shoot!”

"Save your ammo copper! I'm makin' tracks outs here!" Lenny hollered back in a defiant voice. Then he dove off the bridge.

So, Lenny jumped! It was a beautiful dive.

The officers reached the railing and looked down, astounded!

Lenny wasn't making any tracks. He didn't even make a ripple. He smashed onto the surface with a bone-crunching thud.

The river was frozen solid!

Who's the Hero?

"Wasn't he a hero, Pop?"

"Who my boy—Napoleon?" asked Mr. Wills, looking up from his newspaper.

"No, Pop; Tom Flowers," answered Henry.

"Why, what has Tom Flowers done to earn that distinction? asked his father.

"Why, he took Arthur Raymond's part in the fight yesterday with Chub, and Chub was a lot bigger than him."

"But I thought fighting was forbidden at school now, Henry," said the gentleman. His son looked down blushing slightly.

"That's right, Pop," he said; "but the boys can't get on without fighting."

"Really," said his father, dryly, "I wasn't aware they were so quarrelsome."

"Hey, Pop, now you're laughing at me," said Henry.

"But if a fella calls you names, what are you to do?"

"According to you, I guess, poke him in the nose," said Mr. Wills.

"Yea, there's nothing else you can do, unless you want to be called a coward," said Henry; "and I do hate cowards," he added. "I wish Arthur hadn't walked away, instead of fighting Chub, yesterday."

"The Arthur Raymond thinks it possible for the kids to live without fighting, I suppose," said Mr. Wills.

"Well, you see, Pop, fighting has been forbidden since that business with Larry Martin," said Henry; "and Raymond said he wouldn't break the rules. It was very cowardly of him, because we weren't in the playground or even near the school at all!"

"What had Chub done to Arthur that demanded that should fight?" asked Mr. Wills.

"He called him a liar and Arthur should've knocked him down right away. He could've done it easily; but, instead of that, he said he could prove he wasn't a liar."

"And did he?" asked his Pop.

"He's going to bring the proof tomorrow morning; but, of course, the guys don't care because he didn't fight."

"And does Raymond know this?"

"Yea, Pop. We told him what we should do if he refused to fight, but he stuck to it that it wasn't right to break the rules and walked off, and then Tommy Flowers pitched in and hit Chub. Raymond was disgraced."

"Disgraced, you call it?" Well I think he did the honorable thing," said Mr. Wills.

"Oh, Pops!" exclaimed Henry.

"I mean what I say. I call him a true hero," said his father warmly.

"But, Pop, all the boys said it was so cowardly of him not to fight Chub."

"But you say he wasn't afraid of Chub—could have beaten him easily; and yet he braved going against all the kids and not break the rules."

"Then you don't think he was a coward, Pop?" said Henry.

"I hope, my boy, you'll be brave enough to stand by him, though all the rest might think differently," said Mr. Wills. "To stand by those who have dared to do what's right, in spite of all opposition, is true bravery; and I hope you stick by him. It will be much harder than to act the part of Tom Flowers."

For some time after his father left him, Henry sat thinking over what had been said, and decided to stand by his friend Arthur Raymond; but he didn't know how difficult this would be until the next day.

As he was going to school the next morning, Tom Flowers overtook him. He was patting himself on the back saying what a great fight it was and how Arthur Raymond was a blatant coward. Henry wanted to say something in defense of his friend—something of what his father had said the night before; but somehow he couldn't get the words out. But when Arthur came in sight and the rest of the boys turned away, he went over and met him.

"Have you brought the proof you said you would?" asked Henry, wanting to say something.

"Yes, I have it in my pocket," said Arthur, but sighed as he spoke, for two other boys had passed and ignored him completely. It wasn't easy to bear this silent contempt of his schoolmates, although he was upheld by the consciousness of having done what was right.

"Henry, you'd better join the rest," he said, a little bitterly. "They mean to brand me, I can see it."

"Are you sorry you didn't wallop Chub?" asked Henry,

"You might do it, you know. Even now you could walk up to him, show him the proof and then punch him. You're not afraid of him, are you? You're stronger than Flowers."

"No, I'm not afraid of him," said Arthur. "But I'm not going to fight when it's against school rules; it isn't right, and besides, I could get expelled. If I get the chance, I'll let everybody see I'm not a coward, but it won't be by fighting."

By this time they had reached the school and went in; but Henry receives several threatening glances from his companions as he passed to his desk. During school-time the quarrel wasn't mentioned; but no sooner had they got into the playground then Henry was overwhelmed with reproaches.

"What business had you to speak to Arthur Raymond?" said one.

"You're just another sneak like he is," blurted another.

"If you talk to him again we'll brand you too," said a third. And this threat was taken up and echoed by all the rest.

Henry had never yet been treated so badly as this, and he was by no means inclined to accept, especially when he glanced across the playground and saw Arthur sitting by himself with a book in his hand. To be shut out of all the games and ignored was very hard to bear; but Henry remembered his father's words, and moreover, he could not help admiring Arthur's action, although it brought no glory, but a great deal of annoyance. So he said boldly, "Now look here. Arthur isn't a coward, as you guys make out. My father said it was brave of him to stick it out and do the right thing; and I'll stand by him even if you guys don't. So get that straight, huh."

As if a bomb-shell had suddenly exploded in the midst of them, the boys could scarcely have looked more astonished.

"Wills is sure to do as we tell him," had been the unanimous belief until now, and that he should suddenly dare their wrath was almost past belief. They thought they could tease and worry him into compliance with their wishes; but they were sorely mistaken.

Henry had begun to think for himself, and he found that his companions' opinion of things was not always to be relied upon; and, seeing what was right, he determined to act upon it. "Arthur is no coward," he repeated, "and I'm gonna stand by him."

"Oh! Let him go," said one, in a tone of assumed disgust.

"Flowers is our hero. He kept the honor of the school."

Flowers wasn't likely to forget this accolade nor let the others forget it either. He harangued everybody and on the slightest provocation threatened to fight, and still managed to keep up the ill feeling toward Arthur Raymond, whose quarrel he had defended. A kid's opinion is slow to change especially in the case of cowardice and hero-worship;

and their present hero, Flowers, was by no means willing to resign his place, although some of the boys could not but respect the way in which Henry and Arthur behaved, and were more than half convinced that they were in the right, if they had only been courageous enough to admit it!

But one day, as the old sore subject was again being discussed, on their way home from school, they saw a car barreling down the street, while just below a group of children were slowly crossing, under the escort of a deaf woman.

"Look! The children!" gasped Henry.

"Flowers, help them, she can't hear the car coming," shouted two or three boys. But Flowers drew back, pale with alarm at the thought of exposing himself to real danger. At the same moment Arthur threw down his book bag and dashed forward into the road, just in time to snatch several of the children and push the old lady out of the way of the onrushing vehicle. He was clipped on his arm and hurled to the pavement several yards beyond; but managed to save the children and their escort. He wasn't hurt too badly, and the car sped away without slowing down or stopping!

His companions were frightened when they saw this dangerous situation. Everyone else had frozen in fear, but Arthur acted quickly and decisively without any regard for his own safety. His schoolmate gathered around him with great admiration, helping him to his feet. "Arthur, forgive us," said one, "we've made a terrible mistake accusing you of being a coward." They all crowded around him praising his courage and patting him on the back. Henry looked most triumphant, "Now who's the hero," he asked, "Flowers who did the fighting, or Arthur, who did what was right?"

The boys were well pleased to change their heroes. Many of them changed their opinions too, and Henry was almost as highly thought of as Arthur himself, for standing by him when all the rest declared him a coward; and, from that day, to do what's right in the face of all opposition became the settled principle of many in the school.

The Terrorist

(Based on a True Story)

St. Petersburg, Russia—July 28th, 1904. Baron De Plehve, Chief of the *Okhrana*; the Czar's Secret Police, is attacked again by the secret terrorist organization headed by the most feared man in Russia, Ievano Azeff.

All but one of this terrorist cell was arrested by the *Okhrana!* The one who had escaped was Azeff, the terrorist chief!

Later, in his underground headquarters, "They almost got me!" said an exhausted Azeff, grimly as he was addressing his men. "There's an unknown informer…a spy in our midst!" Azeff was tall, dressed in a dull orange colored overcoat, his face was drawn from sleepless nights and incessant fighting. But his voice was sharp, the strength of command still audible.

"I know his police name, Azeff," ventured one of the terrorists seated nearby, "It is Valentin! Our lives are in danger while he lives. We must find him."

Azeff picked up the conversation, standing at the head of the table, "The Okhrana has uncovered our arsenals. We must have more arms, especially explosives!" he said gravely.

"We foresaw that," said a scruffy-looking man, lean with worn shoes, "…and have already put plans into operation." He stopped; his eyes were in shadows under the brim of his cap, his face intensely serious.

Due to the informer, Valentin, the terrorist supplies were discovered. Plan One: the explosives: "Nitroglycerin—hidden in the herring barrel!" cautioned another conspirator, in a low, very clear voice.

Plan Two: arms and ammunition, "The rifles captured yesterday," admitted another man, smoking a pipe. "It was Valentin's doing. The rat!" Azeff felt a flicker of alarm listening to his men.

In another meeting some days later, the terrorists are planning their next assault.

"The plot to attack the Grand Duke Serge must succeed!" began Azeff, "He is the Czar's uncle. But with Valentin to betray us…" his voice trailed off, as if he knew it would fail, his face puckered with suspicion.

"I shall search out Valentin for you," a fellow conspirator said rashly, "I, Burtzeff promise it!" Azeff pushed his hands into his pockets and stared at Burtzeff thoughtfully, as if considering. "How will you accomplish this?" asked Azeff. "I am having a thief steal the private files of the *Okhrana!* We shall find out who Valentin is. And when we do…," Burtzeff retorted with undisguised derision. Azeff looked on and nodded.

Meanwhile the Secret Police where discussing Azeff and his band of terrorists.

"This man Azeff is the head of the terrorists," began the Chief of Police to his colleagues at the Okhrana Headquarters. He was rubbing his hands together in an agitated manner, "We must get him. He is dangerous. Valentin has reported a plot against the grand Duke Serge!"

"Once Azeff is arrested, the terrorist cells will collapse," ventured another official.

Azeff knew they were closing in on him, so he decided to escape to Paris, so while Azeff hurried to make his train…the thief hired by Burtzeff already made his burglary. True to his oath, Burtzeff received the thief and the files on the true identity of Valentin.

At a local hideaway the thief handed Burtzeff the leather file folder—"Here is the secret files I stole from the Okhrana, Burtzeff! Now, my fee!"

"Ah!" responded an overjoyed Burtzeff, "If only Azeff were here! He would supervise the killing of the traitor, Valentin!"

The Burtzeff made a horrifying discovery—"It cannot be!" cried Burtzeff, in an anguished and saddened voice, "According to these secret files of the Okhrana, the traitor Valentin is Azeff himself!" He dropped the dossier and photo of Azeff onto the floor.

Postscript: With this disclosure both the Okhrana and the terrorists collapsed. Having been a high officer of both organizations, Ienov Azeff had betrayed each! Despite the perils of his double-dealing, this deadly daring and successful spy died peacefully in bed in Berlin, on April 24, 1918.

Historical Background:

The prominent feature in Russian life at the turn of the twentieth century was the frequency of violence by the secret agents of the Government. Public moneys have been spread lavishly upon three or four different and rival sections of the State's secret police.

Azeff had been an agent for the Russian secret police for 16 years and at the same time the Chief organizer of acts of terrorism among the Social Revolutionists, including the murder of the Minister of the Interior, Von Plehve, the Grand Duke Sergius, General Bogdanovitch at Ufa, and several plots which denounced at the last moment against Gen. Trepoff, the Minister of Justice Scheglovitoff, the Grand Duke Nicholas and the Tsar.

Azeff began as an informer in 1902; this is officially stated in the act of accusation against M. Lopukhin (formerly head of the Police Department, who had confirmed to the Russian refugee, Burtseff, in the autumn of 1908, that Azeff really was a paid agent of the police). In 1904 Azeff, already then in the service of the police, organized the murder of the arch reactionary Minister of the Interior, Von Plehve.

These events gained Azeff the absolute confidence of the party, and the department of the Russian secret police—the *Okhrana,* whose special function was the protection of the Tsar—did not hesitate to sacrifice Von Plehve and a Grand Duke in order to retain their trusted agent to keep him in the center of the Social Revolutionary Party.

In the first year of the reign of Alexander III, a special police was organized under the name *Okhrana* (Protection) for the personal protection of the Tsar, the head of that special police—Colonel Sudeyhin—entering into relations with one of the terrorists, Dagaeff seriously inviting him to induce the terrorists of the Executive Committee to kill the then Minister of the Interior, County Tolstoy, and the Grand Duke Vladimir and afterwards betray the Committee.

In order to protect the Tsar, the *Okhrana* allowed Azeff to import into Russia revolutionary literature printed abroad, to organize workshops for fabricating bombs, occasionally supplying some money for that; they allowed him to organize plots against Ministers, Grand Dukes, and the Tsar himself! All this time their diabolical policy was designed carefully to protect the terrorists marked out by Azeff against other sections of police, so as to have them arrested by nobody but the *Okhrana*, just at the moment the plot was going to be executed. They might thus be sure of the necessary effect being produced on the Tsar, and the victims might be immediately hanged, before they had time to make compromising revelations that would give a clue to the *Okhrana* conspiracy.

Even escapes were skillfully organized when it was necessary for the *Okhrana* and it agent, Azeff, to spare some active fighting leader, only to had him over later on to a Court Martial to be hanged in twenty-four hours.

Thousands of men were sacrificed every year, only to provide the "agents of provocateurs" of the *Okhrana* with plenty of money.

Source:

***"The Terror in Russia,"* Peter Kropotkin (1842-1921), London: Methuen & Co. 1909 4th Ed.**

From: Part II, Chapter VI *Provocation to Violence and the Participation of Police Officials in Crime*

The Confession

It was nearly midnight when Harold Gedney swung his grey sedan into the deserted street. The beam from the single headlight cut through the darkness illuminating the cobblestone road ahead. Harold strained his eyes and muttered to himself, "That damned busted headlight. I'd better get it fixed first thing tomorrow. Can't see a thing this way!"

Suddenly the loan headlight beam fell upon something lying on the cobblestones ahead of Harold's slowly moving car. He gasped! "Looks like a woman's body—she's hurt." His thoughts were racing. Harold slammed on the brakes and the car squealed to a stop. The figure in the headlight beam lay motionless in a pool of blood. Harold leaped from the car and rushed to the woman's side. There was a slight movement!

"She's still alive! She's been hit by a car—I guess. I got to get help—a doctor!" He tried his cell phone but he had forgotten to recharge it and it wasn't working. Harold looked around frantically! He was an elderly man in his late sixties, white hair, wrinkly face, wearing heavy-lens glasses in a steel frame. His tie was still tight around his neck, when he loosened it. The dark faces of the buildings loomed up about him. This was the factory section. There were very few lights, no phones, none that worked. Harold darted back to his car. "Mustn't move her," he thought, "Have to get to a phone somehow! Have to call an ambulance. Looks like she's dying."

Harold backed his car up hurriedly. The gears coughed as he threw it into drive and sped off down the dark street. At that very moment a police patrol car turned the corner behind him.

"Look, Willie, there's someone lyin' in the gutter," one of the officers said to his partner. "Yea—and that car's speedin' outta there."

The patrol car surged forward, skidding to a stop beside the injured woman. She was strikingly beautiful, full length brown hair spread on the street. Her dress and blouse were bloodied.

"She's been hit by a car," said the excited officer. "See what you can do Willie. I'm goin' after that lousy hit-and-run."

The police officer named Willie leaped from the squad car, "Okay, O'Riley, radio in for an ambulance. I'll wait here—and get that creep!" The squad car roared off in pursuit as officer Willie remained, stooped over the crumpled body. He felt her pulse—"An ambulance," he whispered to himself, "won't do this lady any good. She's dead."

Meanwhile, Harold Gedney sped through the deserted factory section looking for an open diner, a phone that wasn't in shambles, anything that might help him summon aid for the injured woman he'd just left. Behind him the squad car flashed after him, siren blaring! The officer drew up alongside Harold forcing him to the curb. The shrieks of the brakes and the dying whine of the siren echoed off the empty loft buildings.

Before Harold could complete his statement, Officer O'Riley drew his automatic, "Okay, buddy, come out of there with your hands up. Face the car and put your hands on the hood. No funny business." Officer Riley read him his rights and then handcuffed him.

The precinct station buzzed with excitement. Harold Gedney stood before the desk sergeant, his hair mussed, his clothes disheveled. He was flanked by the two radio car officers who'd arrested him. A detective shouted at the dispatcher, others stood glaring at the prisoner.

"Try to locate Lieutenant Anderson, Charlie. Tell 'im we just picked up the hit-and-run. The woman he hit is dead. No ID on her yet."

The sergeant was booking Harold. "What's your name?" he asked grim-faced and angry.

"Gedney. Harold Gedney. But you've got me all wrong. I didn't hit her. I was going for help! You gotta believe me." He began to sob. One of the officers sneered at him, "Crocodile tears. You made a big mistake tryin' to run away, Gedney. A big mistake."

"I didn't do it, I tell you. I was going for…"

Two detectives led him away to the interrogation room. "D'ja hear that Baker?" said one of the detectives to his partner, "This guy says he didn't do it."
"Tell 'im we got ways to make these types confess, Moran."

In the interrogation room, "Why don't you save yourself a lot of grief Gedney, come clean, admit it," said a persistent Detective Moran.

"I swear, I didn't do it, I tell you," insisted Gedney in a meek, quivering voice, "I was just…"

"Here's the Lieutenant, sir," interrupted the dispatcher, "He just got home."

"Hello Lieutenant, this is Moran here. We just hauled in the hit-and-run. Officers O'Riley and Crelock caught him driving away from the scene. He killed a woman."

"Killed her, eh?" came the reply from Lieutenant Anderson, "Got a confession?"

"Not yet, Lieutenant. The creep denies it. We're workin' him over now. Thought you might like to sit in."

"I'll be down in a little while."

The interrogation room was dark except for a brilliant light shinning into the face of Mr. Gedney. The two detectives circled him, firing questions.

"We found glass all 'round the body Gedney. You car's headlight was busted. You still deny it?" Moran said.

A rather shaken Mr. Gedney tried his best to convince them, "I broke that headlight last week…"

"Admit it…" began detective Baker.

Gedney was grilled for what seemed like hours. The bare table and couple of wooden chairs were the only furniture in the room. The see-through glass facing the main office was neatly hidden behind half-drawn Venetian blinds.

"How much did you have to drink Gedney? You stink from it," said Detective Chase, another interrogator, his face not two inches from Gedney's ear.

"I only had two. There was a party at the office. That's why I was driving home so late. You can ask them. I wasn't drunk," he denied vehemently.

"You were drunk," continued Moran, pounding the table, "You couldn't stop in time. After you hit her you got scared and drove off. Ain't that right Gedney?"

"I want a lawyer. I want to call my home," pleaded Gedney, sweating, trembling. The detectives looked at each other, exasperated.

"Sure, sure," sneered Moran, "We'll allow you a call, punk," snorted Chase, "But right now, shut up, you're gonna listen. Don't try to worm your way outta this. We got you dead-to-rights. Admit it. Confess!"

"I'm telling you the truth," whimpered Gedney.

"You're lying," shouted Chase. "You were drunk," he continued, circling round the table, "You hit her so hard, you smashed your headlight."

"Get wise," interrupted Moran, "Save yourself a lot of grief. The judge may go easy on you if you confess. Manslaughter two, maybe. Save us the trouble of getting it out of you. Admit it. Confess!"

The intense grilling went on, and on, non-stop. No break, no let up.

Just then, the coroner himself came into the room and told everyone, that they identified the lady who was killed. It was Lt. Anderson's wife! A shock went through the detectives, especially Gedney, who cringed and sat deeper into his chair. Lt. Anderson's wife! No one recognized her at first because of the condition she was in.

Lt. Anderson, head of homicide, entered the precinct and stared into the interrogation room. Anderson was tall, jet black hair, smooth, baby-like complexion. Watching intently, his face was bleak and strained. He continued to watch unobserved, looking on with intense emotion. He was informed, and led to the Morgue to identify the body.

After a few moments a rather shaken Lt. Anderson entered the room, removed his jacket, rolled up his sleeves and began his questioning, sitting across from Gedney. It went on for another hour, punishing, relentless questioning. Gedney got no rest, no break.

Lt. Anderson was called outside, approached by one of his men, "Lieutenant, we got the lab report, sir. No blood on the car. The dents were old, maybe a week or more. The glass fragments from the headlights didn't match those on the road. I think he's innocent after all!"

"Keep it to yourself for now," said Anderson sharply, "I know this bird killed that girl. We'll force it out of him."

"Maybe he didn't do it, sir," continued the clerk, "Maybe he's tellin' the truth. He couldda busted that headlight last week…"

"Too many ifs, too much coincidence," interrupted Anderson. "The boys will get it out of him. You'll see!" His voice was hard-edged. He lifted his eyebrows, and the clerk walked away down the corridor.

The Lieutenant lit a cigarette and went back into the room. The interrogation continued. Gedney stiffened, his cheeks flush, sweat poring off his face. Moments passed, he felt a tightening around his chest. A pain shot through his arm. He grew pale, ghostly white. He collapsed. Gedney fell dead from heart failure. It was over.

The detectives were stunned. An ambulance was called but, too late, the coroner examined Gedney and filled out the standard form reporting heart failure as the cause of death. The reports from Lt. Anderson and the other detectives were matter-of-fact and brief. They still insisted this was the man and essentially closed the case.

Lieutenant Anderson left the station house after being consoled by all the officers and clerks. He stepped onto the sidewalk into a warm afternoon, lit a cigarette then started for home. Before boarding the bus to take him uptown, he stopped in an automotive store. He rode the bus with his package under arm, arrived home and went directly to his garage, unwrapping the new headlight he just purchased.

After cleaning the blood off his fender, he began work to replace the broken headlight. *"My poor wife never knew what hit her,"* thought the Lieutenant, *"Lucky for me that chump Gedney stumbled on the scene."* He smiled a bit and whistled as he went to work on the repairs.

A Hearty Meal

Bjorn Saknussem shuffled down the busy city street. There was a skip in his step as he hurried home from his job at a consulting firm. His thoughts focused on what he was going to have for dinner. He skipped lunch today, so he was really hungry. He could think of nothing else but what he was going to make for dinner. No delicacies, no gourmet dishes, no fancy settings, just steak and potatoes. It would have to be something simple, something easy to prepare, something quick.

Bjorn stopped in his tracks when he passed a candy store and spotted a Turkish taffy machine. He thought about dropping in to get a snack before heading back home. But that would spoil his appetite. He scratched the back of his neck, his sandy, blonde hair waving in a stiff breeze. *"No,"* he thought, licked his lips and moved on. His mind was set on having that steak. But something was wrong. His wallet was gone! He wondered how that could have happened. He was always careful about where he placed his billfold. Then he remembered bumping into a well-dressed man a few minutes ago.

"That lousy thief must have picked my pocket!" Bjorn burned with indignation and was angry. Instinctively he turned around to glance up the street, hoping to spot the guy again. No good, the man was gone.

Bijorn hadn't thought about using his cell phone to contact the credit card companies to alert them of this predicament. He was starving. That's all he could think about—food! But he suddenly realized he was in a quandary now because he was still ten miles from his apartment and no carfare to get there. What could he do? He began to panic. He looked around anxiously, sweating, biting his lower lip. His breathing became labored. He was short of breath. *"What am I to do?"*

He looked for a cop. Not one in sight. The subway was three blocks away. He thought of jumping the turnstile. The entrance at that station had a gate above the passage so there was no way he could sneak over. If he explained his circumstances to the token booth clerk, he would most likely be ignored. He was never so mortified in his entire life! *"I can't imagine the humiliation in having to tell people I have no money."* Well he had to do just that, swallow his pride, and ask for a hand-out.

In his haste to find a sympathetic bystander, he tripped and fell, ripping a hole in his pants at the knee. He flung his arms out as two passersby came within reach. They were a well-dressed couple who looked rather affluent. *"A perfect touch,"* he thought.

Startled, the couple stopped and asked what had happened. They were staring at Bjorn, waiting for an answer. He swallowed hard, his voice rose as he pleaded his case. They could see he was desperate. And, what do you know, they fell for the story, hook, line and sinker, and gave him the carfare! He shook his head sharply. It amazed him that perfect strangers would come to his aid!

When he finally arrived home a half-hour later, he couldn't get into his apartment. His keys were gone! Now he knew the real meaning of distress. He paced up and down the hallway. He never got a long with his neighbors so he realized they weren't going to be of any help to him. *"I'll have to pick the friggin' lock!"* At least he hadn't lost his briefcase that he carried from the office. He fumbled through it till he found a paperclip.

"This should do the trick," he grunted to himself. His stomach growled and churned as he slipped one end of the paperclip into the lock. Sweating more and more, frustrated more and more, he twisted the slip inside the lock. He jiggled it, contorted it, flicked it back and forth. The lock didn't click open. It was a sturdy deadbolt. He frowned, his eyes hollow, his breathing heavy again. The latch wouldn't budge. The lock was brass, the door solid steel. It would be fruitless to try and kick the door down. Then he had a brainstorm. *"I'll go to the roof and climb down the fire escape and break in through my bedroom window."* Miserable, agitated, but now filled with hope, Bjorn ran to the door at the top of the next landing which would take him to the roof and to the ladder at the back of the building. He felt faint, weak, exhausted. He was white-faced, his whole body rigid, but the knot of anxiety eased within him. He found himself smiling.

When he finally reached the door to the roof, he discovered it was locked. He thought of asking the super to help, but realized he was not in the building. It was his day off. Bijorn was about to despair when, in sheer frustration and anger, he found the strength to kick open the door. He smiled suddenly, widely—and charged to the fire escape. There was only one thing left to do. It was a easy thing at that, break the window and eat dinner!

He drew a breath and entered the apartment. He threw off his jacket, tore off his necktie unlaced his shoes and headed straight to the kitchen. He never got there, he passed out in the living room. His thoughts turned to that Turkish taffy. The night passed, and Bjorn Saknussem rested contently, with a sweet tooth that sung lullabies to sweet dreams.

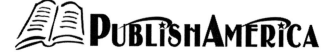

CPSIA information can be obtained at www.ICGtesting.com
Printed in the USA
BVOW022211290212

284143BV00002B/8/P

9 781462 643615